RIC

INSTAGRAM

RICH KIDS *of* INSTAGRAM

A NOVEL

THE CREATOR OF
RICH KIDS OF INSTAGRAM
WITH MAYA SLOAN
COCREATED AND ILLUSTRATED
BY THOMAS WARMING

G
GALLERY BOOKS
NEW YORK LONDON TORONTO SYDNEY NEW DELHI

G

Gallery Books
A Division of Simon & Schuster, Inc.
1230 Avenue of the Americas
New York, NY 10020

First Gallery Books trade paperback edition June 2014

Interior design by Jaime Putorti
Illustrations by Thomas Warming

Manufactured in the United States of America

10 9 8 7 6 5 4 3 2 1

Library of Congress Cataloging-in-Publication Data is available.

ISBN 978-1-4767-6406-1
ISBN 978-1-4767-6410-8 (ebook)

for **Ike**

RICH KIDS *of* INSTAGRAM

PROLOGUE

Todd Evergreen is making his first public appearance.

That Todd Evergreen.

The reclusive, twenty-two-year-old, overnight billionaire whose very existence has put us all in a tizzy.

Todd Evergreen, the notoriously camera-shy cyber-prodigy, is making his official debut.

If you don't know about it, there's a reason.

One day he didn't exist. The next, he was everywhere.

Todd Evergreen, slam-dunking his way onto the *Forbes* "30 Under 30," profiled in the *Times* Business section. Not even a quarter century old, and he's already got panels of experts debating his impact on CNBC, Jon Stewart using him as a punch line.

Trump's offered publicity-worthy sound bites of advice on FOX News, Ashton Kutcher a series of admiring tweets. Elon Musk even asked him to consult on SpaceX. *(Whatever that might be!)*

From what we've heard, Musk could not procure a meeting.

Evergreen doesn't *do* meetings.

But as of this weekend, he does parties. If you were lucky enough to get an invitation.

▪

The media throws around phrases like *whiz kid* and *boy genius* and *visionary*.

Todd Evergreen, we are told, *is trending.*

The only hitch? We haven't the faintest idea who he could possibly be.

There is speculation, of course. Investigative teams digging in the dirt like mangy strays, panels speculating on CNBC. *Nothing.* Does he even have a Social Security number?

The occasional snapshot. Not via the paparazzi, whom he has eluded. Just grainy shots from mobile phones, probably snapped by some NYU students (*do they ever go to class, these kids?*).

Of course, you can't make out his face. But *still.*

Todd on Ludlow Street, a little hunched over, walking quickly with a newspaper under his arm (*the tech guru with a newspaper! How terribly rebellious of him!*). Todd waiting out the downpour under a West Village awning, smoking a hand-rolled cigarette. Todd in Union Square, drinking coffee from a cheap cardboard cup. The kind bought from a street vendor for a dollar fifty, we suspect (*not that we know from experience, mind you!*).

Never without his sunglasses. Not ever. He's like the Anna Wintour of the digital world.

Poser, according to the headlines.

Renegade, say others.

The New Breed of Internet Geek, proclaims a caption, *Rockstar Webpreneur.*

One thing everyone can agree on: Evergreen is way better looking than that Facebook guy. Not much of a feat, we know. But he is a strapping young man, even by real-world standards.

(At least, we think. When we see his face, we'll revisit the topic.)

And to top it off, he's rich. Really, really rich.

▪

They say he signed with Wilhelmina Models. That he's making a documentary. Starting a movie studio. Writing a book. Investing in a publishing company. Recording an album. Buying a label. Starting a theme park, a hotel chain, a line of luxury towels.

He has a billion dollars and buzz. He can do anything he wants.

Billion is an exaggeration, of course, but it makes for great headlines. Most likely, he's in the high nine-figure range (*still, nothing to thumb your nose at!*).

Besides, it just adds to the mystery.

Perhaps he has some friends, we muse, *though they're probably as socially inept as he.* And what are friends, really, but the people you will eventually screw over? *(Not us, of course, as we are loyal to a fault. Good breeding is everything.)*

As for what he's doing with this chunk of change? Well, he bought that apartment. Those floors, to be precise. Two of them, in the top of a nondescript building on the Lower East Side. The lowest part of the East Side, we've been told, though we wouldn't know the difference (*going below Thirty-Fourth* is *such the ordeal!*).

Excellent security and twenty-four-hour concierge service, but *still.* This is no 740 Park.

Immediately following the sales listing, we've heard talk at the club of new real estate ventures. *The Lower East Side is the new Upper East,* they say over the Sunday-brunch buffet.

(We'll believe it when we see it. Which we don't plan on doing anytime soon.)

▪

Where did he come from?

The internet, we are told, is wild with conspiracy theories. *Is it Bali? Kathmandu? Cleveland, Ohio?*

And now that he's sold his company, what will he do next?

Perhaps we should invite him to a cocktail party, we muse over our bridge tables. *A benefit? To play doubles?*

And do you think he'd consider a donation to our various charitable foundations?

(*It's a tax write-off, after all. And imagine the Society Page write-up!)*

▪

Along with the fascination come the inevitable naysayers.

He's not that big of a deal. We've seen it before.

The same story, just plug in new details. We'll call it *Mad Libs for Cyber Success.*

Zuckerberg wannabe, most likely lacking in social skills (*undiagnosed low-level autism, social anxiety*) creates start-up (*social media endeavor, branding enterprise, the mashing of two previously unmashed ideas*) in his basement (*warehouse space, walk-up, parents' garage, dorm room at MIT*). He has a dream, most likely involving strange codes or other stuff the general population could not begin to fathom (*or even want to. At least, we certainly don't!*).

Then it gets a following. The following grows. Before you know it, the young man has gone viral. *(Funny word, this. A virus you long to contract! Like when Mitzi Vanden-Totter's niece got mono the same week as that Rothbart heir. Her Poly Prep popularity ranking went straight through the roof!)*

But we digress.

The rest of the story, of course, is equally familiar: along comes money-grubbing corporate entity, the big buyout, the write-up in the *Wall Street Journal*, the hundred-foot yacht and private beachfront property and days spent partying in Ibiza. With—if asked to harbor a guess—titans of the porn and rap industries.

We hate this story. But we love it, too.

■

Yes, Evergreen is intriguing, on that we are in agreement. But—just to play devil's advocate here—*how much does it really matter?*

Todd Evergreen may be brilliant, but so are many of these young men. He may be attractive, but who isn't? *(And if born lacking in aesthetically pleasing features, there's always that doctor on Central Park West.)*

And as for his site—the Rock Exchange—*Forbes* may project *a revolutionary impact*, the *Times* may call it a *breakthrough in business and music connectivity*, but we are just fine, thank you very much, with Bergdorf online and the SocialDiary.com.

This James Bond act? Lacking in freshness as well. We've already had that Assange character, have we not? And just look what happened to him! (*Hiding out on some tropical island with a harem of underage hula girls, we suspect.)*

What it comes down to is this: it is simply a website. Nothing more, nothing less.

Remember that high school boy in Omaha who got 30 million for his cross-media-e-commerce-integration-thingamajig? It was plastered all over the news and on CNN. *We could have come up with that,* we all agreed, but we were too busy living our lives for such things. So now he's richer than Midas, and we're reading about his fortune in the *Huffington Post* and thinking he should spend some of it on zit cream.

At least we had dates for prom. That's what we tell ourselves.

▪

Evergreen, we are sure, is a perfectly fine young man. But the city is riddled with those, so why him? Why is his the name on everyone's tongue? The face to launch a million Google hits? And most of all . . . *why weren't we invited to his coming-out soiree?*

This, we daresay, will prove *the* event of the season. And Evergreen is only part of the equation.

The host? None other than Gerald Hoff. *That* Gerald Hoff.

1
CHAPTER

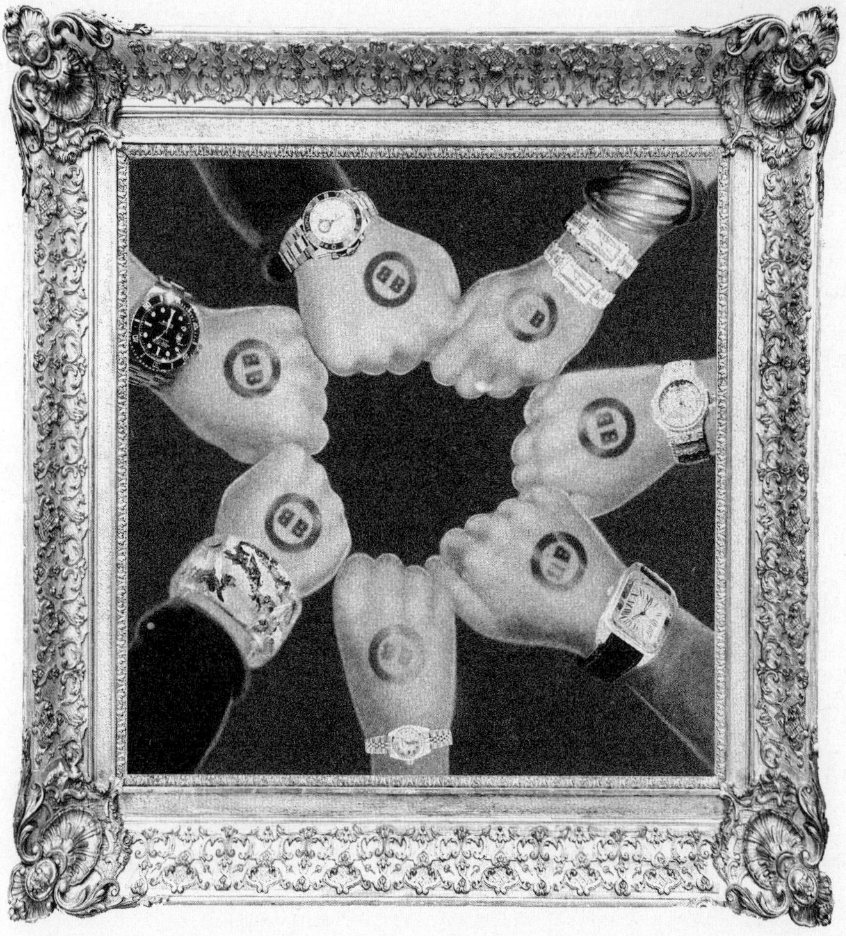

Million Dollar Fist Pump #BBparty @Annalise_Hoff @Miller_Crawford_III @Desdemona_Goldberg @Phillip_Atwater @Christian_Rixen @Cordelia_Derby @April_Holiday by Anonymous

Annalise Hoff

According to Emily Post, the ideal hostess is a cross between mind reader and angel, fulfilling her duties in a flawless yet seemingly effortless manner. I know this to be true, having reviewed the passage myself this very morning. *Etiquette*, Chapter XXV, "The Country House and Its Hospitality."

Now, with forty-five minutes until the guests arrive, the caterer running late, and the booze deliverymen "delivering" only half the order, I have come to a conclusion.

Emily Post is an old, dead cunt who doesn't know shit about here and now.

And where the hell are the monogrammed napkins?

▪

When I was first told who was coming, I'd been surprised to say the least.

For one, Daddy never called unless the matter was of the utmost importance. The moment *Father* came up on the caller ID—from his private line, no less, which was reserved for dignitaries, former presidents, multicorp CEOs, and me, Annalise Hoff, his sole heir and prized possession—I'd raced for the phone. My mind leapt to the most horrific of possibilities: *heart attack. Fed raid.*

But Daddy was as blasé as could be.

"Put together a thing," he'd said offhandedly, and I could picture him reclining in the private jet, or in his sleek midtown office, ice cubes clinking in his tumbler of scotch. "A cocktail party. No big deal. Just a couple of people. Can you throw something together at the East Hampton house?"

My heart soared. We hadn't had guests since Mother's mania-fueled exodus to Palm Beach over a year ago. Not that *she'd* ever been much of a hostess, seeing how her idea of a scintillating evening was a handful of pills, a disruptive state, and an intravenous flow of the Soap network.

"Of course, Daddy!" I'd practically squealed. *Restrain yourself,* I thought, though even my toenails felt giddy.

Then came surprise number two: the guest of honor. Todd Evergreen.

"I want to get the kid seen, make him feel welcome," Daddy said.

"I'll see to absolutely everything," I responded, my voice projecting calm assurance.

"Good. And, Annalise?"

"Yes, Daddy?"

"Intimate. Got it?"

"Absolutely." I said, calculating the square footage of the formal gardens and the placement options for the sailcloth tent rental as I hung up.

A party, planned by me! A real, live social event! This was the moment I had been waiting for. *I have a million things to do,* I thought. *This is going to be the event of the season!* Forget *Guest of a Guest,* this would be a society-page feature! The notoriously reclusive Gerald Hoff was finally opening his doors, letting in the world to see . . . *Todd Evergreen?*

None of this made any sense, and that part the least.

Granted, Evergreen was rich—and even more so since Daddy had bought up the Rock Exchange. The press was having a field day with the whole thing. But why would Daddy finally let down the moat for some computer geek?

I know Daddy thought him a savvy businessman, having heard for myself in the days leading up to the sale. But as Daddy often said himself, "Business is business, kiddo. They're my clients, not my friends."

Todd Evergreen, I thought happily, must be an exception.

▪

The week he closed the Rock Exchange, Daddy had holed up in his study, only emerging to shower, his voice booming all the way from the east wing as he championed the merits of Evergreen to anyone who would listen, i.e., potential stockholders and his board of directors.

I regularly stopped by under the guise of ice restocking, secretly fearing I would find him dead of a aneurysm or, even worse, having lost the deal.

That is what he lived for, after all. The Kill. I understood that. In many ways, I was just the same.

Besides, I wanted to keep abreast of developments, seeing as how this was my legacy he was negotiating. And then there was the décor!

One of the perks to Mother's retreat? Daddy had given me permission to begin an overall revamp of the estate, which I saw as a slow but sure erasure of her very existence. By the time I was done, every remnant would be disposed of, every dead skin cell wiped away.

Daddy had other concerns, I suppose. Inevitably, I would find him pacing the leather-and-mahogany oasis—I had achieved Ralph Lauren meets *Downton Abbey* fox-hunt-with-a-modern-edge perfectly—while ranting into his hands-free.

"Cross-platform, transmedia hub, but take it up a notch. This is Kickstarter with a hitch. You don't just invest, you own a piece." I refilled the ice bucket—hand-sculpted Gucci with rustic appeal, the handles knotted leather—and then straightened up his desk a bit. Daddy didn't seem to notice, he was that worked up. "Let me put this in context. Every music-snob schmuck sayin', 'Listen to this group, I discovered 'em?' Now they really did, even own a piece of the pie. It's like going from groupie to part-time manager overnight, you gettin' this?"

Daddy unbent paper clips as he talked, reforming them into circles. "Those Instagram kids raised fifty mil before they sold to Facebook." He aimed one clip at the elk-antler chandelier. "Evergreen raised one fifty." The metal circle flew, catching on a point.

There had to be forty of them, at least.

"Kid can sell, I'll give him that. But he also knows a sure thing. And imagine what happens when we take that shit public." Then he noticed me. "Hey, baby."

"Hi, Daddy."

"No, not you," he bellowed into the headset. "What, ya think I'm a queer? I'll call you back." He clicked a button and smiled at me.

"You did not need to hang up, Daddy."

"Courtesy call. He'll do what I say."

"How is it going?"

"Not bad." He sat down, stretching back in his walnut, leather desk chair. "But tell me what you think. You Rock Exchange it like the rest of the kids?"

"Some of my friends have invested. But I prefer my interest not dependent on some guitar-playing hippies living out of their vans."

A moment, then Daddy roared with laughter. "You're something else, baby. I'll tell ya."

I grinned. I had not seen him this happy in a long time. One year, eleven months, and twelve hours, to be exact.

The day of Mother's relocation.

Still chuckling, he aimed, shot, and hooked another paper-clip circle.

"I really wish you wouldn't, Daddy. That was handmade."

"Oh yeah? How much it cost me?"

"Ten thousand. Give or take."

"For some fucking antlers?"

"Language, Daddy!"

"I coulda gone on safari for that. Gotten you a whole herd."

"Different species. Besides, it is the craftsmanship you are paying for."

He grinned at me. "I'll close this today, just you see. And, Annalise?"

"Yes, Daddy?"

"This one's gonna be big."

▪

The party, I knew, was about something far greater than some tech nerd with a clever start-up.

After all these years of self-imposed isolation, of battling Mother's mania, Daddy was finally letting the world in.

Daddy is a whiz with the numbers, but the game is my responsibility. And I knew, with Mother finally out of the picture, we would be unstoppable. I'm talking private club invites, Hoff endowments and our name on the side of buildings.

Life would be one long gala, with yours truly hosting.

It wouldn't come easy, but I'd done the preparation. Good, seeing as how I had two hundred years to make up for. Unlike my boyfriend, Miller Crawford III, my ancestors didn't take a little vacay cruise on the *Mayflower*. They were like everyone else, sailing coach class to Ellis Island.

To many, the odds would appear insurmountable. But, as my father is fond of saying, "Odds are for pussies. I don't play them, my baby. I *make* them."

This weekend would go perfectly. Every detail would sparkle with sophistication, from the artfully manicured privet hedges to the gold-embossed place cards. I would welcome people from the veranda, our two-point-seven-acre, six-bedroom, seven-point-five-bath, French-château-inspired estate rising, majestic, behind me.

The party will be held in the gardens, I decide quickly, with the shade trellis dripping over multilevel stone terraces, the squash courts and parterre open to strolling visitors. And yet, I will limit bathroom access to the second level of the house, the route requiring guests to pass the sitting room and the paneled library, the home theater, the billiards room, and the high-tech gym and sumptuously decorated master suite.

The enormous estate was a concession prize, of course, after Daddy forced me to move from the city. *The Hamptons are calm,* he'd said, citing their off-season offering of tranquillity and restfulness.

In other words? *Boring. As. Shit.*

Daddy could not have cared less about the calm; what he wanted was to minimize the opportunity for Mother to make public scenes requiring police intervention. She had already been banned from Bloomies for slapping a salesgirl, Tiffany's for a fit of hysterics that had resulted in several shattered glass displays, and the corner bodega for shoplifting, among other useless items, forty-five Mars bars.

I had found the stash myself and felt a flush of relief. *She's got an eating disorder!* I had thought, elated. *And this nut-job act is just a cover!*

I mean, we lived on the Upper East Side. Binging and purging was practically a hobby, Ladies Who Lunch discussing their various techniques over manicure tables.

Then I found the thirty-eight Bic lighters, eighteen Our Lady of Guadalupe candles, and sixty-six packets of superglue. Mother wasn't just crazy but a kleptomaniac to boot.

This enormous estate, Daddy had believed, would make everything better. Unfortunately, that was to be impossible with *her* inside it.

But now the gates had swung open, the house and I finally allowed to breathe. And this party? The perfect showcase for real estate *and* hostess.

Miller would be reminded of my many charms; Daddy's girlfriend, Candace, affirmed in her decision to be my debutante sponsor.

And Daddy himself? He'd finally see the full extent of my capabilities. Pretty soon, he'd agree to a year off college and a position at *The Set*, even make me a fashion editor. And if anyone blamed nepotism, they could fuck themselves. My father can do what he wants. After all, it's his magazine.

■

At 5:42 a.m., I wake with a confident smile. *The world is my oyster,* I think, *only I'll turn that pearl into a flawless-cut, six-carat Harry Winston.*

At 6:02 a.m., after my brief tête-à-tête with Ms. Post, I review my daily words of inspiration.

To be excellent begins with aligning your thoughts and words. That one is from Oprah, who started out as a crack baby and now has a $52 million estate in Montecito, California, she calls the Promised Land.

I might be wrong about the crack-baby part, but I'm sure it was something equally as sucky. I know the house part is true, though. And despite the tacky moniker, that's the part that really matters.

At 6:22, I spend twelve minutes engaged in yogic breathing, which offers both relaxation and abdominal toning. Simultaneously, I send eight texts and a Snapchat to Miller. Above all, I am a firm believer in multitasking.

At 6:34, I open the curtains and let in the Hamptons. Then I chug eight ounces of water, pop a Zannie, and head toward the bathroom.

You make your own destiny, I chant as I go. *It won't be easy, but it'll be worth it.*

I put Beyoncé on the waterproof sound system, rinse my hair until every strand squeaks, and then have my morning date with the hydrotherapy spray nozzle. I have to give myself kudos for choosing the digital spa, even though Daddy had been a little miffed at the expenditure. In the end, he'd forgiven me, as I knew he would. After all, I have good taste; the oil-rubbed bronze fixtures are completely yummy. And the water pressure? Magic.

Stress relief is a nonnegotiable.

Getting myself off is easy. There isn't much time, so I go to my standby fantasy, the one where my boyfriend, Miller Crawford III, fucks me in a public location. Preferably one that is both unsavory and unsanitary in nature. Where should it be today? A movie theater, perhaps?

No, I think. *A bar bathroom. Some really sordid bar in some waste of a place. The East Village, perhaps. And Miller pulls me inside a stall, hiking up my dress, and calls me an uppity bitch. . . .*

In real life, Miller treats me as though I were as delicate as a rare orchid. In his eyes, I'm the antithesis of those UGG-wearing skank whores in his class at Columbia. I'm worth care because I'm valuable. But sometimes, you just don't want gentle.

Not that I hadn't tried to change that.

▪

Last year Miller and I had been in Daddy's Trump International apartment after a graceful—and early—exit from Winter Formal, which was a disaster of nuclear proportions. My infantile schoolmates could shell out for makeup artists and Privé updos as well as anyone, but the whole monstrosity was still an homage to tastelessness. That's what happens when the decorating committee chair is a scholarship student who favors Express over Prada and the formal dinner is supplied by a midlevel kosher caterer. *Fuck Shannah Rhineberg and her agenda,* I had thought. Since her father had endowed the new Audiovisual Center last Christmas, the administration would wipe her ass if so requested. I mean, I saw her bat mitzvah on that reality show, and I could have sworn I saw a ham on the buffet table.

Anyway, back to the Trump. I don't think Daddy had seen this place since the Realtor bought it. *A tax write-off,* he said, handing me his Palladium. *Go ahead and put some stuff in.* By the time I'd finished, he had a crash pad fit for *Architectural Digest.*

True, the Trump element is a tad garish, and I could do without all that black glass and bronze in the lobby. I'd have preferred Park Avenue, but Daddy is old friends with the Donald, a perfectly nice man even with décor preferences that scream *tycoon compensating for extraordinarily small penis.*

On the plus side were the floor-to-ceiling windows and the spectacular view. From the forty-fourth floor, the city seems laid on a platter, just waiting to be eaten.

It wasn't easy, but I'd convinced Daddy to allow me residence during the school week. His guilt over our relocation had helped. I'd cited statistical averages on New York prep schools versus those in the Hamptons, promising to return every weekend. In the end, he'd agreed, just as I had predicted.

As for Mother, she wasn't even consulted.

Now that she was gone, Daddy had chilled a bit, and I could sometimes finagle a Saturday as well. Especially good since Winter Formal fell on one.

"Do you think my father would donate a wing to the school?" I wondered aloud as I teetered over to the Eames sofa in Daddy's living room. I was slurring but not sloppy.

"No way," Miller said. "He's way too gangster for that. Dude knows how to spend his money. I mean, just look at this place. That sound system is *sick*!" Miller turned up the volume.

Who cares about a stupid dance? I had thought. *This is so much better.* Even if I had to hear some thug wannabe rhapsodize about banging his bitches at a crazy decibel.

Miller's taste in music was questionable, but I had been drunk enough that it did not matter. Neither did some dance more fit for a Hilton off the Jersey turnpike than the Plaza.

What mattered? That my boyfriend was überrich and looked supersexy in his Tom Ford tuxedo. Half a tux, really.

He'd taken off his shirt an hour earlier and was now reciting lyrics and fist-pumping to the beat like some Staten Island frat boy. And still, he was completely yummy. Cut from those years of crew team and tan even in winter. He had lost his gym card but not the six-pack. Just like his pedigree, he'd been born with it.

Miller was perfection. Throw in tackle football, gay him up a little, and he could shoot a campaign for Ralph Lauren.

God, I want to fuck him.

It had been a month since he'd even fingered me, and I hardly saw him since he'd started Columbia. Not that I was sitting around waiting. Between college apps and field hockey and heading up various school organizations, I had plenty of obligations.

Still.

I took a gulp from my drink. I had been waiting weeks for tonight, and it sure wasn't for the Euro-trash DJ.

Only one question remained: *What the hell was Miller's problem?*

Here I was in a fully loaded penthouse with no parental guidance and plenty of sexual frustration. If you didn't know better, I could have been the poster child for *needy rich-girl slut who confuses fucking with affection*. I was a masturbation fantasy and somehow my boyfriend had not noticed.

I leaned on the sofa in a way that was both fetching and cleavage enhancing, so much so that it bordered on nip slip. *C'mon, Miller,* I thought. *Get off your ass and take advantage of me.*

Instead, he popped another beer. Pabst Blue Ribbon. My father had a stocked bar of top-shelf liquor, but Miller thought drinking piss-flavored liquid from cans was somehow subversive.

I could not wait for this "cool" phase to be over.

He chugged the whole thing and reached for another. If he did not get with the game soon, we'd be risking a little stroll into limp-dick territory.

I will not make the first move, I thought. *It goes against everything I stand for.*

Miller is a Crawford. Landing a Crawford takes strategy. And with great goals, you must make some concessions. Waiting for Miller's sorry drunk ass to jump me being just one of them.

"Do all boys go through these phases?" I had asked.

"What phases?" he had said, mid-fist-pump.

"Pretending you are from Compton instead of a Connecticut compound?"

"Baby, this isn't about money. It's about experience. I'm down with the real world, y'know? Life on the streets."

The streets of Westport, maybe.

Well, I thought, it could be worse. At least he wasn't one of those scenesters working the VIP circuit, blowing coke with Kanye at the Boom Boom Room. At least he hadn't turned dandy, like those steel-heir brothers in their lip gloss and ascots, posing for European cologne campaigns, quoting Warhol in *Vanity Fair,* and occasionally referring to themselves as "iconoclasts" in the media.

Some things were irreversible.

Miller would be fine, I knew, emerging untainted from his foray into rich-boy thugdom. There wouldn't be damaging press or drug arrests or reality-show cameos. He could carry on the family legacy, even run for Congress.

I would see to all that.

Miller had never mentioned political aspirations, but I was keeping his options open.

He would outgrow this, just like all his other prep school friends. By the time they hit the Ivies, most readily accept their fate as the future leaders of the free world.

I sipped my Kir Royale. Half ounce crème de cassis, two and a fourth ounces Bollinger. The flute was Glazze crystal, the mix sublime. Identical to the four others that had come before it.

A nugget of morning inspiration rose from my consciousness. *For in war just as in loving you must always keep on shoving.* General George S. Patton, *The Patton Papers.*

Fuck this, I thought, making a decision. I drained my drink and rose from the midcentury Danish-designed sofa.

For a second, I wobbled, then found my footing and demanded everything stop spinning. I had a sexy, half-naked boyfriend, dimmed track lighting, and an innocent-schoolgirl-who-secretly-wants-it negligee under my brand-new Stella McCartney.

Forget the mood music. I was ready.

▪

When I had informed Miller of Winter Formal, I could almost hear his eyes roll through the phone. "I'm in college, baby. I don't have time for that kids' stuff."

"What are you so busy doing?"

"I got a full load, Annalise. I've got a massive paper due next week."

Bullshit, I had thought. *You haven't cracked a book all semester. Your father endowed a dorm and ballistics research lab. You could call in a bomb threat to the president and they would just cite "freshman adjustment issues."*

"I'm sorry, baby. There's just no way."

Granted, it was not really his decision. I could always get what I wanted, the only question being the method.

Never underestimate the power of pouting or blow jobs, and my talents in both are exemplary.

The latter was not an option. A surprise visit to campus would reek of desperation, and I am sure his dorm already reeks of cum rags and dirty laundry. I had never seen it, not that I wanted to. For now, we spent our quality time at Trump. I had even given him a key.

Not to mention, he would want to reciprocate. While Miller has many excellent qualities, being versed in the oral arts is not among them. It's jaw calisthenics, as if he were eating a sloppy joe instead of my pussy.

"You understand. Right, baby?" Miller breathed uncomfortably.

Without realizing it, I'd done half the work already. I contemplated the state of my cuticles, letting him suffer.

"Annalise? Are you still there?"

"Mmmmm-hmmmm." Noncommittal.

"C'mon, baby. Don't do that to me."

"Do what?"

"You know what. I hate when you go all quiet like that."

Another silence. Perfectly weighted, of course.

"I know you're pissed off at me, baby."

"Not at all," I said cheerily. "I know you have priorities."

"So . . . you're okay with it?"

"Of course."

I could practically hear his will breaking.

"But it's, like, really important to you? Right?"

Time to close the deal. Though only to be used on special occasions, the little-girl voice could work wonders. Forget habit; men, I had come to understand, are creatures of obviousness.

"I just miss you," I murmured. "That's all."

Now Miller was the one sighing. "Oh, baby. Okay. I guess I can . . . I mean, if it means that much to you."

I hung up the phone feeling strangely unsatisfied. Occasionally I longed for something more. A man who offers a challenge, perhaps.

Stop it, I told myself. *A trust fund is far preferable.*

▪

One thing about Miller: he was uncomplicated, living up to the expectations I had set for him.

But this time, something was different. Maybe it was his newfound status as an Ivy League student, or perhaps my unexpectedly aggressive behavior.

Maybe it was the Pabst Blue Ribbon.

I did not care the reason; in fact, I did not care about anything. Not that we were rolling around on the crazy-expensive antique Persian or that Miller had ripped the dress I'd practically begged the Bergdorf personal shopper to track down.

Rugs could be dry-cleaned, tailors could work miracles. But what could not be predicted? That my perfect gentleman of a boyfriend would bite my nipples and smack my ass and channel some inner rock-star caveman stud I never knew existed.

This is not how you treat a rare orchid, I thought, reaching into his tuxedo pants like a bulimic going for a carton of Ben & Jerry's. *Control yourself,* I said in my head.

Then I didn't listen.

I was as rough as he, frantically pulling on clothes, then reaching down and gripping him like the StairMaster rail on the steepest incline, pumping him till his wild, glassy eyes were nearly crossing.

He only moaned louder.

I was drunk with black-currant liqueur and power.

Miller growled, pulling me on top of him, gaze unfocused. The rap guy shouted about how good some ho grinded him, but I was pretty sure I'd give her a run for her money.

"You little slut," moaned Miller.

I could have cried it was so romantic.

You can have it all, I thought, elated. "Pull my hair."

Miller grunted, tossing his head from side to side. He reached out like a blind man, gripped me by the roots, and pulled.

The sting was ferocious. "Harder," I ordered. Patton would have loved it.

This time I felt it in my toes. *Again,* I thought, wanting him to rip every keratin-treated strand out by the socket. "C'mon, damn it. Don't be a pussy. Harder!"

He grabbed two more generous fistfuls, the rapper shouting about his Glock and humping. "Now," I hissed. "I want you to hurt me, Miller."

His name is what did it.

Miller froze as if someone had smacked him across the face. With a crowbar. Suddenly, he was scooting backward, sliding off the Persian. He huddled in a naked ball, arms wrapped tightly around his knees, on the imported Italian floor tiles.

He looked like a horrified little boy. *Pathetic,* I thought.

"Oh my God, Annalise. I don't know . . . what I was thinking? Oh my God. Baby. I'm so, so sorry."

No! I thought. *Don't do this!*

Too late. I could see everything in his perfectly symmetrical face; explanations would be useless.

I wanted to scream at him, slap him across the cheek. Tell him to grow up and fuck me like a man.

Instead, I just looked at him.

"I'll make it up to you, I swear it. I'd never hurt you, Annalise. Not ever."

He was right. He didn't have the balls.

I'll worry about physical fulfillment when I'm chairing the Met Ball, I thought. For now, a $500 showerhead would have to suffice.

▪

I know: Freud would have a field day with me. I don't take the short bus, after all. I have a Bentley waiting.

Refreshed, I turn off the water, squeeze the excess moisture from my hair, and cover myself head to toe in La Mer.

Wrapped in a fluffy towel, I stare at myself in the mirror.

The girls at school may think I'm cold and calculating, even scary, but the boys think something else entirely. I drop my towel, observe myself naked from every angle.

My boobs are on the larger side of B. Not huge, but perky, the nipples pointed upward like they're smiling at you. My butt is round and tight from all the field hockey, and my hair naturally glossy, a proven indicator of health and vitality.

A hot piece of ass, that's what guys think. And for that I am eternally grateful. Still, I go by the use it or lose it theory. Self-maintenance is an imperative.

Another case in point: my mother.

In preparation for today, I had every hair waxed off my body, even the ones I didn't know existed. On Tuesday, I had my arches done by that Fifth Avenue eyebrow guru, who'd run his fingertips across them for half an hour, as though hypnotizing the follicles. In the end, he'd plucked four hairs and charged my father's Centurion $200. *Magic.* A waste of time, even if Lady Gaga is a client.

On Thursday, a new dress from Escada and a French manicure. The dress is classic, the polish subtle. Sexy is overrated.

I sigh. The reflection staring back at me is purely my own, and utterly satisfactory.

Tonight I will put this to good use, I think. *Tonight I will make everything happen.*

At 6:45 a.m., the Hamptons morning was ripe with promise, my calendar painstakingly scheduled. Now, I'm aware that I missed a notation:

3:37 p.m. Commence with Shitfest of Epic Proportions.

▪

Now, with the guests nearly here, I'm on the edge of a nervous breakdown. I contemplate popping another Xanax. Then I do it.

I'm in the kitchen, frantically cutting crudités and hating everyone. Especially the caterer, whose car had an issue. *The muffler,* she texts me. *On my way.*

You better be, I think, *or have a good lawyer.*

Outside, the tent is erected, the servers wasting time until the food arrives, probably ashing their cigarettes in the koi pond and dipping into the liquor. The half order, since the booze-delivery guys fucked up, insisting there is a Dom drought in the greater Hamptons vicinity and thereby forcing me to send Dimitri, Daddy's security guy, to fetch resources.

Four hours later, Dimitri has not returned and I'm chopping limp, moldy vegetables to the faint strains of Beethoven.

At least the string quartet showed.

I know exactly whom I can blame for the state of the vegetables: Renata, who does not consider food shopping to be part of her household responsibilities. In fact, her sole obligation seem to be leading an online chat group for sexually confused Latino teenagers and ordering shit off the Home Shopping Network.

As for her sexuality, I'd rather not think about it. But all arrows point to bull dyke with a big-ass attitude and ax to grind.

"Renata!" I yell through the chopping. It's the fifth time I've called her, and I know for a fact the bitch heard me.

"*Sí*, Missus Annalise?" Renata says sweetly. I glance up and nearly hack off a finger. I can see she's disappointed that I didn't.

"Have you seen the monogrammed napkins?"

"*¿Qué?*"

"The napkins. The cloth ones? With the initials? I've looked everywhere."

She stares at me blankly.

"Never mind. The caterer is late. Have you seen to the flower arrangements?"

"*No comprende*. Speak more slow."

"Forget the flowers, okay? I'll do it. But what about the guest bedroom?"

She just opens her eyes wider.

I know her game. She speaks English as well as I do, and I'm pretty sure she's to blame for the wine-cellar shortage. The reason I had to call the delivery guys after the weekenders had already wiped out the selection.

One thing about the Hamptons: besides tennis and deep-sea fishing, boozing and pills are the preferred pastime. "I asked you to make up the guest room. Yesterday."

"No, I do not think so."

"Yup, I'm pretty sure."

She sighs. I'll bet she's never even been to Guatemala. Probably born and raised in Hoboken. No matter how many times I ask, Daddy refuses to fire her. He feels guilty, I figure, since Mother adored her. As much as that agoraphobic, drugged-out whack job was capable of loving anything besides her pill collection.

I feel the heat rise to my face and wonder, for the gazillionth time, if crazy runs in the family. Maybe it's already laser-cut into my DNA, and one day it will bubble up from inside. Just like that, I'll go from Junior Class Prefect with a 3.87 GPA (*fuck that granola art teacher. B-minus? She wears Crocs, for fucksake. What does she know about aesthetics?*) and morph into *Girl, Interrupted.*

Don't get distracted, Annalise. I glare at Renata, trying to keep focus.

I feel the fury boiling.

One of the tests by which to distinguish between the woman of breeding and the woman merely of wealth, is to notice the way she speaks to dependents.

Post again, that deluded ho-bag. Easy to say when the help doesn't harbor murder fantasies about you. Renata blames me for my mother's leaving.

She's right, of course. *Still.*

This is a test. Everything is a test. Fuck Emily Post. What I need is a real-live role model, not a cold, dead corpse, pinkie still pointed while six feet under.

Then it comes to me: *What would Kate Middleton do?*

I place the knife gently on the counter, forcing my lips into a placid smile. "Now, Renata," I say with a firm, regal calmness. "As I'm sure you are well aware, my father has put a great deal of trust on those serving in his employ. And if he became aware of their neglect, I am sure he would be most unhappy. The same is true of their misuse of his generosity."

She stares at me blankly.

"Meaning," I hiss, "I tell him you don't do shit around here except watch TV and drink all our fucking liquor. And that you took the La Perla bras from my mother's closet."

A pause. Got her on the bra one. I'd been saving that for a special occasion. "Where you put the sheets?"

I knew she understood English.

"To the left of the bed. Brand-new, still in the package." *One-thousand-twenty-thread-count sateen,* I think. *Woven in Italy. For what I paid, I could buy your illegal Guatemalan cousins. That is, if you weren't from Jersey.* "And don't forget to mop the adjoining bathroom and put out fresh towels."

She glares, lips pinched into white lines. Then she turns on her heels and exits. A loud buzz. The intercom. A high, childlike voice.

"Annalise. Could you come up here, please? I need you."

I can hear Renata snort all the way from the foyer.

Regroup, Annalise. Don't lose it.

I stabilize myself on the edge of the counter and attempt to ward off the impending panic. *What you need is some positive fucking self-talk. Or do you want to throw away years of planning, loser?*

You are a Hoff, Annalise. There are expectations

I will do this because there is no other choice. I will do this because it was destined.

■

R*ockefeller, Astor, Vanderbilt, Hoff. Rockefeller, Astor, Vanderbilt, Hoff. Rockefeller, Astor, Vanderbilt, Hoff.*

I chant with each heel click to the French-limestone staircase.

At the top, a cry rings out. "Are you coming, Annalise?"

Candace.

While the little girl voice can be effective on select occasions, as a lifestyle choice it is only fit for B-list actresses and strippers. "Annalise?"

I forgot one. *Lilliput.* And when a Lilliput beckons, you have no choice but to follow orders.

Candace Lilliput is wearing a push-up bra and thong bikini. The thong part is in front and consists of a strand of pearls pushed into her Brazilian-waxed coochie.

"Will he like it?" she says, biting her bottom lip and posing for me. Sometimes I wonder if my future stepmother wants to fuck me. Then I remember I'm not special; Candace Lilliput is equal-opportunity slutty.

She's also heir to an international-banking fortune and sponsoring my debutante status. At least, she says she is. As of yet, I haven't received the official invitation.

Glad I took that second Zannie.

"Of course," I tell her, forcing myself not to turn in disgust. "It's adorable."

"The pearls are from Tahiti."

"An excellent use of their most valuable export."

"Oh, Annie, you're so funny."

"Please don't call me Annie."

"Sorry, darling," she says flippantly, then stands in front of the three-way vanity carefully examining every angle. "I just want to make your daddy happy."

"You do." *You're low-maintenance, sexually available, and have double-D titties. He's rich and busy. OkCupid couldn't have worked this better.*

Then again, I'm the one who introduced them. And, yes, I knew exactly what I was doing.

"Especially tonight," she says. "This is the first time he's introduced me to a client. Do I have cellulite?"

"You have to have fat to have cellulite."

"I don't know. I see something. Maybe I should get that Pilates pro from the club. All the girls say he's a genius."

Probably because they're all fucking him, I think.

"But getting an appointment is near impossible."

I nod sympathetically. Since the squash pro gave everyone HPV, the Pilates guy has been busier than ever.

"I just don't want him to lose interest."

"He's utterly infatuated with you, Candace."

"I don't know. He hasn't paid as much attention as usual."

She stares at herself, waiting for me to speak. Waiting for my advice. My mind has gone blank. Perhaps the second Xanax is kicking in. "I just want tonight to go absolutely perfectly," she adds hopefully.

Just then, I do something I never do. Something I find wholly reprehensible.

"Annie? Why are you crying?"

Then my eyes are blurry. All I can make out is flesh rushing at me. She's got me in her vise grip and is leading me to the bed, wrapping her stick arms around me. I almost forget she's naked, that's how embarrassing this is.

Don't be a pussy, Annalise. Tears are for little girls and weaklings. Get it together!

I try to stand, but she pulls me back down. She's pretty strong for someone with borderline anorexia.

"I have so much to do," I tell her, nauseated at my own blubbering. "That's all. And it's only forty-five minutes until the guests—"

"It'll be fine, darling. I promise." She rocks me in her arms, which is thoroughly clichéd and disgusting. And for some reason, I don't mind it.

"I just want everything to go as planned. The caterer is late and I haven't done the table and—"

"Why are you so worried?" She holds me by the shoulders and stares at me. Instantly, her confusion turns to a knowing smile.

"I know what this is about. It's Crawford, isn't it? You heard the rumors."

"What rumors?"

She looks like I smacked her. Then she rushes over to the mirror, giggles, and nervously applies lipstick.

I don't have time for this. I don't care if her family name is on esteemed institutions, I do not have the energy for my vapid, possibly inbred future stepmother's imbecilic behavior.

"What rumors, Candace?" I shriek. If Kate Middleton heard, she'd find me terribly common. And she can go fuck herself, right along with Candace and the caterer and everyone else who has turned my triumphant day into a big shit-a-palooza.

"He's been spotted with quite a few other women," she says matter-of-factly. "The dismissible sort. And of course, that's only gossip. But these rumors tend to have some truth to them, and I've heard from quite a few sources." She does not turn from the vanity. Her reflection is one of regal disinterest. I've broken a rule and I know it.

Society Rule Number One: *Never lose control of your emotions.*

"But not to worry, sweetie. Men have these silly proclivities. Which is why you must work hard to keep their interest." She turns her head from side to side, examining her work. "Let me finish my face. Then I'll help you clean up the little hostess mess you've made. It will all be just fine, Annie. Things have a way of working out exactly as expected."

She turns and smiles, lipstick applied with razor-sharp precision. "Pearls are Tahiti's main export, you say? Isn't that just fascinating?"

2 CHAPTER

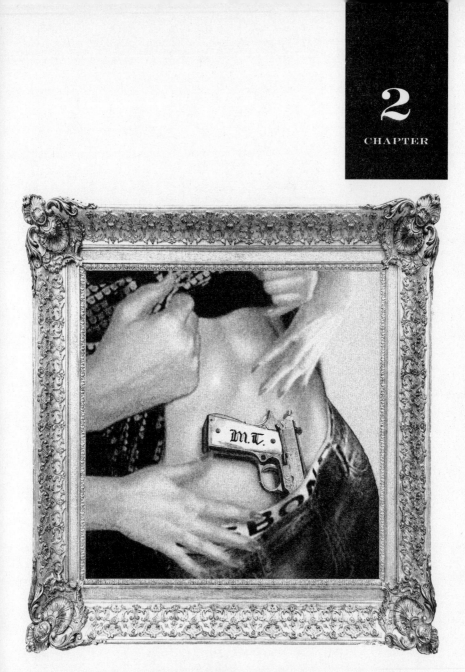

Say hello to my little friend @Miller_Crawford_III #badass #T4L #bitchesloveme by Anonymous

M.C.

"Who the fuck are you?"

A total stranger is on the floor in front of me. He groans and rolls over.

I'm sitting, but everything is spinning. I don't remember getting here. I force my eyes to focus. I know this place. This is my place. Still, there are questions.

Why is the bed wet? Did I piss myself? And how the fuck did I get here?

But most of all, who is this dude on my floor?

No, not piss. Just sweat. Booze sweat. Like a police outline, only a wet one. Good. But there was something else. Something important.

"Fuck!" I yell.

The asshole wakes up. His eyes flutter. "Hey, man." He rolls over again and starts snoring.

I hate mornings like these. Afternoons? I grab for my phone: 3:42. *Shit-balls-piss-ass-Jesus-on-a-fucking-crutch-I-hate-my-life*. I've got forty minutes, and there's no way in hell I'm gonna make it.

Too bad that isn't a fucking option. I'm brushing my teeth with one hand, splashing water in my pits with the other. Desy's on speaker.

"There's someone on my floor!" I say. "And I've never fucking seen him!"

A peal of laughter. Peal. I'd never heard one before Desy. I thought it was cute last night. I thought she was, too.

That was before the part I don't remember.

"Should we brunch, muffin? I know a fabulous place—"

"Are you kidding? I'm late. But what the fuck happened?"

"M.C., *sweetheart.* I do find your blackout episodes endearing." I'm inside the walk-in closet now, still dripping. I'm digging through the dirty laundry. When does the maid come? I thought this place was full-service.

Though it's pretty great, I gotta admit. Massive Tribeca loft with multiroom sound system and sick view of Manhattan. Concrete and steel with a chrome makeover. A real panty-dropper.

Which is why I haven't told my girlfriend about it. She thought I was living in the dorms like the other freshmen. First year, it's required.

But I don't do required. And I'm not living in some shitty dorm. Especially one with my last name on it.

Lucky my girlfriend wouldn't go near a dorm. She'd be afraid of catching something.

I find the least wrinkled khakis available. "It wasn't a blackout," I tell her. "I remember . . . most of it."

Besides, sometimes I don't want anyone here. Don't want strangers touching my shit, sitting on my sofa. If I'm going to hook up, there are always other options. This crib is all mine.

Except last night, I guess. How fucked-up had I been?

"But seriously, Des, who is the fucktard on my floor?"

She laughs. Again. I wish she'd stop. I'm busted up and late and some dickhead is on my rug and might have ass-raped me in my sleep for all I know. I don't have the time for Desdemona Goldberg.

"Does he have brownish hair?" she says. Finally.

"Blond."

"Tall?"

"I guess."

"Ironic facial hair?"

"What the fuck does that mean, Desy?"

"Muttonchops? A goatee? A flavor savor? Don't you know anything, silly boy? That and vests are all the rage in Brooklyn."

"What the fuck do I know about Brooklyn? I don't do Brooklyn."

"You did last night. We took a taxi to Williamsburg right after the Sexpot."

"A taxi? You gotta be kidding me. And what the fuck is Sexpot?" I finish buckling my belt. Shit, I missed two loops. I pull it out and start from scratch.

Desy sighs. "If you don't remember, that's devastating. The beauty-salon bar? You sat under a hair dryer, M.C.! Is this ringing a bell?"

"You're making that shit up."

"*Silly!* You adored every minute! Totes bonded with Helga!"

"Helga?"

"The Russian drag queen who gave you a manicure, sweetcheeks!"

I look down. "What is this gay shit on my hands?"

"Homophobia is so nineties, M.C. But isn't it presh? Lollipop Sprinkle. And the glittery finish? *C'est magnifique!*"

"How do I get this shit off?"

"Polish remover! But why would you want to take it off? It's so glam rock! Besides, you were the one who wanted a manicure. Practically begged them to fit you in—"

"Wait, I paid for this?"

"Of course! Forty dollars. And you tipped a hundred!"

"Seriously? What a fucking scam! A whore would have been cheaper. And a better use of my money."

Silence. Even scarier than the laughing. Then screaming. "Is that how you see me, too, M.C.? *Another hundred-dollar whore?*"

Shit. I pressed the crazy button.

"You know that isn't what I meant—"

"You sure couldn't get enough last night! Why the fuck am I wasting my time on you? You snort *all* my coke at Marquee, then go on and on. All your plans for me. The tour, the record dropping. *Blah blah blah.* Is everything you say utter bullshit?"

"Wait, Desy—"

"I can't believe I let you touch my pussy! My pussy is *sacred*, you asshole!"

No way. Wait. Just a second.

The unisex bathroom. Track lighting. Auto-fogging stalls.

Red walls. Desy. Pushed up against one of them.

I'm the one who pushed her.

It's all coming back. Only problem? Now I don't want it to.

She's still shrieking. I turn down the volume on my phone. That whacked-out bipolar bitch. She must have forgot her trazodone again. Or just didn't take it. Does it on purpose. Says it makes her more *interesting*.

Did I really fuck her? I guess I really care about this record label. Took one for the team. She's hot, but you get a side of hot mess right along with it.

I look at the clock: 4:10. Already texted for a ride. Now I

gotta get outta here. Volume up again. Desy still shrieking.

"—don't need you or your bullshit wannabe label. My father knows *everyone*! Producers. *Real ones.* You can just go fuck yourself up the—"

"Desy!" I shout. "Shut up! Just for a second!"

"I don't take orders, M.C. Especially from you!"

This time, I use my sexy voice. The I'll-be-your-daddy-and-give-you-a-spanking-you'll-like-it one. "I just want to tell you something, okay? Something important."

Silence. Always works on the crazy bitches. "What?" she squeaks.

Charm, thick as peanut butter. "I think . . . *you are completely adorable.*"

Silence. Peal.

"Only thing—I gotta make my appointment. I hate it, though. It'll hurt me, not hearing your voice. I love your voice, you know that? So . . . can I see you soon?"

"Maybe." All sweetness. Hooked and reeled.

"Good. Just let me ask you something. Baby, will you tell me who the guy on my floor is?"

"Jermaine. He's an electro-funk DJ."

"Electro-funk? That's the lamest thing I ever heard of."

"You loved him last night." She giggles. "Said he really *got* you. Said he could be your long-lost brother."

"Well now, I need him to get the fuck out of my place. Thanks, Desy. You and me, soon. Bye, babe."

"Too-da-loo!" Dial tone. Merciful silence.

Wallet, *check*. Sunglasses, *check*. One quick glance in the mirror. Pretty good. I can work this.

A few quick breaths, a couple of bounces. Punch the air in

front of me like a badass. I'm Muhammad Ali, I'm Mike-fucking-Tyson.

You can do this, man. You can do anything. You, M.C., are the motherfucking shit.

▪

After I've half-dragged/half-carried the half-asleep douche bag down two hallways and in and out of the elevator, I deposit him on the Hudson Street sidewalk. Immediately, I jump in the waiting Benz.

"Call me," he says, just as my door is slamming.

I take off the sunglasses, check the time. Thank fuck for tinted windows.

Four twenty-six. I just might make it.

The privacy partition rolls down.

"Tough night?" Rodney's grinning.

"You know it. Can you get me there in time?"

"Maybe, depends on traffic. We'll have to make that Tower pickup—"

"Tower pickup? Oh, yeah. *Fuck.*"

The Hollywood douche. I forgot. "Okay, Rod. Do your best. But can you make a pit stop at the Duane Reade? I need some nail-polish remover."

He raises his eyebrows.

"Don't even ask," I say with a smile.

"We'll hit up the one on Broadway, Mr. Crawford."

"Fuck. How many times I have to tell you? Mr. Crawford is my father. Just call me Miller."

"That's your father, too."

"I know. Sucks, doesn't it?"

He smiles again. Partition rolls up.

I send a text to Annalise, sigh, and lean back into the leather.

I got it under control. Just like always.

▪

We pull over on Fifth Avenue. Trump Tower. I scan the front of the building. Just the doorman bullshitting with a ratty dude in cargoes. A fucking white kid with dreads. Probably his dealer.

"Where is he?" I mutter. "She said he'd be right here. Waiting."

"You know what this guy looks like?" asks Rodney.

"No idea. Just his name. Phillip something." I check out the area. Always liked this place. Makes no apologies. "Just look for the Hollywhore. He'll be all tan and shiny."

A minute passes. Nothing. Just the doorman and the kid laughing.

"Want me to go inside?" asks Rodney.

"Nah, I'll do it." I reach for the handle.

I made a promise long ago: I won't be *that* guy. The kind who orders staff to do petty bullshit. Sure, there are emergencies. Scoring coke for an after-hours, buying last-minute condoms. As for the rest? I can get my own double latte, thanks. And I can find this Ryan Seacrest wannabe Annalise wants carted to the Hamptons.

I open the car door and groan. The sunlight jumps my ass. I think I singed my eyelashes. "Fuck," I say, reaching for my vintage snakeskin Cazal616s—same as Diddy. "I just had them in my hand." I dig in the seats, check the floorboards.

"This blows anyway. What am I, a carpool service? *And where the fuck is that Hollywood douche bag?*"

"Hey."

I turn. Guy with the cargo pants. *Great.*

He smiles at me. Rumpled Polo, beat-up loafers. Dude's got West Side hoodrat written all over him. Prep school expulsion, I'd put money on it. Little poser peddling shit cut with aspirin and powdered sugar. I'd never score from a guy like this.

I've grown up a lot since high school.

"Thanks, man. But I don't want any."

"Want any what?" A lopsided grin. Got one of those trust-me, I'm-your-buddy faces.

"I said I'm fine, man." This time I'm serious.

Not a flicker. Just stands there, smiling. At least he's blocking the sunlight.

"Seriously, dude, I'm looking for someone, okay?"

"I know. The Hollywood Douche Bag." He shrugs, extends his hand. "Phillip. You found him."

3
CHAPTER

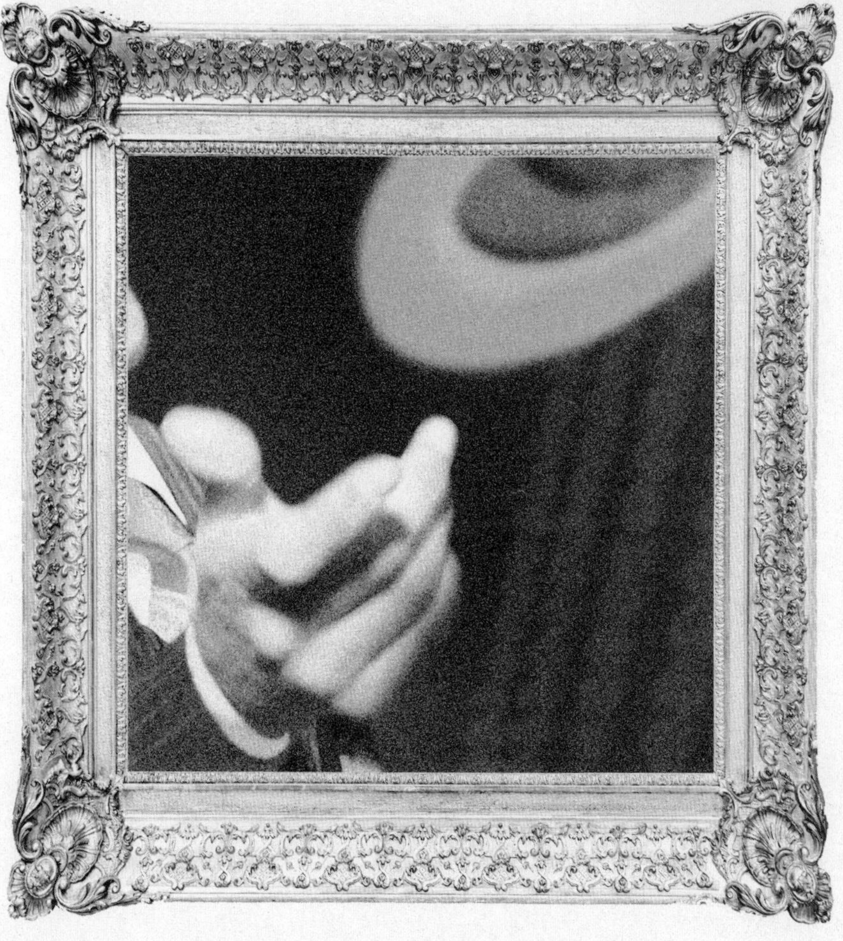

Anal Ring Toss #myfavoritegame @Phillip_Atwater

by Anonymous

Phillip Atwater

Now is the time for apologies. He speaks of his stress, his burdens, his hangover. His demanding classes and demanding girlfriend and family obligations. What is expected of him, and how he cannot meet those unrealistic expectations, and how, ultimately, this moment of failure sums up all the shortcomings in his brief yet overburdened life.

He uses the word *fuck* a lot.

He wrings his hands and taps his feet and fiddles with his sunglasses. The ones that have been on his head the whole time.

He apologizes for his very existence. "It's just been a fucked-up day, man. I mean, I don't know you. But Annalise likes you. And she doesn't *like* anyone. But I've met industry guys, right? And they're asswipes. Not that you're . . ."

Better than a thousand hollow words is one word that brings peace. "Here." I hold up the baggie.

He stops midsentence, eyes wide. Then he smiles.

▪

We pass the miles and the *sebsi* I bought from a wrinkled, old man outside Tangier. The smoke curls up around us, the tinted city flying past, morphing into a smaller city, then only pieces of city, then no city at all. With the push of a button, the driver dissapears. Now it is just the two of us in this cloudy, black-leather cosmos.

Make an island of yourself. Make yourself a refuge.

Though I do not subscribe to a set belief system, Buddha's got some pretty rad pointers.

"The Hamptons." Miller tokes, then leans back and laughs loudly. "*I fucking hate the fucking Hamptons.* Wait, where'd you get this stuff again?"

"Morocco."

"This shit is *sick*. And you brought it back . . ."

"In a can of coffee beans."

"That. Is. Fucking. Insane."

"Best in the world. Roasted over charcoal fires, ground up with mortars. Very ritualistic art form, goes back generations."

"The hash?"

"The coffee."

"Fuck, dude. I meant the hash!"

"Yeah," I say, laughing. "That's pretty good, too. Got the herb from some bros outside Taghazout."

"What were you doing there?"

"Surfing. Trying to figure it all out."

"And did you?"

"Yes. No. Maybe." I suck in, letting the elixir work its magic. "Snagged some killer waves, that's for sure."

We grin at each other. I pass the pipe.

"Like your nails, man," I say.

"Fuck!" he says, reaching for a Duane Reade bag. "Totally forgot about that shit."

"Very glam rock," I say.

■

"Wow, I was expecting—"

"A Hollywood Douche. I know."

"I figured Annalise had her reasons. Wanted to impress her dad, prove she's got contacts. She wants to run his new magazine. And since your mom's, I dunno . . ."

"The most powerful woman in Hollywood? Or so says *Variety*."

He looks uncomfortable. "Shit, this stuff makes it hard to control my mouth."

"Tibetan monks can control their body temperature through mediation. Drop their fingers' and toes' by seventeen percent. They can lower their metabolism, too."

"You're a trip, man."

"It's true, Harvard did a study. They took them fifteen thousand feet up in the Himalayas in the freezing winter, monks wearing nothing but thin shawls. Little guys bedded down right there on the ledge and slept like babies, not even a shiver."

"No fucking way."

I take another toke. "*Tummo* mediation. I tried it myself a few years ago in the sequoia backcountry."

"You wore, like, *a robe*?"

"Nah, my boxers." Now we are laughing. "But I only lasted half an hour. I mean, it was *snowing*."

Somewhere far away someone honks a horn. I pack another bowl.

▪

Are your eyes still closed?"

"Yeah, man."

"You still picturing the hollow tube?"

"Sure."

"This time, let the air travel up into the crown of your head, then down to your navel. Ready? *One. Two. Three.*"

"Okay. I did it."

"You feel anything?"

"I don't know. Maybe. Do that chant thing again."

"*Humee hum too hee too wahe guru.* So . . . are you warmer?"

"Could be. Hold up a sec. Wait . . . yeah. I think I am. For real. Seriously, dude . . . that is . . . *weird as fuck.*"

"I told you, my friend. Inner fire."

▪

There's a buzzing and a bodiless head levitating in the cloud of smoke. "We hit weekend traffic," says the driver. "Want me to crack a window, Mr. Crawford?"

"Call me M.C., you asshole," he says, and the driver chuckles. The screen rises and the windows unroll and I am once again reminded how little we control, how the universe is a series of unexpected events and unseen forces.

I inhale deeply, then watch the smoke spiral upward.

"He drove me to elementary school," says Miller with a wistful smile. "I'd eat the Oreos out of my lunchbox on the way. Never ratted me out."

"That's beautiful, man."

"Yeah, I guess. I mean, he kept me company. Sucks to be an only child. You got sisters and brothers?"

"Three."

"What are their names?"

"Dahnay, Ye-Jun, and Dulcina."

"Say what?"

"They're adopted. Dahnay's thirteen, just starting seventh grade. I'm teaching him to surf and he shows real potential. Stands out, that's for sure. Probably the blackest kid in Malibu. Who isn't on a gardening crew."

Miller starts to laugh, then looks uncomfortable. "It's okay," I tell him kindly. "I meant it to be funny."

He laughs again, though I strongly suspect he's forgotten what was funny in the first place.

"The girls are crazy for him, though, calling and texting all hours. This one sent him a topless picture. She's *eleven*."

"Are you kidding?" Miller says, suddenly alert again. "That is fucking insane. What did you do?"

"Called her mother and said, 'I think your daughter might be dealing with some emotional issues.' And she starts crying, babbling how the father left her for a Penthouse Pet and the girl probably saw her picture, was emulating what she knew, and on and on, about how she'd done everything humanly possible to keep him from leaving her, the new boobs and daily Pilates and fat transplants from her ass to her face, but he'd gone anyway and now she had an eleven-year-old porn-star-in-the-making and had never felt so lonely in her life." I sigh. "And then she asked me to come over and fuck her."

"And?"

"I went over and fucked her."

He stares at me, wordless.

"But afterwards I made her promise to get a child psychologist."

"That is the craziest shit I've ever heard. You see them much? Your siblings?"

"No."

Miller is suddenly uneasy, shifting around on his seat. "Do you want to talk about—"

"No." I smile. "I want to smoke this bowl."

■

"This traffic is bullshit," says Miller. "Gonna be late. And I wanna meet this guy, Evergreen. Dude is a genius. I mean, his site is a game changer." He sighs. "Not to mention, Annalise is gonna bust my balls. Hey, where'd you meet her?"

"Annalise? In the elevator. She just smiled and said, 'You must be Phillip Atwater! I've heard loads about you.' Never met her before in my life, but she seemed sweet."

"*Annalise?* Fuck, I love the girl. But *sweet* isn't the word. . . . I mean, she's hot as shit. And, like, *smart.* Cares about real stuff. Not like those bitches who go crackass 'cause you don't text every second. Talking about their fucking hair for five hours. Their purses. *I got this one before all my friends, Miller! Isn't that amazing?* And I wanna say, 'Don't you get it? I don't give a shit about you, or your fucking purse either.'"

His words are coming faster, his voice growing louder and more agitated.

"Annalise is different, right? She's like, top-shelf. She's Macallan thirty-year and these other girls are, I dunno, Bud on tap. I mean, sometimes you want that. At a bullshit club, maybe. DJ pounding, dance floor full of Jersey chicks in stripper heels. But do you want beer every single day of your freakin' life? Do you want, like, a wine cellar full of kegs?" He pounds the seat with his fist, red spots blooming on each cheek. "You know what I'm saying, man?"

I have no idea, but I'm pretty sure it has nothing to do with beer.

"We are not going in circles, we are going upwards," I recite. *"The path is a spiral; we have already climbed many steps."*

"Lyrics?"

"To life, maybe. *Siddhartha.*"

He stares at me, face screwed up with concentration, jaw clenched. I breathe deeply, sending rays of calm in his direction. I've often been the one to nurse others through the torrid waves of bad-tripdom, once reviving a Finnish girl from a mushroom overdose at a Scandinavian rockabilly festival using this very method.

Under my gaze, his body relaxes, and for a second, I can almost feel his heart rate grow slower, steadying itself to an even tick.

"Are you for real?" he asks.

"Nothing is real."

"How come I never met you? I'm at the Tower all the time."

"I don't go out much."

I pass him the *sebsi,* and he inhales deeply, coughs, and then laughs. "With this shit, I wouldn't either."

"Moroccan hashish. Kif. They grow it in the Rif Mountains. *Kif from the Rif.*"

"Kif from the Rif." He grins. "You're better than *Wikipedia*, bro."

▪

He tells me he never talks this much, not about real stuff. He tells me I'm a good listener.

He has stopped apologizing.

He talks about his music, and it is like a switch flipped inside him, the wattage oozing from under his skin. *I've been scouting the clubs,* he tells me, *got the drop on these guys. The real deal. Straight outta the Queensbridge projects.*

I nod and listen and watch the smoke rise, the spirals unfurling between us.

None of this plasticized, slicked-over bullshit, poser mofos saying they got a message and never seen shit, spouting off how they're down for the hood and served hard time for poppin' some nigga, but they're really straight outta Cornfuck, Iowa, pullin' down shifts at the TGI Fridays . . .

I inhale, lean my head back, and allow my flesh to melt.

No pretty-boy wannabe Justin Timber-flake, not these guys. I mean, who the fuck is Drake, tell me that? Some teenage Canadian soap star, gets himself some bling and grill, and boom, he's the voice of a generation?

He's excited now, gesticulating and tapping out beats on the tinted window, and I'm thinking how something matters to him, how he wakes with a purpose. How that is a beautiful thing.

I'm talking the real raw shit here, man. These guys are like that, right? The hustlers, the pimps. Corner boys fighting the power. When it meant something.

I think of beautiful things. That girl I met at the hostel in Kauai, the one with the wild hair who never wore shoes, or was it Costa Rica? No, that was the French backpacker, but she didn't wear shoes either.

I'm talking Run-DMC, slayin' suckers who perpetrate . . .

It was Kauai, I remember now, that bonfire on the beach, the local boys sharing their herb. And there she was, parting the darkness like a curtain. Calling me pretty white boy . . .

Kool Herc. Bro. Changing the course of history with two turntables . . .

When she smiled, her teeth glowed white in the moonlight. I remember now. Rolling across the sand, her body slippery from the ocean, her skin shiny brown like a beetle shell. Her calling me haole and straddling me. I was so baked, but I remember . . .

"And that's what I plan on telling him." The voice, intense, pulling me back. Miller. Leaning toward me, his eyes focused. "He's got the capital, I got the goods. I'm gonna say, 'Evergreen, take a look at me. This is your future right here, man. You dig?'"

Miller stares at me.

"Yes," I say. "You have a vision."

■

We have nearly reached our destination.

"It's all marketing," he says confidently. "You know, you're from Hollywood. Strategy. So Desy, she's got star power, I'm talking pop potential, total bubblegum, dismissible shit. But the kind of shit that sells. And Evergreen's got the pull. He's got the capital. So get him on board, launch her . . . boom, we got a label!"

He looks at me expectantly, like he's waiting for something important.

"And that's the beginning of everything."

A huge grin spreads across his face. "Exactly. *Living life without fear.* Just like Biggie said. *Putting five carats in my baby girl's ear.*"

I'm glad he didn't quote that part about the Twin Towers.

He looks at me with awed respect, like I hold all the answers. Unfortunately, he's right.

I was just like you once, I think. *Living in my happy little house with my happy little dreams and never seeing the bars on the windows.*

Then I broke out, and for a few transcendent moments, everything was perfect.

Until that castrating, narcissistic Nazi mother of mine

froze my bank account. Until she sent a PI to drag me kicking and screaming back to her dungeon.

Hope is a beautiful thing. Until you lose it, that is.

▪

The day I planned on leaving was like any other Tuesday.

I woke at 4:45 a.m. knowing I was ready. I'd made the arrangements, written the letters. Then I opened the curtains, thinking, *One thing left to do*.

I smoked a bowl, pulled on my wet suit, grabbed my board, and headed for the patio. Dialed in the alarm code and quietly eased the sliding doors open. After all, the kids were still sleeping.

As for Mom, she was somewhere else, maybe a film festival or the house in Vail. Could be Spielberg's ranch or the Star Island estate or the Hills hacienda she kept to be nearer the studio. She might have been alone or with someone she was fucking, like D-Girl Dacee or the cokehead pottery heiress or the new Vassar intern.

It could have been the wealth manager. Spiritual guide. Personal stylist or personal assistant or personal psychoanalyst.

Most likely, it was just Eduardo, her best friend and stylist. The one who pencils in a lip mole and has wanted to fuck me since my fourteenth birthday.

Bottom line, she wasn't around. In that moment, it was just me and the ocean.

I stood on the porch and took in the morning.

The sky was eerie dark, but it didn't matter. Not at 5:00 a.m. with big surf already. Perfect wind, the waves rising to greet me, as though they knew and had conspired for my epic send-off.

I headed down the sand toward my favorite spot, passing Jasper, who waxed his board with a blissed-out smile. Sometimes we shared a pre-swell bowl, and I listened to his Old Carp stories. He rhapsodised on about days before Billionaire's Beach, when the real girl-midget Gidget caught air with Tubesteak. The days when you could claim this very sand with a beachwood stake, build a shack, and take up residence.

A time I could hardly imagine, before Malibu popo and rent-a-cops, before the Man was there to permit and zone you out of existence. In those days, this was Jasper's kingdom, though he's spent the last twenty living in a van off Venice. Still, he was here every morning like clockwork, parking by the PCH before daybreak. He'd climb through the paparazzi-clipped fence hole, scope the surf, and resume his lifelong quest: to carve the perfect wave, to catch the ultimate air and go flying.

Sometimes, I was jealous.

He nodded at me with a half smile, then went back to the waxing.

I kept moving.

A half mile farther, and Sean Penn sat in lotus, his longboard laid out beside him. He barely noticed me, lost in contemplation, perhaps ruminating on the nature of the universe or his next movie role or whether the southwest waves would offer suitable momentum.

I appreciated his disinterest.

A respectful bunch, the true devotees. The sunrise riders. You speak or you don't, and to each his space and moment.

Of course, there were exceptions. The biweekly McConaughey cameos, where he'd pose shirtless, board in hand, for an entourage of snapping photogs. Since the day surfer guys went ballistic on his crowd of trailing paps, he'd chosen the freezing morning water over further lawsuits.

That day he was MIA, maybe put off by the unflattering lighting. Again, I was grateful.

I passed Sting's house and Leonardo's, Tom Hanks's and Bill Murray's. A few miles up the beach and I'd hit Dealmakers' Rock, where moguls sealed fates on handshakes. Carbon Beach, where the truly powerful had migrated, the execs and money-men in their multimillion, multilevel beach homes. Mom had threatened to move us for years. *I won't live with the Talent,* she hissed, adding she refuses to be shown up by that asshole Geffen.

Lucky for me there was never time between awards season and adoptions. My brother and sisters are the best things she'd ever produced, that's for sure, and she sure paid enough for them. *Adoption is the right thing to do,* that's what she said. *I mean, just look at the press it got Angelina.*

Finally, I found my spot.

I waded through the beach break, then stopped for a moment and stood there. Let the water splash my ankles, the sand ooze between my toes. Let my eyes rest on the spot where water and land meet.

Light was just breaking.

Despite the cesspool of industry types, the Colony had its attributes. Hollywood cred is one thing, but no animator could 3-D an ocean this magnificent, no matte painter render a horizon so perfect.

I climbed atop my board and began the journey to meet it.

■

W*eed, women, and water,* that's the surfer mantra. But the real ones know that's only half of it.

Pure meditation. A solitary experience. Even with friends, you're still by yourself, hours spent looking out toward the ocean, land growing farther and farther behind you, but you never turn back. Not ever.

You paddle. You wait. You hope the big one is coming.

And when it does, you ride to the beach. Or go crashing. Then you do it all over again, right back to the beginning.

This day, I wouldn't make a choice.

I didn't vibe on the word *suicide*. That was for movies and emo bands. Instead, I preferred *mission of chance*. Besides, suicide had only one ending.

This could go either way.

Today the waves will decide, I told myself. *To embrace or suck me under.*

■

Hair still wet and backpack loaded, I slipped the letter under Dahnay's door. Ten pages, handwritten.

Either way, he would have found it. But this way is better.

For Ye-Nay a pencil drawing tucked in her Dora lunchbox, right next to the tuna fish sandwich wrapped in tinfoil, crusts removed, just how she likes it.

A scrawled little girl prancing her pony across a rainbow. *I love you* curling through the clouds above them.

Stupid, but she was only seven. Besides, she was totally crazy for horses.

Xoxoxo, Phillip.

Nothing for Dulcina. She couldn't say my name yet, so she wouldn't have known the difference.

Five minutes till the nannies come. Two for my exit.

One last thing, this time for my mother. A neon-yellow Post-it slapped to her MacBook monitor.

M—
Back when I'm ready. Don't come looking.
Phillip

PS Ye recital on 15th. Be there. And make sure she has a costume.

■

A buzzing, and the driver's head again, only now he is serious: "We'll be there in ten, but I'll stop at the Exxon first. Get you boys some coffee."

Across from me, Miller gives a slow, languid smile. "So, first time in the Hamptons. You ready?"

"I'm sure I can handle it. After all, I've been to six continents."

"That's nothing. To these people, the Hamptons is the only continent that matters."

4
CHAPTER

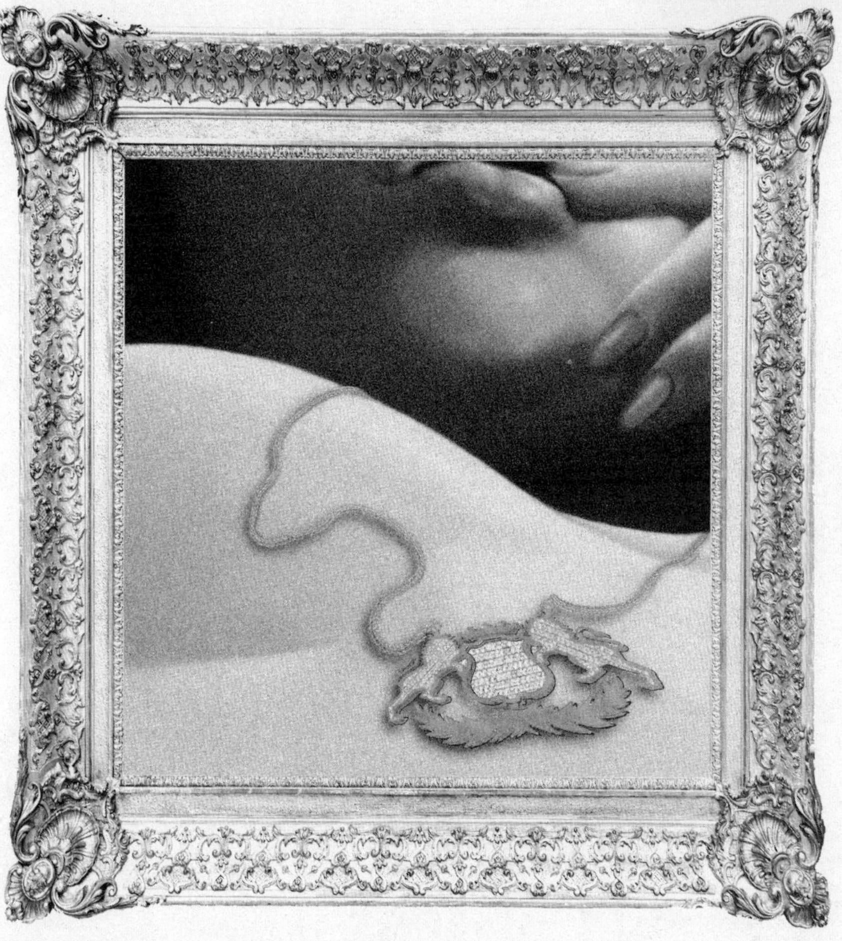

The Royal Crest! #booblicious #theroyaljewels #princesscut #diamonds #gold @Cordelia_Derby @Christian_Rixen by Anonymous

Christian Rixen

"Which shall I pack, sir?" asks Balthazar.

I survey the forty dress shirts meticulously arranged across the formal dining table. The garments are pristine in their plastic sleeves, each box laid out with razor-sharp precision. I know the family seamstress has altered each with a surgical attentiveness, the results meant to streamline my posture and accentuate my overall pleasing physical makeup.

The very sight of them fills me with annoyance. "I am only going for the weekend."

"Never underestimate the necessity of thorough preparation." Balthazar smiles knowingly.

"Duly noted," I mutter.

He ignores the sarcasm, as he does most things he deems inappropriate or improper.

"They are all satisfactory. Just choose the ones you believe most adequate."

"Adequate is fine, sir. But personal taste is far more important."

I sigh. Naturally he picks the day I have a pressing engagement. With less than forty-five minutes until my departure, nonetheless.

I know this routine well, having acted a part every day since my arrival in New York. In fact, I could recite his responses for him.

The script goes something like this: If I do not indulge his queries, I will incite Balthazar's distress. Once distressed, he will choose to extend said task. If he extends said task, I am prone to a lapse in tact, which will only serve to incite further queries, more distress, and, if pushed far enough, a call abroad. To discuss, of course, my impatience for mind-numbing tasks and tendency toward tactless outbursts.

It is hardly worth the effort, I think.

I will myself to contemplate the shirts, and he watches with satisfaction, every inch of him radiating smugness. Balthazar's life, I have come to understand, is an experiment in ceremonious banality.

I suspect he apologizes to his shit before being so rude as to flush it.

Needless to say, this is precisely why my father chose him: to deter behavior unbefitting one of noble heritage. Or, as the Americans are fond of saying, act the buzzkill.

Despite the years of elite English tutoring, slanguagedictionary.com has become a trusted resource. After all, I came to the US with a mission, and cultural adaptation is the key to the realization. But how do I escape the castle confines with forty dress shirts and a manservant intent upon royally cockblocking me?

He watches intensely, awaiting my decision. Today is integral to forwarding my mission, so I haven't the time for meaningless frivolities. Who is he, after all, but the hired help?

"The blue, I suppose. And now, if you do not mind, I must excuse myself."

For the thousandth time since arriving in the US, I wish he were Johan.

■

At first, I had not been keen on Johan's arrival. I had been distraught to lose my nanny, even though I knew thirteen was too old for such things. And indeed she could act the twat with her endless chastising, her annoyance over unfinished tutoring assignments, and my *inability to follow the simplest of ground rules*, but I still felt a childlike attachment. After all, she had been around since I was a baby, nursing me through nightmares and fevers. And, I suspect, nursing me on her breast as well.

The Countess may have birthed me, but she was far from maternal. Nevertheless, I adored her, as one would a fun-loving, immature sister. She spent her days flitting around the master suite, trying on her vast selection of finely made dresses, doing her hair into strange, complicated styles, and experimenting with makeup she had especially imported from America. I often spent hours observing these rituals, listening to her airy, nonsense prattle. Even as a near-adult, I would sprawl across the four-poster bed and listen to her read from gossip magazines and embark on lengthy, thought-provoking analyses.

It was rather dull on our isolated estate, and she offered much-needed entertainment.

George Clooney is terribly handsome, yet strikes me as untrustworthy, do you not agree? Something about his hair perhaps, she would say, or *Queen Margrethe was seen smoking again! Everyone is in an uproar, my dear. But had I married a man like Henrik, I would relay vice as well! I see he escaped to his French castle again. . . .*

I enjoyed these interludes, during which, more often than not, I was stoned. One of the stable boys, Hans-Jakob, offered up an excellent selection of weed.

The Countess had been the one to relay the unfortunate news. *You need structure, my sweet Christian. And thirteen is appropriate to acquire a butler.*

Translation: the Count had put his foot down.

We have chosen the most wonderful applicant, she added. *Exceptionally qualified, I am told. Worked wonders for Prince Frederik's ne'er-do-well fourth cousin.*

Translation: the Count had found me a personal slave master.

▪

The Countess and Count rarely spoke, their interactions limited to formal dinners and the rare entertaining of a visiting dignitary. Half her life was spent in the east wing, the other half attending benefits and social gatherings, most of which he refused to attend. I would await these glamorous entrances and exits, her kissing my cheek and sweeping out the door, a cloud of chiffon and diamonds disappearing into the night.

I was sure she had a lover. I was unsure if the Count had emotions, let alone a penis.

If the Countess was akin to a fun-loving older sister, the Count was a cold, distant stranger who, for some odd reason, lived in my home.

As the Count of Hirschenborg, he oversaw the estate. Thousands of acres, including the castle, gardens, stables, and outlying properties; not to mention the holiday retreat in Rio and the beachfront hideaway on Strandvejen.

His sole responsibility, from what I have gathered, is the signing of documentation. Otherwise, he is left with inordinate amounts of time to contemplate new additions for his rare-stamp collection.

He rarely acknowledged me, and over the years I had grown not to care.

What I did care for, and deeply, was the impending arrival of a personal prison guard in the guise of a butler.

▪

I had one fond memory, though I had begun to wonder whether it was a figment of my imagination. A few years earlier—was I ten, eleven?—Father had gotten drunk on vintage wine. He had been celebrating, if I remember correctly, some honor bestowed on him by the royal family. These things mattered a great deal to the Count, in fact, made his very existence worthwhile.

You have a legacy to uphold, my boy, he had slurred. Why was he talking to me? He had unexpectedly showed up at my door, though I could not remember his ever coming to my wing. It was late, past midnight, and I was stretched across the floor next to a pile of comic books, shoving Matador Mix in my mouth and amusing myself with the Playstation.

A legacy to uphold? What the fuck was he talking about?

Okay, I had said.

Follow me.

He led me through the sleeping house, my every footstep echoing across the marble. I followed him through the cavernous great room and atrium. I passed the library, a plush magenta haven I often visited, though less for the rare books and more for the Count's wet bar. As much pride as the Count took in this extensive periodical collection, I had never seen him in there, except on the rare occasion when he showed it to a dinner guest.

He stumbled a few times.

Down the narrow staircase, into the pitch-dark cellar. Excepting the vintage-wines room, I took care to avoid the place. In the movies, this is the location where a serial killer prepares his victim.

The Count clearly knew this labyrinth well, leading through narrow passageways and around sharp corners.

The whole thing was odd, to put it mildly. I barely knew his eye color, let alone his interests. Perhaps he did not have a personality at all, as I had never been privy to one before that moment. Yet now, he would barely shut up.

I always knew of my obligations, my boy, he had said, as though through a mouthful of mush. *Upholding our heritage? Nothing matters more.*

I kept my my own lips tightly shut, afraid to break the spell. This was the most exciting thing that had happened in months, maybe years.

Then, just like that, we were in a tiny room lit by a single bulb. The Count slid open a panel in the wall, revealing a safe. *Cool,* I had thought. *Very James Bond.*

A code, a click, the metal door squeaking open.

This is your legacy. He smiled at me perhaps for the the first time ever. *Go on, boy. Look inside.*

The black-opal brooch, the pearl-drop pendant, the Edwardian sapphire with seed-pearl borders. I held each with a gentleness I had not fathomed was in me. The pin of pinkish-red rubies, the ring of square-cut emeralds. The marquise diamond-drop necklace.

Piece after piece, blinding me.

Never had I imagined anything so perfect, let alone held such a thing in my hand.

One day, all this will be yours, he had said, holding his balance on the wall. *Generations of history. Do you understand?*

I nodded, though I did not.

A great deal to live up to, he had slurred. *And failure is not an option.*

▪

The Count never mentioned that night again, once again retreating to his distant, vaguely disapproving demeanor and stamp collection.

There were perks to having absentee parents, especially those with an inheritance dating back to the Vikings. The Countess suffered occasional fits of guilt, immediately compensating for her lack of parenting with a barrage of expensive goodies.

Could she buy my love? *Absolutely.*

Father had his hobby, mother the social circuit. To that point, I had been left with a pushover nanny and my own devices, which had served me well. Within a few years I would be off to boarding school, and until then, what was rebellion but performance art for an audience of paid household employees? A butler was unnecessary, not to mention idiotic.

Additionally, my behavior seemed warranted. After all, the country could be boring as hell, even in a castle.

True, I had become a tad unruly, as well as immune to punishment. Restrict me to my quarters? *Jeg er sgu da lige glad!,* I would think, then shrug and retreat to my weed stash, Bang & Olufsen speakers, and forty-two-inch flat-screen television.

But now everything was to change; I had been assigned a keeper. And if he was anything like the Count's butler, Balthazar, this turn of events would prove unfortunate.

I prepared myself for the worst, imagining a domestic with Nazi tendencies and portable whipping post.

Johan was the last thing I ever expected.

▪

Upon the day of his arrival, Johan found me in the stable, a half-naked baroness beneath me. Seeing him in the doorway, the baroness squealed and crossed her arms, attempting to hide the massive *store patter* for which she was infamous.

I stared up at Johan defiantly and awaited the flagellation. Instead, he raised an eyebrow. "Your meal is ready," he said calmly. "And do join him, Baroness. Though, if I may be so bold, you might consider dressing for the occasion." With that, he turned on his heel and exited, his strides measured and graceful.

"He saw my *babser*!" the baroness yelped, arms still crossing her goose-pimpled flesh. "He saw them, Christian!"

"So? Everyone else has."

That was followed by a slap, a slew of degrading insults, and a huffy exit.

This was not my finest moment. A bed of hay is unrefined, even by rebellion performance-art standards, and even more so with a lounging partner widely known as Miss Royally Slutty. Easy access, though, in more ways than one, with her estate nearby and her lineage approved by the Count himself. *Maybe you will marry her one day,* the Countess had once said. *I believe your father is hoping for such a match.*

Fat chance, I responded. *She is dumb as a doorknob.*

That said, I was not above socializing with her, as I found parts of her to be of great interest. The breasts part, to be more accurate. In certain circles, they were as highly regarded as her family crest.

In regards to Johan, I was testing him. And the biggest surprise was his lack of any.

Yet, I saw his true feelings right there in his expression. Forget surprise; he simply did not care one way or another.

I could relate. On may levels.

■

Johan would be the first person to treat me as something other than a bloodline. He would not question my judgment or chastise my ineptitudes or call me sir when not in the presence of others. If he found me in my room, engulfed in a cloud of smoke, he would simply unlatch the windows to air it out and ask if I would like crackers or macaroons with my tea.

He was not friendly per se and revealed little of himself, seemingly immune to my pestering. His favorite technique? Answering a question with a question.

Did you want to be a butler as a child, Johan?

Do you believe a child would aspire to be a butler, Chistian?

I do not know, that is why I asked you. Had you many girlfriends?

Do you believe girlfriends to be of great importance, Christian?

Oh, just shut up.

I knew he had interests beyond butlering, as he spent free hours in the library. *What do you do in there all that time?* I had asked. *Drain the wet bar?*

It has already been depleted, he had said with a slight smirk. *But I am certain you know nothing of that.*

In truth, I already knew of his specific library activities, having spied on him. I returned later to examine the books he spent hours poring over, his forehead wrinkled in concentration. I was hoping for a revelation that would illuminate his inner workings. Perhaps he was obsessed with Nazi propaganda or fighter jets, the psychology of the mind or Indian mysticism.

Watches? This was not the secret passion I had been expecting.

Antique Timepieces and Their Makers; *Vintage Luxury Wristwatches*; *A Hundred Years of Watchmaking*; *The Pocket Watch: A Self-Winding Legacy*.

What a bore, I had thought. Yet, on infrequent occasions, I would find myself back in the library, drawn to peruse these materials myself.

Only when he took a rare holiday, though, or was fast asleep.

▪

Whether Johan offered the "structure" my parents sought was up to debate, but they both seemed pleased with my turnaround. And true, with Johan's arrival I was less apt to act out. Not that I smoked less weed or drank less stolen wine or had less frequent interaction with those of slutty, regal status; I simply no longer saw the need to flaunt such things to the household staff.

The Count seemed especially relieved, as his belief in proper child rearing had always been that of the seen-and-not-heard mode. Now he was free to sign documentation and poke about for new stamp additions without his worrisome son entering into the mix.

As my boarding-school departure grew closer, I came to understand that he had simply been biding his time until he could pass me off. I would be exported to Norway, just as they did with pork and cheese, and there I would be versed in Scandinavian history and royalty-approved etiquette. I would take high teas with the headmaster and mingle with the rest of Europe's upper echelon, the future barons and other counts-to-be and perhaps—though this was more my hope than his—a wide selection of slutty baronesses. I would be exposed to a vast array of new people, my father believed, acquiring the skills necessary for my resounding future success.

Translation: *I would socialize with others just like me and cultivate some equally asinine hobby as his.*

This, in his mind, was how you formed a man.

What my father had not realized was that after all those years of isolation, he was offering up the world on a tray. Whereas he had been a model student, serious about upholding the dignity of his legacy, I saw another kind of opportunity.

Forget performing for the household staff; I was getting an even bigger stage.

■

I was finally free of the castle confines. The only problem was being unsure what to do with such liberation. With no Johan to keep me grounded, I went with my natural impulse: extreme.

There were always others willing to join me, be them titled or not. The vast array of people my father had hoped for—*others like me*—also had vast resources.

By seventeen, I had been kicked out of several boarding schools, eventually managing to graduate from a Dutch institution noted for their liberated approach to academic standards.

Translation: *a holding pen for burned-out heirs whose filthy-rich parents had run out of options.*

By twenty, I had left university, reentered university, and left once more. I finally returned at the Count's insistence and graduated despite a rather checkered attendance record. His generous donation had been the determining factor.

The Count's main concern was damage control. The damage being, of course, me.

By twenty-two, I had seen the world, having engaged in meaningful exchanges with a diverse range of international personas.

Translation: I had gone on drug-fueled benders from Monte Carlo to Mykonos; snorted cocaine with Lindsay Lohan on a Saudi prince's private island; fucked every available baroness from Copenhagen to Finland; accidently set a fire to the yacht of a Greek shipping heir; unknowingly impregnated a Dutch socialite and a British publishing heiress, whose subsequent abortions I learned of much later; fallen in love with a French It girl, accompanied her family on holiday to Crete, and subsequently realized I was really in love with her former-model mother.

The father and husband, as luck would have it, approached life from a rather open-minded perspective.

Not until my stint in an exclusive Swiss rehab did I understand that I had not loved either of them, or anyone else for that matter.

Least of all, myself.

■

Over the years, I had often revisited that night with the Count, imagining those jeweled pieces in my palms, the light reflecting off their many planes and facets. I would think of them at odd moments, the cool aquamarine emeralds while having a champagne-and-coke-fueled tryst, the sharply cut diamonds while coming down from another debauched weekend.

During an especially frenzied night on a beach in Mallorca, after ingesting a hazardous mix of eight balls, poppers, vintage chardonnay, and truffles, the medics were called. The evening is a blur, except for one moment: picturing the sharply cut planes of that marquise diamond as they pumped my stomach on the sand.

I had never returned to those jewels, as I feared a reexamination would prove them less vibrant, the memory of their perfection more powerful than the actuality. No matter the women I used, or the drugs—the faces on which I had incited disappointment—those heirlooms would remain unchanged. In my mind, they would be eternally perfect.

■

Following my second stint in rehab—this one in a Tuscan villa where we engaged in grape-picking therapy—I returned to my childhood castle. My daily schedule vacillated between bong hits and *Grand Theft Auto*, the chef sending up plates and the maids not meeting my eyes when tidying up my wing.

My parents barely acknowledged my presence. And for that one consistency, I was thankful.

My father need not die for me to inherit his title, I realized. I had earned my own: *loser*. Albeit a loser with excellent bloodlines.

Johan had been kept on as a general butler, and I avoided him like the plague. I did not like what I saw in his eyes; mainly, my own reflection.

Late one night, after lonely hours spent stalking the darkened grounds of the estate—this was a time of day when I could move about without eyes shifting quickly away in judgment—I found my legs, seemingly independent of my body, leading me on a familiar downward path.

I had watched the Count drunkenly punch numbers all those years prior and, for some reason, chosen to burn them to memory.

The code was the same, as was my legacy.

The jewels were just as I remembered them.

■

What do you know of antique jewels?" I asked Johan. He was carrying a tray of tea upstairs to the Countess, who required nourishment during her lengthy preparations for whatever social event she had planned for the evening.

I took great pains to avoid her, just as I did Johan.

Yet he had not seemed surprised at my sudden query, simply setting down the tray on the antique side table.

"A great deal, in fact."

"As much as watches?"

"Even more, perhaps."

"And will you teach me?"

He stared at me for a moment, his face unreadable, and I was taken aback by how much older he seemed, lines around his eyes and graying at the temples.

"Do you want to be taught, Christian?"

I had not answered, only nodded.

■

Johan began with the basic mnemonic device: cut, color, clarity, and carats. He taught me of grouping, specie and variation;

mineral structure and grading system. From there we moved on to historical context, sitting in the library for hours at a time, Johan patiently charting the evolution of each crown jewel. *The Emerald Tiara,* he would say, tapping a page with his fingers, *the sapphires believed to have been a wedding gift from Napoléon to the Bavarian princess Augusta when she married his son, yet arriving in Scandinavia via Josephine, Augusta's daughter. These are not to be confused with the Leuchtenberg Sapphire Parure, of course.*

Of course, I would say, leaning forward and nodding, Johan watching me with a vague smile.

Johan taught me what the jewels represented: the alliance of peoples, the union of formally disaffected cultures, the spurning of one legacy for another in the choice of bestowing. This was not about signing estate papers in a study, this was innate, the legacy of nations, the genetic makeup of historical DNA.

My DNA, I realized.

And it was not silly or dismissible as was a stamp collection, but something painstakingly designed to highlight symmetry and beauty. *Eleven sapphires in a frame of diamonds,* Johan would say. *Do you see how the leaf and honeysuckle motif accentuate the blue of the gemstone?*

Yes, I would say, nodding. *I see everything.*

■

Johan called in a favor, securing me an exclusive internship at the exclusive Jewelry Academy of Copenhagen. He vouched for me, somehow convincing the Count to allow my attendance.

Johan, I am sure, suffered equal disappointment in the outcome.

I would make it up to him, I decided, both for his sake

and my own. When my father agreed to a year abroad—his last effort at damage control, perhaps—I saw a second chance.

You may go to New York, he had said, *but there are stipulations. One year, and it will be spent wisely. You will meet with schools and decide upon the most appropriate. Which will be Harvard, of course, the same as Prince Frederik. Then, once graduated, you will return to Denmark and take up your duties as the future Count of Hirschenborg. Do you understand?"*

Yes, sir, I had said, though my plans differed a bit, as further schooling was not among them. I would find investors, I had decided, and launch my jewelry line in the land of free enterprise, Mickey Rourke, Kanye, and Bruce Springsteen.

And the best part? Johan would accompany me on the journey.

Unfortunately, my father had other ideas.

Johan has proven inadequate in your proper development, he had said from the desk in his study a week before my departure. He was working his way through a stack of documents, signing the bottom of each page with a zestful flourish. *He suggested this jewelry-internship nonsense in the first place and is therefore partly to blame for this mess. So, no, he will not be going.*

He had lifted his mother-of-pearl pen and dipped it in ink.

Balthazar will be your chaperone, he had said, resuming the task, his voice full of unwavering finality. *And that is the end of that.*

Unfortunately, it was not.

And Christian, he had added, as I neared the doorway. *Upon returning, you will be in need of a suitable mate. The young baroness, I believe, has already expressed an affinity for you. You shall speak with her on the matter, proclaim equal affection, and, once graduated, go about setting up a life with her.*

But, Father, I responded, *I do not love—*

Love is beside the point, he said. *And if you wish for this American excursion to proceed, you will do as I say.*

▪

Two months later, and I have finally arrived in New York, where my innermost hopes will manifest into reality. That is, after Balthazar is satisfied enough that my time has been wasted.

"The blue?" repeats Balthazar.

"Yes. Absolutely."

Despite my father's stipulations, I am hopeful for the future. New York is full of investors, and I am sure one will be willing to fund a talented young designer, especially one with charm and a royal lineage.

"Midnight, periwinkle, or azure?"

Not that I would be meeting them anytime soon.

"Azure, I suppose."

"The periwinkle goes well with the white linen pants, sir."

"I am not taking the white linen pants."

"I saw to repacking, sir."

I stifle a sigh, reminding myself of my father's final words to me before boarding the plane: *Be wary, Christian. Balthazar will regularly update me on your progress, and I will demand transparency.*

Translation: one wrong move and I was right back where I started.

If I could not have Johan, I would have preferred no butler at all. In fact, I would have preferred another residence entirely, one less ostentatious than this Park Avenue monstrosity my father has purchased solely for me to inhabit, this six-bedroom triplex with marble floors, a formal dining room, prewar moldings, and wrought-iron fixtures.

While perfectly nice, I had hoped for something more youthful. An expansive, open-air loft in SoHo, perhaps, where I could host hip parties, charming potential investors with my modern, sophisticated edge.

Instead, I am in a building of crotchety, aged socialites who, despite their lavish dwellings, loudly discuss the exorbitant price of tomatoes while riding the elevator.

With the ever-present butler, coupled with the antique furnishings—Father saw to having the place decorated in a *style befitting one of your station*—I have simply traded one castle for another.

And now Balthazar is seeing to my packing as well. "I had concerns as to your selection of waterfront attire," he says curtly.

"Waterfront attire?"

"The Charles River. I did a bit of research and gather that it is quite the recreation destination."

In the month prior to our voyage, Balthazar saw fit to verse himself in the art of Google search, a newly acquired skill that he uses to spit even more useless information in my direction. "They had a variety of images on the Harvard website. The students by the water, and I did not want you to feel out of place. Some even lay out blankets and eat their lunch."

"And I suppose you packed a blanket as well."

"Yes, sir." He reaches assuredly across the table.

"Naturally. Well, you just think of everything."

"One of my duties is seeing to your needs before they have arisen."

"I will take the periwinkle."

"Excellent selection, sir. I am sure it will prove most flattering."

▪

Square-paneled, pavé-set black sapphire or white-gold bezel with diamonds? Ten minutes later, I am in my room pantomiming lifting a flute of champagne to observe each cuff link in action. While the sapphire is cut to highlight the artistry, the diamonds offer that elusive wow factor, the bling so desired by North Americans.

Both pieces are impeccably designed, but that is to be expected; I am the designer. But virtuosity will only take me so far, which is why I always consider my market. In Denmark, we count centuries over carats; in America, Kim Kardashian's 15.9 D-cut makes headlines.

Razzle-dazzle over sophistication, I tell myself, settling on the diamond.

I consult my watch, knowing our three o'clock rendezvous is imminent. For a moment, I am lost in a dream, marveling at the timepiece. The grainy face is partially composed of moondust, the mechanical insides sprinkled with bits of Apollo 11. Limited edition, firmly held on by a strap woven with space suit and crocodile. I am jealous it is not my creation.

Some pieces achieve transcendence, I think, *but this one is literally otherworldly.*

I will just have to do better, I tell myself, just as the doorbell chimes.

For helvede*!* In my meandering over the watch, I failed to check the time.

Three on the dot, just as agreed upon. And no one else could possibly have come for a visit. Only why is she here? She agreed to meet in the lobby, a request I was firm on.

"I'll see to it, Balthazar!" I yell, already sprinting down the hallway. I am just in time, intersecting his path to the foyer. "Please, let me," I say pleasantly. He steps back, nodding curtly.

Balthazar has a plethora of nods. As I am not a butler linguist, I would never presume to attempt decoding all of them. Yet this one, I am certain, falls somewhere between *You exhibit behavior unbefitting a young man of your stature* and *Stop doing my job, you retard.*

I swing open the door and there she stands, grinning, her lips a disconcerting shade of fuchsia. "Christian!" she squeals, then launches herself upon me. I attempt to untangle her in a swift yet gentle manner.

I will never understand this American need to embrace virtual strangers.

"We were to meet in the lobby," I say, my voice low. "Were my directions unclear in this matter?" I speak slowly, as though she were the foreigner.

"Oh yeah! Duh. I totally forgot!"

A falsehood, to be sure. She peers over my shoulder with a distinct lack of subtlety, her eyes greedily consuming my Park Avenue residence.

"Sir? Shall I arrange tea, perhaps?"

"You are a student at Harvard," I tell her in a frantic whisper. "Do you understand?"

"No problem," she whispers back. "I took a class in improv!"

I turn to Balthazar, who contemplates us from the arched

foyer. "Thank you, Balthazar, but we haven't the time. Our schedule requires a hasty departure."

"Of course, sir." He looks pointedly at the young woman behind me.

He cannot leave well enough alone, I think. *Why am I not surprised?*

"This is Miss April Holiday," I say, stepping aside to reveal her. "She is a Havard alumni but now resides in New York. The administration appointed her as my tour guide and was kind enough to have her escort me to Boston. They have been terribly accommodating."

I can see Balthazar question the validity of the story, but before he can open his mouth to speak, April has bounced forward with a squeal. "I just love Harvard!"

"Welcome, Miss Holiday." A flash of his eyes—so quick as to be nearly imperceptible—and he has sized her up. Taken in the long, lithe body, the perky nose, the dimples, and the blond hair piled on her head. He has assessed the clothing, deeming the dress too pink, yet acquiescing that the garments are well made, if a bit overt for his taste.

He strongly suspects, if does not outright know, that the closest she has been to Harvard is a layover in the Boston airport.

"Oh, wow, look at this place! Totally old-school. I just love the furnishings!" says April, and I wonder if loving everything is also an American trait, or simply a publicist one. "I mean, this antique table is *to die for*! Where'd you get it?"

"A gift from the French royal family, I believe," says Balthazar.

"For real?" She reaches out, her hand gliding across the polished mahogany. "I was sure I saw it at Restoration Hardware!"

"A different variety, perhaps," says Balthazar, watching her movements with thinly veiled horror. "This is an Empire gueridon, most likely from the 1900s. Which therefore accounts for the intrinsic *delicacy*."

"Wow!" Her hand is still firmly affixed to the surface. "You know a lot about design! Where did *you* attend school, Mr. Balthazar? Is there, like, a class for butlers?"

"The Royal Institute for Domestic Management," he says coolly. "Before that, I received my degree from Oxford."

As with most British butlers, he fancies his birthplace the height of butlering artistry. Unfortunately, most agree with this assertion, my parents included. A British butler is a sure sign of class, even if he is, thank you slanguagedictionary.com, an utter dickwad.

"Well, I'm happy to give Christian a tour of the campus. Harvard is the best, after all!"

Balthazar smiles politely, but I sense he is wary.

"I mean, it's real exclusive and all—"

"Which is exactly why we must be departing," I say, cutting her off. "So I will make a good first impression."

"Okey doke!" says April, lifting her hand from the table, and Balthazar practically sighs with relief.

"Your bags are in the lobby, sir. I had the porter fetch them."

"Excellent," I say, guiding April toward the door.

"Nice to meet you, Balthazar!" she calls over her shoulder.

"Yes," he says, adding nothing further.

■

It's true!" she says in the elevator. "You really are a royal."

"You were in doubt of the fact?"

"This is America, sweetie. For all I know, you worked the register at Royal Dry Cleaners." She laughs loudly. Do all publicists laugh at their own jokes? *No,* I decide, *this inappropriateness is hers alone.*

"For what you charge, a dry-cleaning position would hardly prove suitable."

"A joke, Christian. Ever heard of one?" Once again, she finds herself terribly amusing. "Is all this yours?"

We have reached the lobby, the porter racing forward with a cart of baggage. At least four Louis Vuitton travel pieces, one of them a trunk.

"I suppose," I say.

"We are only going for the weekend."

"Never underestimate the necessity of adequate preparation."

"Whatever. I'm just glad we upgraded to the limo *van.*"

We are on Park Avenue, standing in front of an enormous vehicle. Part limo, it seems, and part bus. A hulk of a man slides open the door for me. "This is Rocky," says April. "He will be serving as your bodyguard." Rocky grips my hand in his large one, my teeth practically chattering with his firm shake.

"A pleasure," I say. I move to sit but nearly bump into a metal rod.

"A stripper pole," says April apologetically. "This was the only limo van available."

Rocky chuckles. "Maybe April will give us a little show." He winks at me. "Welcome to New York, Chris."

"I prefer Christian, thank you."

"But that's only half of it! Tell him the whole thing, Christian. *Puhleeeese?* Rock, you have *got* to hear this."

I sigh. "Christian Vincent Knud Valdemar Guadeloupe Rixen of Hirschenborg," I say, feeling akin to a private circus monkey.

"Ain't that something?" says Rocky. "What's with the Guadeloupe thingy?"

"My great-grandfather was stationed in the West Indian islands during the period of Danish colonization," I respond matter-of-factly. This is not something we advertise, my father often leaving out the surname purposefully.

"What does that mean?" asks April, eyebrows pinched in confusion. Harvard student indeed.

"Great-Granddaddy got himself a little case of jungle fever," snorts Rocky.

Finally, the van-slash-limo-slash-strip-club begins moving. "On our way," says the driver.

"Okay," says April. "Then let's get down to business." Instantly her voice is deeper, her tone taking on a seriousness. She flips through pages on her clipboard with determination, and I wonder what she did with the seemingly vacuous April who was only recently sitting across from me. "In a debriefing, it is best to start at the top. First off, the host. Gerald Hoff, you might have heard his name. Corporate giant. The press has coined him the Master of Media. . . ."

5 CHAPTER

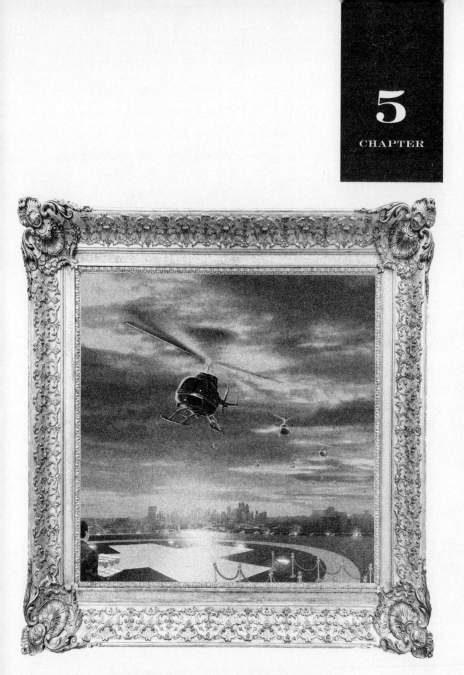

The party has arrived. #BBparty #crooklyn #superchopper #sunset by Anonymous

Cordelia Derby

Be a light to the world. That's what it says in the book of Matthew—5:14, if you take your Bible specific.

Like every good Southern girl, I know my Scripture, even if I don't go advertising it on a billboard like those mega-churches off the I-40. I'll never be one of those come-to-Jesus types, and you surely won't find me saving souls outside the JCPenney.

Truth be told, you wouldn't find me at a JCPenney for any reason. I'm a Saks girl myself, just like my mama.

Still, no one would dare question my devotion, seeing how my papa runs the most powerful Christian-based poultry empire this side of the Mason-Dixon and my people go by Derby.

Not that I'm uppity. *Treat everyone you meet with unwavering respect*—that's the motto I live by. Last year alone I mentored precious little black children, led our chapter's weekly prayer circle, and served as philanthropic chair for the Kappas. The blood drive I organized brought in a record forty-two pints, and our annual Watermelon Shindig raised more than $3,000 for charity. Everyone agreed it was the best event ever, despite those Phi hooligans spiking the melons with vodka.

I don't practice the word, I live it.

I'm the one pledges come to when they're tore up over some sorry mess of a boy, and the one my sisters rely on to turn hissy fits and catfights into giggly gossip sessions. Unlike my brethren getting their knickers in a bunch over trifles, I don't aim my gospel like a loaded weapon. Believers come in all forms, and sure enough I am one.

The other thing I'm sure of? The last thing Jesus wants is for his lights of the world to be shut up in some dusty old cupboard.

Which is why, riding high over New York City in a Luxury Elite helicopter with one of the most powerful men in the free world, I am not surprised by the sudden turn of events. Pleased as punch, no doubt in that. But shocked? Surely not.

Jesus wants us to shine. Just read your Bible.

▪

Set up a meeting with the Boston hedge-fund guys," roars Mr. Hoff. "And get someone from risk assessment. What's his name. That little Yale prick I hired."

"Stephan Englander?" says Eleanor.

"Yeah, that one. They'll eat up that Ivy League shit. They can compare clubs, yada yada. Then he shuts the hell up, got it? Brief him."

"Yes, Mr. Hoff." Eleanor, bless her heart, stumbles to keep up with his big strides. Lucky for me I was practically born in heels. "I'll pencil in Tuesday at four," she adds, making a note on her yellow legal pad.

"And I want those mergers projections."

"Already sent to your in-box," says Kate, swiping her iPad.

Eleanor narrows her eyes.

"The rundown for Monday?" says Hoff.

"Eight fifteen, Strategy Team," she says. "Ten forty-five, conference with Dubai; eleven fourteen, interactive media briefing. Noon, the trainer—"

"The blonde with the big rubber bands?"

"The German. Tae Bo."

"Cancel it. I'll do the elliptical."

Eleanor nods, out of breath, and I give myself a little pat on the back for all those Zumba sessions. I'd considered Pole-Dancing Pilates, but only for a hot second. After all, my mama runs Hallelujah! Fitness Enterprises, and reputation is everything. While Jesus may want his army of soldiers strong for the fight, I'm pretty sure he doesn't want them sliding on poles like tramps to get that way.

We step into the private elevator and I head to the back, the designated location for lowly interns. "Hello, Miss Cordelia," says Gil as I pass him.

"Hello, Gil," I say.

Eleanor and Kate simply ignore him.

"What floor, Mr. Hoff?"

"The roof, Gil."

Gil nods and presses the button with a white-gloved fingertip. "Takin' a little trip, sir?"

"Got a thing with the daughter," says Hoff. "You know how it is. I just take the orders!"

They both chuckle.

Eleanor pays no mind, drumming her fingers like she's got somewhere better to be, Kate not bothering to look up from her screen. For the umpteenth time, I wonder who taught these Northern ladies their manners. Embarrassed, I catch Gil's eye, then bestow on him one of my patented Cordelia Derby smiles. I think he blushes, but it's hard to tell with black people.

Excuse me, *African-Americans.*

In the past two months I've learned that Hispanics prefer *Latino*, *handicapped* is for parking spaces, and *Oriental* only applies to carpets. *Dwarf* is bad and so is *queer*, unless you're studying it in college, which seems an odd choice for a major, but who am I to judge? As for Eleanor and Kate, they are not secretaries, but *first* and *second administrative assistants.*

Up here, folks care a lot what you call them. How you treat them seems less important.

"You scheduled Barry?" booms Mr. Hoff, right back in Big Boss mode.

"Yes," says Eleanor, jumping to attention. "Eight o'clock dinner on Monday. His assistant requested a plus-one. Less request and more order. Said Mr. Diller insisted."

"Oh yeah?" Mr. Hoff snorts. "A new pretty-boy assistant, I'll bet. And he sure don't hire 'em for their typing skills."

I stifle a giggle, knowing Eleanor'll have my hide if I let loose with one. Not that I care what she thinks, but I'd rather not spend the next week sealing envelopes.

"Tell him drinks instead. Mafioso bar on Mott, the one full of tough old bastards." He laughs to himself. "He can bring the pretty boy along, but I'd strongly advise against it."

"Got it," says Eleanor. "I'll let him know—"

"Already texted his people," says Kate, looking up from the send button. Eleanor glares at her.

Eleanor's been around forever, but Kate only eight months. And while Eleanor has the prestige of time, Kate has got speed and youth, which sure counts for something.

What neither of them has, *bless their hearts*, is even the bitiest sense of style.

For a split second, I imagine how we look, three women-on-the-go trailing the CEO with determined expressions. Real working ladies, only two in black and gray suits, their hair pulled back in tight knots and their sensible heels going clickety-click.

As for me, I'm dressed to the nines in the sweetest new little Lilly Pulitzer pink-and-blue shift, my bun flawlessly messy, my Hermès bangles gently tinkling. I am chimes in a gentle summer breeze, my every arrival a cloud of iris blooms and Casablanca lilies. Chanel No. 5 is just fine, but I'll go to the grave wearing my top-secret signature. That and my false eyelashes.

We have come to a stop. "Move along, ladies," booms Mr. Hoff, striding out before the doors have fully opened.

We exit and Gil tips his hat to me in the most darling way. *What a lovely man,* I think. Impeccably groomed, and his uniform always freshly ironed.

These little things matter, and so does noticing them.

"How about the Kid?" says Mr. Hoff, his voice softening a tad, hardly enough that anyone would pick up on it. "Have we got all our ducks in row for his arrival?"

The others may think it's a strategic business move, this little Hamptons hootenanny, but I know better. Mr. Hoff longs for a son, and this boy genius is as close as he's probably getting. There's his little girl, of course, and word is she's a handful. But in his heart of hearts he longs for a strapping male heir, one to carry on his glorious legacy. And as luck would have it, he went after a deal, and Jesus saw fit to bring this boy wonder right along with it.

Mr. Hoff may be a media mogul, but he's a man, just like every other. And every Southern girl worth her salt knows the truth: men are simple creatures. Unless they're homosexuals, I suppose, in which case you'd have to consult one of the Yankees majoring in homosexual studies.

"Your VIP is in transit," says Eleanor. "His jet arrives at the Hamptons airport in forty-five minutes. A driver will be waiting."

Now is the moment I've been waiting for. "Actually, sir," I pipe up, "I went ahead and upgraded him to a limo." Three faces turn in my direction. "You said you wanted him to feel right at home, and I figured that would be a more hospitable welcome than some old town car."

"And I took the liberty of putting together a basket of munchies," I add cheerily. "Just a little something. After a flight, I'm always positively famished!"

There's the teeny-tiniest pause, Kate looking at me like I'm crazier than a loon, Eleanor like I'm not worth the time it took to look in the first place.

"Mr. Hoff," Eleanor says, her sneer transforming into a mask of apology, "I hadn't approved—"

His grin stops her cold. "Cordelia, I like how you think," he says, smiling like he's never seen me before. "In fact, I got a great idea. Why don't you come along? The Kid'll appreciate a pretty little thing to welcome him. At least I woulda at his age. Not that I remember much from twenty-two."

"Oh, Mr. Hoff, that's just silly. You're *so* not old! But if you'd really like me to—"

"I would."

"Then of course, I'd be absolutely delighted!"

He bows ever so slightly and puts out his arm to beckon me, Eleanor and Kate stepping aside with their mouths gaping open like codfish.

Lift your chins, ladies, I think, taking my sweet time. *Or your faces just might stick that way.*

■

If I've learned anything in the two months since taking the semester abroad, which is what I call this sudden relocation, it's that women in New York are nothing like *Sex and the City*. At this point, I'm pretty sure Carrie Bradshaw won't come waltzing down Fifth Avenue in some fabulous frock and invite me out for cosmos. Women like her don't exist, not really.

At least, not at Hoff Incorporated.

The women here are hard as logs. They lack in basic social graces, view their chests as burdens instead of God-given accessories. It didn't take long to understand: instead of competing with the men, they've decided to just become them.

These ladies don't want to bond, they want to eat me. Southern-fried intern on a big old platter, maybe even two helpings.

That's not how I imagined it would be, of course. Not for one itty-bitty second.

▪

"The new intern," said Eleanor on my first day, looking me over like Maw Maw does porcelain figurines at the Antiques Fair.

"Yes, ma'am," I said, giving her my most gracious smile. "I'm so excited! It's such an honor, I can't thank you—"

"It wasn't my decision," she replied curtly, turning her back to file something in a metal cabinet. "In fact, I'm not sure what we'll do with you."

"Well, I can type fast, nearly sixty words per minute. And I'm a wonder with a coffeemaker!" I kept my voice light. *I'll win her over,* I thought. *In no time we'll be getting lunchtime blowouts at Drybar!*

Enthusiasm is infectious, everyone knows that. It's the first thing they teach you in pre-K etiquette, even before proper utensil placement.

"Look, Cordelia." She whipped around in her slick leather chair and fiddled with papers on her desk. "I realize your father knows Mr. Hoff, but we don't usually take interns."

"Yes, ma'am. I understand that. I know it was real sudden. And it was supernice of you to consider—"

"As I said before, it wasn't up to me." She tapped her stubby, bare fingernails on a legal pad. *Forget the blowout, we'll go for manicures.* "And here's what you must understand: Hoff Incorporated is one of the, if not *the*, most important international media conglomerates in existence."

She kept emphasizing phrases, like I'm touched in the head, or maybe she thinks Southerners are dumb in general. The Kappa house scored the highest GPA in the whole SMU Panhellenic system, I'll have her know.

"And Gerald Hoff is *central* to that infrastructure. In fact, he *is* that infrastructure. So he is a busy man. *Very busy*. Right now he's got several ventures—"

"The Rock Exchange, I know! I love that site, so smart of him to snap it up! And I heard that young man who started it is moving here, isn't that just lovely? And Mr. Hoff is starting a fashion magazine as well? That's so exciting. I know all of them inside out, every publication. *Cosmo*, *Vogue*, *Bazaar*, even the European—"

"Cordelia," Eleanor interrupted.

I pretended not to hear her. This was my chance and I refused to waste it. "The editors, the makeup of each section . . . I'm majoring in fashion merchandising, after all. I even started a style blog at SMU, and we get thirty thousand visitors a month. Isn't that something? So I'd love to help out there if Mr. Hoff could use me!"

I ended the speech with my own flourish, the kind of smile I save for special occasions. The one that works wonders on pageant judges, even landed me a front-page photo after the Daughters of Confederate Heroes Annual Diamonds and Rosebud Cotillion.

It worked a lot better on the Society-section reporter.

"Let me be clear, Cordelia." She looked me in the eyes for the first time since I'd entered her office. "Your father may have dealings with Mr. Hoff, may even have socialized with him. And this relationship opened the door, *my door* to be exact, to your presence here. But this is not *the country club*, this is *business*. And your sole job at Hoff Incorporated is to be seen and not heard." She raised her overplucked eyebrows, like two commas rising. "Have I been perfectly clear?"

"Yes, ma'am. Crystal."

She need not have elaborated. Her first look said everything. In Eleanor's eyes, I was a cowlick on church Sunday, a wine stain on a wedding dress. I was that mangy old dog that keeps showing up on your porch no matter how many times you shoo it.

I'll just have to prove myself, I thought, smiling even harder, *and you bet I'll be sweet as pie when I do it.*

I firmly believe in manners, even dealing with a plug-ugly Yankee B-word with a bad attitude.

"What would you like me to do first, ma'am?"

I'd seen Eleanor's type before, only with far better taste in accessories. I'm a Kappa, after all, so I'm used to being envied. Those Thetas and Deltas with their wet-T-shirt nights and pimp and ho parties would talk smack till the cows came home, but in the end, they couldn't touch us.

You can't touch what doesn't acknowledge your existence.

Sure, we were the good girls who wouldn't put out and never threw keggers, but everyone knew we were the prettiest on campus, not to mention some of the richest.

Do a Theta, marry a Kappa, that's what they say. Should I spread my legs for every good old boy this side of the Mississippi, or should I bear his children and run a fashion label from my multimillion-dollar neoclassical estate? I preferred my dignity, not to mention true love and Jesus's eternal salvation.

There is no condom for the heart. That's what I tell my sorority sisters.

I'd prove myself without changing, of that I was certain, except for a minor wardrobe update and downgrade of Aqua Net. From what I'd seen, the-higher-the-hair-the-closer-to-Jesus did not apply to New Yorkers, probably due to the large population of Jewish citizens.

In the end, I'd keep my sass, self-confidence, and social graces, just like my mama taught me. And my mama should know, seeing how she owns a successful fitness franchise, oversees a staff of sixty, and has her own secretaries.

Excuse me, *administrative assistants.*

▪

"I like the Kid," says Mr. Hoff, booming even louder than usual, probably 'cause of the wind and propellers. "So I figure, no effing around. 'You got this great product,' I say. 'I want it. How much we talking?' And he says, 'Give me a number.' So I do, and what do you know? *He takes it.* No haggling, doesn't want to control a thing. Just a check with his name and, *boom,*

TheRockExchange-dot-com is a Hoff acquisition. He didn't even want the stock options, but I insisted. And just you wait till we go public. Think the Kid is rich now? That's nothing. He's gonna be one loaded eff, I tell you!" Mr. Hoff smiles to himself. "But it's worth every penny. This site is gonna be a monster. It'll change the face of the music industry, just you wait!"

"Such a brilliant acquisition, sir! I mean, everyone follows the Rock Exchange. I remember my sorority sister Linette going goo-goo for this alt-country group, putting in all her au pair savings, and her mama kept saying, 'Are you a ninny?' But now they've got a top ten and she made herself a pretty penny, paid off credit cards and then some—"

"And that's just the beginning, Cordelia. Grassroots is fine, but wait till my marketing guys sink their teeth in. Product placement, MTV tie-ins. This thing is an explosion waiting to happen."

He leans back and grins, the stress falling from his face, and drinks his second martini. I mixed them both, the first before we'd even done liftoff.

Let me, sir. After all, I'm the intern! On the rocks with a twist? My papa's not a drinker, but every lady knows how to mix a proper drink up.

I'd never been in a helicopter before and hadn't expected the built-in wet bar, let alone the buttery-leather seats or the flat-screen set to CNBC.

Below us, the buildings and cars look like toys you could pick up and rearrange, like how I did with the furniture in my Barbie Dreamhouse.

It didn't take long for Mr. Hoff to open up and start jabbering. One of my God-given gifts, having this effect on people. Men people especially.

"I respect the Kid. Just sell and move on. Want to know the best word in the English language? *Next.*" I nod and smile encouragingly, and he takes another gulp. "As for the rest, he's a mystery. My guys did a full vet, couldn't dig up a thing. Not much of a talker, either. But he's sharp, maybe the sharpest twenty-two-year-old I've ever met. So I said, 'Move here, Kid. What have you got to lose? I'll bet you got more ideas, and I sure got the capital. Besides, New York is the center of the free universe."

"And you're the center of New York, Mr. Hoff."

"Well, I wouldn't go that far." He winks. "Then again, maybe you're right, kiddo."

"You are! That's why I practically begged my papa to call in a favor. Know what he said? 'You don't need that big old city. Why don't you just intern for me, honey?' And I said, "'Cause as much as I love you, Papa, poultry just ain't my thing.'"

Mr. Hoff laughs. Not just a snort or a chuckle, but the real thing. He drains his glass, sets it down, and I get him freshened up before he's even noticed.

"Good man, your father," he says. "And one hell of a negotiator. When I went to nail the sponsorship deal, he took me to that spread you guys got, whaddaya call that place?"

"Dove Hollow Ranch? With the horses?"

"Lots of trees—"

"The Texoma Lake House?"

"Nah, the place in the woods—"

"Oh." I smile. "The Lodge. He musta really taken a shine to you!"

"Craziest way I ever closed a deal. Rifle in one hand, shake with the other. And then ya go kill something! Well, your father did, and I shot the air a coupla times. Got the picture pretty quick. I'll keep my killings to the boardroom."

"You just need practice!" I say encouragingly. "I got my first rifle at seven, after all! The prettiest little .22, pink camo with Swarovski crystal. Shot my first whitetail a month later!"

He stares at me for a second. "You're somethin' else, Cordelia. Chip off the old block!" He reaches for his glass, now full instead of empty. For a second, he looks confused, then he glances at me and chuckles. "Somethin' else, I tell ya."

"Well, I sure appreciate that, Mr. Hoff. And I must have got Papa's negotiating gene. After all, I got myself a heck of an internship! What did they call you in the *Post*? 'The Master of Media,' wasn't that it?"

Mr. Hoff doesn't answer, just leans back, tipsy and swole up with his own brilliance. No man can resist being praised, and that's just a fact of nature. And coming from a pretty girl? Well, that's even better.

I take a moment to run my hand across the baby-soft leather seat and stretch out my legs, knees together of course. I wiggle my toes, admiring the fresh pedicure in newly purchased Louboutins. The turquoise straps and the Blue Sparrow polish are a match made in heaven.

Everything works out in the end, I think, *as long as you put your faith in something bigger.*

Amen.

I turn to Mr. Hoff, whose cocktail glass is once again empty. "Another freshener, sir?" I ask pleasantly.

"Cordelia, you are a peach." He holds out his glass to me.

"With all due respect, Mr. Hoff, girls from Georgia are the peaches. Now me, I'm Lone Star through and through! And there's nothin' soft about a Texas girl." I give a tinkling laugh, and I can see, in that very moment, he thinks I am the most charming thing in existence. And in all honesty, I just might be. Sure did work for it with all that cotillion training.

"So I hear you're starting a magazine, Mr. Hoff?" I say, daintily unplugging the Grey Goose bottle. "Tell me all about it!"

"Oh, yeah, that thing. My daughter won't leave me alone about it!"

This is news to me. I file it away, like any good intern. "You know, it's a personal passion of mine." I hand him the beverage. "I'm just plain crazy for fashion periodicals. . . ."

▪

"What have you done?"

"Isn't it lovely, Daddy?"

"I said intimate, Annalise. What the hell is this monstrosity?"

She opens her mouth to speak but gets all choked up. From the look on her face, this is a new experience.

It's only five minutes after our arrival and Mr. Hoff is in full meltdown, his daughter looking like she got smacked upside the head with a two-by-four. *Thank the Lord I got fair warning,* I think. Deer in a headlights sure isn't pretty, even if that deer happens to be wearing Escada.

Such a shame the tulle doesn't suit her figure.

The second the driver pulled through those electronic gates, I'd known hellfire and brimstone were to follow. "What?" said Mr. Hoff, eyeing the rows of shiny vehicles.

A parking attendant came jogging over with an ear-to-ear smile. "Can I get you a spot?"

"I live here, you dumb fuck," said Mr. Hoff, his car door already open.

Thank the Lord I'm a wonder in heels, because I had to run. That's how fast he was marching.

Now he stares at his daughter with fury. He's fit to be tied, but the place is fetching. The grass is so green it sparkles, the tent a big white poof above it. Guests drink champagne and mingle, the women dressed to a tee in floaty sundresses, the men turned out in crisp shirts and pastel jackets. A Texas boy wouldn't be caught dead in pink, that's for sure, but I find the whole thing charming.

A quartet plays something sweet, and the vases are full of long-stemmed ivory orchids. I would have gone with a pop of color, but that's just me. After all, these are her stomping grounds.

At least, that's what she must have been supposing.

"Two hundred strangers, Annalise," booms Mr. Hoff. I never approved—"

"There aren't more than eighty, Daddy, and they aren't strangers—"

"I don't know them. So, *strangers*."

Her smile is back, and it looks painful. Frozen as a second runner-up's when she's forced to squeal for the winner.

"They're all the right people, just like you said. And we're having the loveliest time imaginable! Rumor has it there's even a royal coming!"

"Royal pain in my ass, maybe. And where the fuck is Candace?"

"Language, Daddy!" Annalise hisses, glancing over her shoulders. "I assume she's mingling, but she's helped me enormously. And she's absolutely thrilled with the outcome, just as I assumed you—"

"Get her now."

"Lower your voice, Daddy. You're making a scene!"

Mr. Hoff stares at her and I know what he's thinking. *Is she too big for a whupping?* He's got a temper, that's for sure, but until now I've only seen the boil. Now he's fixing to blow, and forget the gasket. This time it'll be the whole dang engine.

Instead, he turns sharply. He's looking right at *me*. "Cordelia," he says, using his Big Boss voice from the office, "you know what I just decided? I'm making you an editor on my magazine. Think you can handle it?"

"Yes, sir! I'd be absolutely delighted."

Then comes hollering, but this time Mr. Hoff isn't the one doing it. Men are pushing through, their cameras flashing, not caring a whit whom they barrel into. "Watch it!" says one, nearly running poor little me over.

"What the fuck is this?" says Mr. Hoff.

"The royal, I assume," Annalise says quietly, though she isn't paying a smidgen of attention. Not to Mr. Hoff or the flashing bulbs or the nervous babble of her guests.

She's looking at one person, and her eyes tell me everything.

Fixin' to lay a hurtin', just like my paw paw used to say when vagrants trespassed on his East Texas farmland. Then he'd clomp out the door, *Jesus rest his sweet soul*, the old .243 Winchester cocked and ready.

Just like my paw paw, I've got an arsenal. The only difference is the choice of weapon.

I lift my chin high, look her dead-on, and shoot my biggest, glitziest Cordelia Derby smile. "Lord Almighty," I say giddily, "isn't this just *terribly* exciting!"

6
CHAPTER

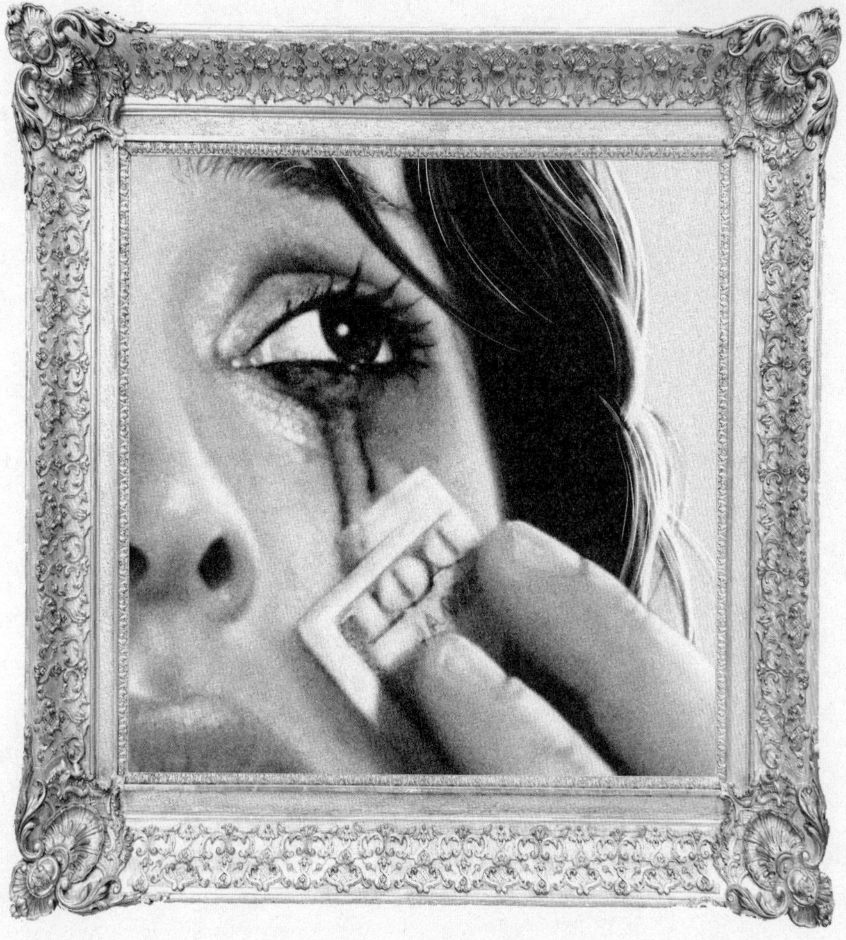

Cry Baby #hissyfit #hundred$hankie
@Annalise_Hoff by Anonymous

ANNALISE HOFF

According to Emily Post, the ideal woman follows the rule of four S's, exuding sincerity, simplicity, sympathy, and serenity.

I got them covered.

I stare at this girl serenely, even with a twinge of sympathy; *I will simply obliterate her,* I think, *and I mean that sincerely.*

Emily Post may be an old dead cunt, but I can follow her rules to the letter.

Of course, there are the lessons Post never covered. For instance, how one is to calmly exchange niceties with a ho-bag Scarlett O'Hara wannabe who, forty-five seconds earlier, jacked your lifelong dream while wearing a big, shit-eating grin.

One, I might add, she is still flaunting.

"Isn't this jus' tar-rah-blee excitin'?" she repeats, as though I missed it the first time.

"Terribly," I say, my voice finally returning.

"Ah real-life roy-yal, cahn you believe it?"

"Yes." My smile is sharp enough to cut her.

Perhaps her accent is less pronounced than I imagine, but I cannot be certain. Through my filter of fury, she is practically a Beverly Hillbilly—and somehow appointed to an editorial position on a glossy publication marketed to high-level clientele.

Keep it together, Annalise. Keep it to-fucking-gether.

"And you are . . . ?"

"Mah-grit Cordelia Deh-by. Your papa's new intern!"

I will bitch-slap that smile off your smug little face. Run a magazine? The girl is wearing blue polish, for fucksake. Blue polish perfectly matched to her rip-off Canal Street Loubies.

Do not. Lose it. Annalise. "His intern, I see. Well, how lovely."

"And yer papa jus' insisted I come with him!"

"Did he? Well, he certainly is kind." I look her dead in the eyes. "Especially to those beneath him."

"Bless his heart. Isn't it just the silliest thing! Him making lil' old me editor of a fancy new magazine!"

Silly? How about insane? Absurd? Verging on mental instability?

Wait a minute. What if Daddy is the problem?

Perhaps he is sick. What other explanation could there be? I try to remember the symptoms of early-onset Alzheimer's from *Psychology Today*. Impaired judgment was one of them, I am pretty sure of it.

In truth, I only skimmed that column, finding the ones on mind control and manipulation far more interesting. Of course I would prefer *Harper's* any day of the week. But as any actualized socialite is keenly aware, a wide breadth of knowledge is key to successful societal interchange. Not that this bitch can read.

"Well, I think this whole durn gatherin' is jus' dee-lightful!"

I mean, she hardly speaks English.

Daddy must be sick, I think, relieved. *What other reason could there be? I told him to drink more water, the poor thing.*

But even as I think it, I know it is not so. Daddy has never punished me, at least not in any way I could not dismiss. No

Black Card? No biggie. I still got that AmEx you forgot existed.

The truth is painfully obvious: Daddy isn't diseased, he's pissed.

The Chitlins Princess and I face off, eyes locked. *This was a mistake,* I want to tell her. *You are a mistake, do you get it?* "I like your blue polish," I say instead. "It matches your shoes to a tee."

"Louboutins. The fall line, jus' released. Got 'em today at Lord 'n' Taylor."

That is when I see it, what was there the whole time. That wholesome, corn-fed smile of hers? *Laced.*

Fine. If she wants to play, I am game. But chickie better watch her back; my checkmate spews more blood than a *Saw* franchise. *You're going down, you white-trash yokel. Right after I get through this fuckfest of a party.*

▪

Of course, the wheels had started coming off the bus hours before Daddy showed up with that redneck ninny. I'd trace it back to the moment when my stepmother casually told me that my boyfriend was a cheating liar.

I managed to hold it together while exiting Chez Vapid and did not even stumble down the grand staircase. Though my knuckles were white on the carved railing.

Only in the privacy of my bathroom, the titanium locks bolted and fans turned to full capacity, had I allowed for precisely two minutes and forty-five seconds of unadulterated sobbing.

He's been spotted with quite a few other women. I've heard from quite a few sources.

How could I have missed the signs? There were no physical cues, no nonverbal indicators. None of the telltales you read about in scientific journals or *Cosmo* quizzes.

Perhaps it is just a rumor, I had thought through the sobs, mascara, and mucus. I pinched a red welt on my arm. "Don't be an imbecile, Annalise."

Gossip is different in the Hamptons, a game with an agenda. Elucidate, demean, bond, or destroy, but never just for shits and giggles.

Though not always entirely true, most rumors had a truth to them. Hamptons leisure offered ample time for decadence and illicit indulgence, the discussions of which were of equal importance. *Who is sleeping with whom they shouldn't be sleeping* being a foremost topic of interest.

But *Miller*?

The thought left me flabbergasted.

Had I been blinded by his endearing naïveté? Or my own in believing he loved me?

And most important: *Who in the fuck could he possibly be fucking?*

He did love me, it had to be so. Beyond my beauty and intelligence and obvious oral stylings, I had the quality you could not quite pinpoint, the one you would never find in those horsey Connecticut heiresses his mother seemed to favor. While placing third in Walk/Trot at the Hampton Classic is quite a feat, Brittany Dupin's pony Bon-Bon had more sex appeal than her in his right hoof. And Eleanor DeWitt's Plymouth Rock ancestry was obviously pure; her weak chin practically screamed inbreeding.

Besides, my daddy's wallet was bigger than all their daddies' wallets.

Je ne sais quoi, I thought, rising shakily from the sheepskin bath mat to a standing position. *An indefinable quality, but you know it when you see it.*

And in that moment, I did. It was staring right back at me.

I wiped my eyes, blew my nose, and contemplated my reflection. Despair added a healthy flush to my cheeks, my swollen lips taking on an attractive, Jolie-esque bee-sting quality.

I suppose it comes down to one question, I told the devastated yet still alluring face. *What would Kate Middleton do?*

Upon her dumping by William Mountbatten-Windsor, the attractive-despite-premature-male-pattern-baldness Duke of Cambridge, Kate had not succumbed to public displays of whimpering. Instead, she channeled an unparalleled reservoir of strength and poise. The subsequent photographs—Kate carefree and fabulously attired, an attractive suitor always within camera range—had sealed her future.

Great Britain may be behind in hair-transplant technology, I pondered, *but there were lessons to be learned from their future queen.*

I knew it came down to this: *mental breakdown* or *graceful resurgence*?

Choice? *Please. I am a Hoff. Failure is not an option.*

The issue settled, the girl in the mirror had cracked the tiniest of smiles.

Immediately following, I engaged in fourteen yogic inhalations, ran a boar-bristle brush through my hair, and touched up my mascara.

As for Miller, I thought, *I can deal with him later.*

I applied a final coat of Dior Addict Lip like a soldier straps on his helmet.

Ten minutes later I emerged, prepared for battle. I surveyed the grounds, noting the vivid green grass, the exquisitely shorn privet hedges. The rare orchids had been transplanted, the tent erected, the infinity-pool water dyed to suggest a turquoise oasis.

If so asked, I would have guesstimated the air temperature a pleasant seventy-five degrees Fahrenheit.

The locale was perfect, with one small exception. A slight breeze, I always thought, added a subtle dash of drama.

The battlegrounds are prepared. Now the troops must be rallied.

I checked my watch: 4:05 p.m. Less than two hours to get this shit moving.

A morning inspiration popped into my head, as they are apt to do in moments of necessity. *All things are ready, if our mind be so.* Shakespeare, William.

Within moments, I had gathered the serving staff and begun firing orders. "Redo the champagne-glass pyramid. And the tablecloths require ironing."

Even Renata appeared, probably hoping for my Telemundo-level meltdown and was forced to pitch in despite her best efforts to be useless. "Not this one," I told her, tossing out a lackluster orange. "I want the cocktail garnishes *vivid*."

She chopped well, I had to admit. Even with her eyes narrowed.

The bartender watched me, a smirk on his lips. *Was he stoned?* I wondered. Luckily, I made a point of preparing for inadequacies.

"You have the cocktail list?" I asked.

Next to him, Renata chopped and muttered in Spanish. I did not speak her language, but *rich white bitch* seemed a likely translation.

"Yup." He held up a hefty folder. "You even laminated the pages! This thing is *sick*."

"Are you on some illicit substance?"

"Uh—"

He was saved by Candace, who floated in with an Anna Sui dress and Gucci shades that practically drowned her face, fresh drink firmly affixed to hand. Vodka, judging by her breath. "Isn't this lovely!" she trilled. "You must let me help you, darling!"

For once, I was glad to see her.

Now, in my time of need, I pushed those negative thoughts away, reminding myself of her positive attributes.

Foremost being her stellar hostessing reputation.

I launched myself upon her. "Should I have the attendants park cars behind the squash court?" I asked, slightly repulsed by my own eagerness. "And shall I light up the parterre? The spiral hedging is still in progress, but perhaps the dusk will mask the lack of symmetry? And what about—"

Behind the immense dark lenses, I sensed her eyes glazing over.

"I would love any advice you could offer, Candace," I practically begged. "As you know, I respect your opinions deeply."

"My opinions?" she said, as though just noticing my presence. "Hmmm. Well, dear, I only have one . . . you're doing *splendidly*, Annie!" She lowered her sunglasses slightly. "Kudos, my dear! Now just give me a moment to grab an itsy-bitsy drinky-winky."

Judging by the red in her eyes, she had partaken of a few already.

And just like that, she had skipped off. Seconds later she was flirting with the obviously baked bartender and downing bing-cherry mojitos.

Oh well, I had thought. *At least he can follow my drink guide.*

In that moment, the truth became painfully obvious: this would be my war to wage, and all commanding would be solo.

Five fifteen. Less than forty-five minutes, hardly a dent in the task list.

A thought crossed my mind. *Every commander has a second, do they not?* "You," I said, beckoning the solitary unoccupied figure, a young man who leaned against the tent pole with a bored expression. He raised his eyebrows, stretched, then strolled in my direction as though life served as his personal runway.

One of those model-slash-hired-help hybrids, I thought. *The kind who appear every summer season.* Though lacking in service-industry experiences, these types compensated with pectoral development and, as many middle-aged Hamptons women were well aware but would never publicly attest, their ability to assist with a rather diverse range of capabilities.

This breed of House Boy was a hot commodity, especially during the inevitable rite of passage: i.e., the Hedge Fund/Investor/Chief Exec husband leaves you for a twentysomething Nanny/Personal Assistant/East Hampton Barista.

Once arrived, he cocked his head, jutted his hip, and hooked a thumb in his black serving pants. "Yeah?"

I looked him over. *Relatively attractive,* I thought. *If your tastes run ethnic.* And for Hamptonite women in midlife crisis, they often did. "Are you engaged in any tasks at the moment?"

"Tasks? Just chilling."

I sighed, feeling the initial telltale tugging at my temples. A migraine was coming.

For the fifteenth time since leaving Candace in her pearl thong, I longed for a Zannie. Right after my bathroom breakdown, I had searched my usual stash locations—the toe of my left Prada, my knee-high boots, the lining of that Burberry coat I had not worn since eighth grade—but *nothing*. Desperate, I had even checked the pockets of my mother's leftover vintage Chanels, sifting through the garbage bag of them I kept meaning to donate.

No way I took that many. *Senora Bane of My Existence finally found my stash,* I had thought, not that I could ask her.

In that moment, reduced to seeking the help of a wannabe Gap cover boy, I had less faith in my fortitude sans chemical enhancement.

"You looked stressed," he said, a slight curl to his bottom lip.

"Insightful."

He gazed provocatively from under half-closed eyelids and I wondered if this was pointless. He thought I was looking for another kind of assistance. *Five twenty-two*. Thirty-eight minutes until cork pop.

"I need someone to direct the parking attendants in exactly twenty minutes. And to help reset the stage for the band around seven fifteen p.m."

"Anything else?"

"Yes, and your tip will be generous. That is, if you can handle it."

"I can handle it." He smirked as if to say, *What do you really want? 'Cause here I am, laid out pretty on a platter. Now whatcha gonna smear me with, chocolate or ice cream?*

I rolled my eyes. "Never mind. You are wasting my time. I will just find someone—"

"C'mon!" he piped up. "I'm smarter than I look. Lay it on me."

I sighed, thinking beggars and choosers and all that nonsense. "A check-in with the quartet." I ticked off the tasks on my immaculately manicured fingers. "Then I need you to gather staff for a quick rundown, re hors d'oeuvres rotation. And regarding the flower arrangements, I have one word: *rearrangement.*"

"No problemo. I'm a sucker for a chick in distress."

"You can remember everything?"

"Sure thing, ma'am."

"And do not call me ma'am. Call me Annalise. Miss Hoff is even better. And you are?"

"Pablo."

Whatever. Bet he goes by Pete back in Long Beach or Pine Bluffs or whatever flyover hometown he hails from.

"Hey." His brownish-green eyes opened wide. "Don't worry, okay? I got your back."

Perhaps it was the sympathy in his voice, or the unfortunate events that day. Perhaps it was the lack of Zannies. Whatever it was that set it off, there it was.

Why couldn't my mother have fucked him, just like every other normal Hamptons housewife?

Don't you dare, Annalise. Do not go there.

But this is her fault. Admit it. She's the one to blame.

Here I was, a soon-to-be senior in high school, and treading treacherous social waters. And the only life preserver? A Hamptons boy toy disguised as a waiter.

That, and my slutty pseudo–future mother. Who, at that moment, was showing the pothead bartender how to tie a cherry-stem knot with her tongue.

The outcome was obvious. I could throw around orders, but throw a garden party worthy of the Society section? Not a chance.

Not to mention your boyfriend is fucking half of Long Island.

Oh, God, Annalise. Just stop it!

But everyone knows. Everyone.

Forget about debutante balls, this would be my debut of humiliation. *Poor thing,* they would whisper. *So naïve. Isn't that just like new money? Just parading around, like Mr. Trust Fund hasn't put his schlong in every Lululemon-clad tramp within a ten-mile radius.*

Five thirty-three.

I had to admit what was obvious. Those invitations I sent? Suicide notes.

I spotted Candace's forgotten double vodka unattended on the table next to me, grabbed it with a trembling hand, and choked it down. Behind my eyes, I felt a faint prickling.

"Hey, are you okay?"

The voice brought me back. I looked up, surprised. Pablo was staring at me, his eyebrows pinched in concern.

Fuck his concern. I wanted to puke all over it.

"Seriously, Annalise. Are you?"

"I told you *Miss Hoff* is better," I spit.

His arm reached out to touch me.

I don't want your comfort, I thought. *In fact, it disgusts me.* "You want to know what would help me?" I snapped. "A fucking Xanax."

His arm dropped to his side, the impulse subdued. Unfortunately, the same could not be said of my words.

Just like that, they were spewing. Coming quick and uncontrollable as a Learjet skydive from two thousand feet of altitude.

"No? No Zannies? Okay, then how about an Oxy? No? Prozac, a bottle of whiskey, just about anything will do. Maybe just a knife. I could cut myself like one of those emo freaks, anything to relieve the stress of this *fucking shipwreck*." My words surprised me, each new one quicker and more scathing than a slipped flatiron. "If you could do *that*, Pablo, well, maybe for a single minute, no, a *millisecond*, this entire day would not feel like a suckfest catastrophe of epic fucking proportions."

I forced my mouth closed. *What did I just do?*

I looked around, my eyes darting frantically. Under the tent, the little Hamptons soldiers rushed here and there, caught up in their own pressing obligations. No one had noticed, it seemed.

Still.

Even with this hired-help pretty boy as the only witness, my monologue had been an unforgivable, abhorrent lapse in control.

Pablo grabbed my hand, swiftly pulling me away from the tent.

"Well," he said as we moved across the grass, "I can't help with the Zan, but the Oxy is no problem. I have a few Valium, too, and a ton of X. But that might be for another time. MDMA and violins? Not so much."

We reached the far side of the pool house and stopped. I faced him, stunned.

"You've been crying."

Got me there. I chose not to answer.

"Here, take an Oxy."

"Give me two."

"Not a good idea."

"Do it, Pedro. I pay your wages."

"Minimum wages. Gonna threaten me over six bucks an hour? Good luck with that, Miss Hoff."

That is when I stopped thinking and started reaching out, putting a hand on each cheek. *He needs to shave.* I kissed him. Hard. For a while.

When I came up for air, he said, "That wasn't, like, required. I mean . . . I was gonna hook you up with another pill. I already decided."

"Of course you were. I just wanted to see."

"See what?"

I sighed. "You know, you could be my type. In an alternate reality where you had a real job. And a green card."

He snorts. "A green card? My parents are from California. I grew up in Long Beach, you racist."

"Long Beach? Ha! I knew it. Now give me another Oxy."

"I got something better. But I want the forty-five bucks up front. Cash only. I don't take Gold Cards, even from the rich bitches."

"Fine. Besides, Gold Cards are passé. Daddy does Palladium."

"Be right back," he said. Instantly, he was gone.

I had been completely wrong in my assessment. Forget physical fulfillment, this industrious young man offered goods even more highly valued among elite society.

Across the yard, the tent was a hive of buzzing activity, the energy only seeming to build by the second.

Strains of Bach intermixed with clinking ice, clanging cutlery with chairs being scraped across the dance floor.

They better not leave marks, I thought.

I noticed a gentle breeze had risen.

Well, I suppose I shall just have to tell them. I headed over to those engaging in improper chair placement, a tiny smile playing on my bottom lip.

The key to success, after all, is proper delegation by an authoritative entity. Or, as Daddy puts it, *Let the bastards work for you. It's why you pay 'em, isn't it?*

Five forty-five. Fifteen minutes. Not much time, but still plenty.

Random acts of kindness are bullshit, of course. But a sign? That was something else entirely.

I will pull this off or die trying. Besides, dying won't get a spread in Social Life.

Last I checked, they covered parties, not obituaries.

▪

By the time the first guest arrived, I had pulled it together. With the aid of pharmaceuticals, of course, as well as Pablo.

I had misjudged the poor lad; he was absolutely lovely. In fact, by 6:30 p.m., everyone in the world was.

The party was off to a splendid beginning. The string ensemble heavenly, the blue cheese and pear tartlets perfection.

Even the burnout bartender's summer cocktail mixers were a hit. *The sliced fruit-wedge garnishes,* I noted with satisfaction, *add a pleasant burst of color.*

Most successful of all? The hostess herself. I took stock of my reflection in one of the Victorian-scrolled sterling servers and was pleased to discover the very prototype of the refined lady of the house.

My skin was glowing, my lips glossy. With slightly flushed cheeks and ever-so-tousled hair, I could have been a pre-Raphaelite maiden, sans the unkempt peasant dress and frizzed-out split ends. I had achieved freshness without the boho infusion; Mary-Kate Olsen minus the sloppy.

Not that I was the only one to notice.

That's her. The daughter.

Pretty, isn't she?

Yes, that Hoff.

I worked the room, but I never stopped watching or listening. Even at their lowest volumes, these sorts of voices traveled. The topics remained the same as ever, but the players were ever shifting.

There was Real Estate (*"The Richard Gere home. Two bedrooms, six acres. Lovely views, but sixty-five million? Perhaps Buddhism makes exceptions for materialism, but also price inflation? Not so Zen*) and New Arrivals to the Community (*" . . . a Real Housewife, can you believe that? . . . Yes, the TV show. I think New York, but it might be Jersey, I'll have to do the Google. . . . I know, another one! Between her and that Dina Lohan character, what is this place coming to?"*). There was Gossip (*"She soaked all his Brooks Brothers in bleach and spread them across the solarium. What a scene! And there she is, playing doubles at the Hills Club, just happy-go-lucky as ever. . . . Yes, a restraining order"*) and Fashion (*"Balenciaga, two seasons ago. Probably consignment, that cheapskate"*) and, inevitably, Self-Improvement (*"The Flesh Regenerator. Horrid name, I know, but these quantum lasers actually rejuvenate on the cellular level . . . six thousand, plus the shipping fees from Dubai"*). And last but not least, Political Matters (*"Oh, Obama"*).

But most of all, there was the party itself. People Who Matter discussed the projected arrivals of People Who Really Matter. "I heard Phyllis Atwater is coming," said one.

"The head of Prototype Pictures?" said her friend, toying with a blond extension. "Unlikely. She usually spends August at the Vail Château. But her son just moved to Trump International, I heard. Drugs, *tsk-tsk*. But even better . . . did you hear about the royal?"

"Royal?"

"Yes, from Europe. But not one of those little, swarthy countries . . . one of them with the blond Amazonian types."

A royal? My barely contained smile risked bursting. This was better than I could have imagined. And still, the best was to come. Foremost among the People Who Really Matter discussions? Two specific individuals.

One being Gerald Hoff, my elusive father.

"He bought a twenty-five-thousand-dollar VIP table at the Hampton Classic and didn't even show!" said one of the Bottom-Feeders in a not-so-hushed whisper. "A tax write-off, I suppose." The other BF just shook her head at the blatant audacity.

How did they get in here? I wondered, having paid an inordinate amount for security provisions. Then again, those of BF status were notoriously skilled in crashing.

When my Really Mattered father finally arrived, he would be flabbergasted. I smiled at the thought while finishing my watermelon concoction. I imagined his entrance, the barely contained awe upon his face. *You did all this?* he would say. *Well, guess you're just a chip off the old block, kiddo.*

But even more than Daddy, discussions centered around He Who Mattered Most, the guest of honor. His name being repeated and re-repeated in frantic whispers.

Todd Evergreen, can you believe it? The *Todd Evergreen.*

Now, only one questioned remained: *Where the hell were they?*

By six forty-five, several facts were glaringly apparent: first, the party was a raging success; second, my father and Evergreen were officially late.

Circulate, mingle, kiss-kiss, banter. The sound of my own laughter was disconcerting.

The circulation part sucked, but it had to be done. That way Miller could see how perfectly happy I am. When he decided to show up, that is.

So lovely of you to come! I said through a tight-lipped smile. *What a lovely dress, a lovely night. . . . Daddy? Oh, haven't you met him? . . . How lovely of you to say, he is a wonder. And the moment I see him, I will make the loveliest of introductions!*

Miller? Oh, I haven't a clue. Around here somewhere, I suppose. You know how boys are!

Absolutely. Evergreen will be here in a jiff. Just a delay. . . . I know, more exciting than words!

A stilted act from the jilted Hoff, like a CW star playing Lear on Broadway. My lines read by rote, the smile so forced my cheeks ached.

That is, until Little Miss Redneck showed up. That's when I decided to bring in the reinforcements.

■

Adorable, I had said to Pablo with an eye roll when he showed me the tiny yellow capsule stamped with a peace sign. *But what happened to violins and MDMA not mixing?*

You could use a lift, he said with a snort. *And your version of ecstasy is probably just, like, slightly less pissed off. You're not like other chicks, Miss Hoff.*

No shit. And you might as well call me Annalise. Since your tongue was in my mouth and all.

He needn't have given the dissertation. I had no idea what I was missing.

■

Within fifteen minutes of taking the pill, I have entered an alert yet dreamy state, floating the tent length as though gliding through tufts of clouds.

Beyond the flaps, the sun has dropped, the stars rising and aligning. Inside, someone raises the artificial lights, a warm, diffused glow shimmering off bare shoulders and sharp clavicles. *Good choice adding the track lighting,* I think, the warm tingle spreading. *Five grand is nothing for this kind of ambience.*

The place is packed, voices and champagne bubbling. Not a crow's-foot in sight, not a misplaced freckle. Everywhere I look are toned bodies and flawless faces.

My feet are bare, I think abstractly. I am the nymphet Lolita, Kate Hudson on a beach shoot.

The quartet has been replaced by a band, the guitar licks reverberating through me. The lead singer has the only wrinkles in sight, his skin as weathered as his leather pants. And not in a purposely distressed punk-chic way, either, just a needs-new-leather-pants way.

Somehow, he works the look. He's uncomfortably sexy, like Michael Douglas or Harrison Ford or one of those other grandfather-aged actors.

Famous in the eighties, says a woman to my left. *Ate a cockroach while playing Madison Square Garden.*

Crack cocaine, whispers another. *And now teaching guitar out of a basement in Southampton.*

Not an act in high demand, but he was all I could find this late in the season. And yet, why had I been so worried? He has a gift. Each song is more enthralling than the next, his cigarette-and-phlegm warble practically inspired.

"Doo doo doo doo doo doo doo doo doo doo . . ."

The final notes, big finish. "'Walk on the Wild Side,'" he says in the mike. "That was for Lou, who saved my life once. Nineteen seventy-five, speedball overdose. And now for some Eurythmics!"

How adorable, I think. *How kitschy! Sophistication and local flavor!*

This is the best garden party ever!

A quick hacking fit and he launches in. *"Sweet dreams are made of this . . ."*

"I love this song!" I say to nobody in particular. "We should all be dancing!"

I head for the polished portable dance floor, weaving through the crowd. From a distance, I can see the usual suspects have beat me to the punch, already shaking and swinging themselves into oblivion. In half an hour, others will join them, of that I am sure. But for now, the only thing missing? *Me!*

The familiar faces, always the first dancers at any party. I know everything about them instantly.

The Russian models stand in a circle but do not acknowledge one another. They stare off into space, their faces cold, their moves taken from Beyoncé videos. Though never officially invited, they never fail to show at functions, their shimmies and twerks performed solely for prospective investors.

At a noted distance are the fortysomething premenopausals. With husbands still closing deals in the city and children overseen by the rare breed of Swedish nanny—the homely kind—their days are free for chemical peels and philanthropic endeavors. They are renowned for their book clubs and volunteering; the cocaine binges and yoga-slash-sex-retreats are discussed with less frequency. During the season, they travel as a desperate pack, their moves as ferocious as their dresses are age-inappropriate.

"Some of them want to be abused. . . ."

Off by herself and not caring one bit is the infamous former-stripper-turned-billionaire-wife, who, rumor has it, met her Wall Street prince when he hired her to entertain his Korean clients. Now she writhes and grinds, her adoring audience consisting of paunchy middle-aged men in button-downs. Though long ago having traded her fishnets for Versace, the pole has never really left her.

Bad news, every last one of them. Of this, I am well aware. At least, the logical part of me.

As for the other part? It does not give a fucking smidgen.

I race for the center of the floor, my bare feet slapping the wood with each leaping step.

That is when I see him.

Miller who? This guy is so much better.

His majesty *indeed*. The royal seated at a table nearby. His suit cut to elegant perfection, his leg crossed in that way that only European men can pull off without the gay factor. He leans forward, engaged in what appears to be a fascinating conversation.

With Honey Boo Boo the Hillbilly.

I'll show him American royalty, I think, feet already moving in that direction. Because, with Kate Middleton as my witness, I know he won't find it in her double-wide.

"Hold your head up, keep your head up, movin' on . . . movin' on . . ."

▪

"You're making a spectacle of yourself with that royal!" Ten minutes later, and Candace has pulled me away from his highness, practically dragging me across the tent. Now she has me in a darkened corner by the generator.

Nonetheless, I continue to dance.

"Oh, there ain't no other way," croons hot-grandpa lead singer from the stage, his leather-clad ass shaking. *"Baby, I was born this way. . . ."*

"I was having fun!" I squeal, gazing longingly at the now-packed dance floor.

"I see. And your version of *fun,* I take it, is a sweat-soaked attempted dry-humping of a young man with royal status?"

"C'mon, he's European!" I say, though *whine* would be more apropos. "He thought it was funny!"

"Amusement and humor are not the same. I thought, after that horrific scene with your father, you'd at least try to keep from creating another disastrous scene."

"Where *is* Daddy?"

"Around here somewhere. It took a great deal of effort, but I was able to calm his nerves."

That is when I notice the red smear at the corner of her mouth. "Oh, yeah? How did you do that? Wait, I can guess. Speaking of which, your lipstick is a *mess.*"

Eyes darting around, she digs for a compact in her blue croc Hermès clutch.

"Ewww, I was right. Is *that* how you calmed his nerves?"

Her eyes flash. She glares, mussed lipstick all but forgotten. "You know nothing about being a woman, Annie. Men are intricate creatures with many complicated needs."

"You think a blowie is complicated?" I say, my mind-to-mouth filter having dissipated long ago. "I mean, I have always found them pretty damn easy."

Maybe it is her attempt at seriousness or the piercing of her eyes. Maybe it is that the upward smear of her signature color—Yves Saint Laurent #9, Rose Stiletto—makes her look like a circus clown half smiling.

Whatever the reason, I start to giggle. And once I start, it feels like someone turned on an internal spigot. I could not stop even if I wanted to.

She lifts her hand to slap me.

I catch her wrist, digging my fingernails in the flesh. "I dare you," I hiss.

I have been down this road before, after all. And she isn't even my real mother.

She pulls away, trying to get a grip on her emotions. Digs in her bag again and finds the compact.

"Let me ask you a question, Annie." She gazes in the mirror and runs a finger along the side of her mouth. "Do you believe this to be debutante-worthy behavior?"

"Absolutely not. But I suppose it does not matter."

"Oh, no?"

"'Oh, no?'" I squeak in imitation. "No, not at all. Because—and here's the crazy thing, Candace—*I have come to a revelation.*"

"Have you?" she says, still working on her lips. The excess color is almost gone.

"You never intended to sponsor me in the first place, did you? Just wanted to get in good with your boyfriend's daughter."

Snap. The compact closes.

A response is not needed, as we are obviously in agreement.

The truth was there the whole time, clear as Waterford crystal. I should have gotten the invite months ago. I was clinging to hope, for some insane reason.

I wanted to believe, I suppose, in fairy tales.

"And my name is Annalise, not Annie," I hiss, the giggles long gone. "Do you understand, you vacuous, slutty interloper?"

Before she has a chance to answer, I see Miller striding up the lawn, flashing his flawless smile.

Perfect timing.

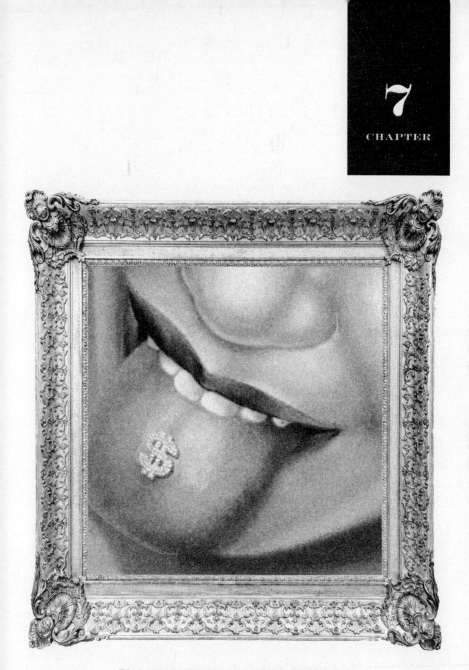

Diamond tongue-lashing #jacobthejeweler #iceprincess #piercing #bling by Anonymous

M.C.

"What have you done?" she yells, pushing me. I stumble back, hands up.

Who is this crazy bitch? *And what did she do with my girlfriend, Annalise?*

"What do you mean?"

"I knew it the minute I saw you! It's true, isn't it, Miller?"

Annalise's hair is tangled, her cheeks red. She's so loud that people have started to watch.

It's kinda hot.

"You egotistical man-whore!" she shrieks, pushing me again.

She's starting to freak me out. "Hey, chill out. Fuckin' Hamptons traffic, baby—"

"You just use people, don't you? You use and you use—"

"Fuck, baby, it was back-to-back—"

"And you reek of pot!" she screeches.

"Okay now," says Phillip, all low and soothing. "Annalise? Just look at me for a second, okay?"

She keeps glaring at me, biting her bottom lip. Fuck, she's scary as hell. So why is it kinda turning me on?

"Please, Annalise?" says Phillip, like how you talk to a kid bawling over a skinned knee. She finally looks at him.

"Annalise," says Phillip quietly, moving in close to her. "I'm worried about you."

She stares at him, the anger slowly dripping off her face.

This guy is good.

Suddenly, Annalise smiles. A weird one I've never seen before. Like she thinks he's the sweetest mofo in the world. She puts her hand on his cheek.

If I didn't know her, I'd think she was on something.

"You are the best guy ever, Phillip," she says. "And your skin is so soft!"

She's totally on something.

The music stops. "Hope you dug on that," says a voice. We all turn to the stage, where a douche in leather pants is talking into a mike. He's older than fuck. "And now for a classic," he says, the band—if you can call them that—starting the intro chords. "Reminds me of that time I woke up on the floor at CBGB's in my own puke. Let's get our groove on, Hamptons!"

"There's a loving in your eyes all the way. . . ."

Cheesy as hell. I hate this fucking music.

"I love this song!" squeals Annalise, finally taking her hand off Phillip's face. "I'm going to dance!" She does a little bounce-turn toward the stage. She's about to run, then stops. Turns to me with a sneer. "I will hate you for eternity, Miller Crawford the Third," she hisses.

Then she's gone, skipping off toward the packed floor.

"Karma karma karma karma karma chameleon . . ."

"That was crazy," says Phillip. "What did she take?"

"I don't know, man, but it freaked me the fuck out." I'm already headed toward the bar. "I *really* need a drink."

Three shots and two beers later, I'm even more pissed. Make that four shots. In front of me, some chick I call my girlfriend is going nut job. Dancing like nobody else is around, flipping her hair, doing some weird-ass grind like a stripper on her off-hour.

And the worst part? It's sexy as shit. And other guys think so, too. All these fat Wall Street bastards watching from the sides, smirking with drinks in their hands.

"Refill," I say, slamming my glass down on the bar. The bartender frowns but reaches for the whiskey anyway.

"Slow down," says Phillip.

"Fuck you. Hey, thanks for having my back. Bros before hos, mofo." Wait, what the fuck is she doing now?

Annalise is sitting on some dude's lap. Giggling.

"Who is that piece of shit?"

"Hey," says Phillip. "Don't worry about—"

"I'm fucking serious, man!"

"Lower your voice."

This time I yell. "Who the fuck is—"

"Christian Rixen," says a woman next to me, all perky and teeth. She smiles, happy as can be. "A royal from Denmark, he's a very well-known jewelry designer!"

"So he likes dudes?" I ask, momentarily relieved.

She looks confused. Her dress is way too pink.

"That's kind of homophobic, my friend," says Phillip.

"Oh, no!" she chirps. "Christian's not *gay*. In fact, he was just flirting with Cordelia Derby for an hour."

"Cordelia what?"

"Derby? New editor at *The Set*? I wanted to talk to her myself, but she's been surrounded all night." Her lips are moving too fast, her face a little blurry. "See, she and Christian were totally clicking, then that girl came over and scared her off—that one. Sitting on his lap."

"So he's not gay?"

"Not at all! By the way, I'm April—"

"I'm gonna kick that dickhead's ass!"

I'm already headed for her, but Phillip grabs my arm. "Wait, M.C."

"I fucking mean it. Who the fuck does he think he is?"

"Well," says Pink Dress, backing up, "maybe we can catch up later?"

"If you do that," says Phillip, "You'll make everything worse. You're trashed, and so is Annalise, and I don't think now is the best time—"

"I don't care what you think!" I pull my arm away. I take a step, then stop for a second, dizzy.

It might have been six shots. Or seven. It doesn't matter, I think. I can still whup that pussy.

I take a step and there's a loud crash and a bunch of yelling. *Did I make that happen?*

"Get off me!" says a voice.

I look where everyone else is looking. In the corner of the tent, a big-ass security guard has his grip on some dude in a hoodie, twisting his arm behind his back. "Let go of me," says the kid.

"Stop struggling or I'll hurt you," says Security Guard. He's totally jacked-up, upper arms the size of small children.

"You're hurting me already. Let go of my arm!"

"You shoulda followed directions," barks 'Roid Head. The kid tries to get away, but the guard pulls him in a lock.

Next to him, two other guards watch, arms crossed.

"What directions?" says the kid, face still hidden by the hood. "You can hardly put together a full sentence!"

With his free hand, 'Roid Head grips the kid by the back of his hoodie and lifts him, the veins on the guard's neck throbbing with the effort.

The band has gone quiet and so has the party. Everyone is watching like they'd hired these goons to put on a show. I look for Annalise, but she's gone. A new girl has taken her place next to Ass-Munch. I squint, wondering if I imagined it all. Maybe it wasn't Annalise. Maybe it was this little girl with blue shoes the whole time.

Fuck that. It was Annalise. *Sitting in his lap.*

Back in steroid corner, one of the other guards has stepped in. "Maybe you should back off, J.J.," he says, real low and weak. "You look like a bully, y'know?"

'Roid Head whips around, the kid going with him. "What did you say to me, you little bitch?"

No time for the little guard to answer. Another voice, this one roaring. "What the fuck are you doing?"

Everything freezes. Heads turn, the crowd parting.

Mr. Hoff, feet planted, stands near the stage. He looks crazy pissed.

"This guy tried to sneak in, Mr. Hoff!" says 'Roid Head. "He pulled up in a taxi, was talking all this nonsense—"

"Let. Go. Of. Him." This time, Mr. Hoff doesn't need to be loud. *"And get the fuck off my property."*

'Roid loosens his grip, the kid stumbling forward. 'Roid backs up, holding his meaty hands open in front of him.

The hooded kid does not even look at him.

"Come here, son," says Mr. Hoff, then reaches up for the lead singer's mike.

Old Man Leather Ass hands it over before Hoff's arm is outstretched.

The kid straightens himself and sighs. Then he walks over, real slow, like no one is watching. Like he has all the time in the world.

He stands next to Hoff, tapping his old-school Converse.

"Ladies and gentleman," Hoff says into the mike. "I would like to introduce a true visionary." He puts an arm around the kid's shoulders, his face full of pride. Mr. Hoff's never looked at me like that. I mean, he hardly looks at me at all. "The future of interactive media and our guest of honor, Mr. Todd Evergreen."

A few surprised claps, then a shitload of them.

Mr. Hoff hands him the mike. "Say something, kiddo."

With the other hand, the kid pulls down his hood. It is so quiet you could hear dust particles falling.

He clears his throat. "So, this is the Hamptons."

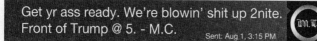

Get yr ass ready. We're blowin' shit up 2nite.
Front of Trump @ 5. - M.C.

Sent: Aug 1, 3:15 PM

M.C.

Phillip Atwater

"That's it?"

"That's it. 'This is the Hamptons.' Silence."

"Good line. And then?"

"Chaos, my friend," I say. "Total chaos."

Beamer doesn't look at me, but I'm used to that. I know he's hearing every word.

"A siege. One minute, the whole place staring at this guy, this massive security dude going ballistic, threatening to kick his ass—"

"Amateur," Beamer snorts.

"—whole tent watching with mouths open, like the kid was some terror suspect sent on a jihad jet-set mission—"

"You're a poet, man."

"*Fuck off.*"

Just another day on the steps of Trump International. I lean into the rail, lift my chin, and let the sun warm my face.

"But soon as they know the truth? He's the Second Coming. They're on him, like white on rice." Something occurs to me. "Hey, is that a racial slur? I always wondered."

"For white guys who chase Asian pussy, maybe," says Beamer, then gives a low chuckle. "Nah, just fuckin' with you."

Beamer is my go-to source on race relations, seeing he's one of the only black guys I've spent a significant amount of time with. Except for my brother, that is. And Dahnay knows even less about his cultural heritage than I do.

Fucking Malibu.

"Asian pussy," mutters Beamer, still laughing.

Unfortunately, half of Beamer's insights serve solely to mess with my head. I give it back the best I can, but we both know the truth: he's playing in the Majors and I'm still gunning for a spot in Little League. Not to mention he's got twenty years, one hundred pounds, and a mixed-martial-arts title on me. I glance at him from the corner of my eye. That's one of the rules. No eye contact and we can hang.

Despite his amusement at my idiotic questions, his expression remains unchanged. This does not surprise me. From what I've seen, he's only got two of them: Pleasant yet Detached Hospitality Consultant and Scary-Ass Black Man You Don't Want to Fuck With.

Pleasant Professional or Scary Mofo, he's the epitome of four-star upscale doorman, an immaculately uniformed guy who will carry your bags, get you a car service, and, if need be, scare off trash attempting to infiltrate your pristine kingdom.

My expression? Doesn't matter. Everyone who passes thinks one thing: delinquent punk with nothing better to do.

We make no sense, Beamer and I. Like a buddy-cop movie my mom might shit out between awards seasons. He's the wizened badass in the precinct who was raised on the mean streets of East Harlem; I'm the spoiled rich kid who had a beach for his backyard and somehow fell into the job. Box-office gold written all over it.

But it's kind of true. By fourteen, Beamer was running drugs for the local gang; at fourteen, I was stealing my first spliff from the B-list sitcom-star father of one of my Harvard-Westlake classmates. He's done a stint in Iraq, got a private investigator license, served in high-level security, and can kill a man by placing one thumb to his pressure point. Okay, maybe not kill, but at least cause massive internal damage.

I'm a 2.3 GPA high school graduate with no foreseeable future other than holing up in his power-dyke mom's Tower apartment until the trust fund is unfrozen.

If it were a police-buddy movie, you could call it *Coppo-sites*, or something equally stupid. The setup is perfect: we bicker, I prove myself, he teaches me to be a man. Life lessons all around. Cue the music, do a Subway tie-in, and we got ourselves a hit.

Beamer's most prized possession is his gold-plated Beretta. *A gift from an influential Italian business associate,* he once said vaguely. Mine was a vintage balsa longboard—extra kick in the nose, single box fin, sick blue thunderbolt on the tail—but someone stole it from the youth hostel in Bulgaria.

Who surfs in Bulgaria?

Right now, Beamer wears Pleasant Face, scanning the one-block domain of which he is ruler. He doesn't miss a thing. Knows the apartment of every person who lives here, the make and model of the resident's car, and, if chauffeured, the ethnic origin, temperament, and navigational skills of the hired driver.

115 K, he'll say, *2013 Beemer S550. Russian dude with an attitude. Parks like shit, too.*

What are you? I once asked. *The Rain Man of Trump International or something?*

Never seen it.

It's a classic!

Never seen it, man.

Of course not, I said. *It doesn't star Tyler Perry in a dress. That's what your people are into, right?*

I see the glimmer of a smile. This is Beamer's favorite game. *Shut the fuck up, you little trust-fund white boy. What's up with those dreads, anyway? You think you're Bob Marley?*

This is our version of bonding. Though nobody would have any idea if they saw us standing there. They'd never know we had conversations, let alone liked each other.

I was grateful either way. I'd take his friendship, even with stipulations.

There were more lonely hours in a day than I could ever have imagined.

▪

At first, Beamer had been wary of my loitering, asking what I needed. *Directions to the museum? A restaurant recommendation?* Then he'd just ignored me.

One day, he'd finally turned to me, exasperated. *Why you always hanging out here?*

Nowhere else to go.

Don't you have friends?

I shrugged, and he'd gone back to pretending I was another decorative plant lining the lobby steps.

I'm not that kind of brother, he said.

What kind of brother is that?

The kind who runs favors for little white prep school boys.

That's cool, I said. *Since I'm not that kind of boy.*

He stared at me for a moment, then went back to scanning his turf, as though we'd never spoken in the first place.

Not much he could do about my presence, even if he wanted to. I might look like a street kid on hiatus from snorting bath salts and hooking up in abandoned buildings, but we both knew I was a resident and could sit any damn place I pleased.

I had been telling the truth with the shrug, though. I didn't have friends, not really. Except for Annalise, and that was more friendly banter. A cursory *How do you like New York? Settling in nicely?* and *What is your mother working on now, Phillip?* as we passed in the hallway or shared an elevator ride.

Those first weeks, I'd made an effort to venture beyond Trumpdom, doing a few hits on the bong and wandering the MoMA, but my brain just felt scrambled by the Warhol faces and starry nights and circles of naked girls dancing through teal.

I tried Central Park, even engaged in a whole conversation. If you could call it that. Her name was Pixie Dust or something like that, one of those free-spirit street urchins who spent her days in Sheep Meadow, all unwashed hair and too-baggy clothing. *Wanna hook up?* she'd said, gazing at me. Her pupils were huge black spots through smudgy liner, like a little girl scrawling on cat's eyes for Halloween with a marker.

Okay, I said. Because I was horny, felt sorry for her, and had nothing better to do.

She'd led me to a hidden spot between the boulder piles and dropped to her knees. I gazed into the trees as her chapped lips went to work. *You're cute,* she said after, wiping her mouth. *Hey, think you could loan me a couple of bucks?*

In the end, I stopped leaving the Trump International biosphere altogether, my days spent circling the huge, empty apartment. I kept the place meticulous, not that it was difficult. Just straighten the sheet on the futon and clean up the take-out cartons.

For a while, I attempted a routine of study, meditation, and yoga, but it quickly devolved. Five minutes in lotus, then I was surfing for porn on my laptop or staring out the window at Columbus Circle. That weird concrete and bush island floating in traffic, the official marker they use to measure every distance in the city.

If I was stoned enough, it looked like the big-city version of an alien crop circle.

I couldn't do this forever, that was clear, so I forced myself to leave the apartment at least once a day. Sometimes I'd stand outside Annalise's door awhile, daring myself to ring the bell, which I never actually did. You'd think I was a psycho stalker in love with her.

Wrong. For so many reasons.

In the end, the pilgrimage always ended the same: with Beamer. But the day he'd asked if I had friends? That was the turning point.

Hey, I'd said, right after he'd turned away. *Want to smoke a joint?*

That'd get me fired, he said, still looking toward the street. A moment later, he sighed and reached in his pocket for something. *When I get fucked-up, I gotta keep it covert. You dig?*

That's when I knew: he had so much to teach me.

Where you been? He smirked, holding out a vaporizer in his cupped hand. *This is the future, white boy. Wall Street guys, housewives, the asshole sellin' pretzels on Fifth Avenue. Out in broad daylight, doin' their regular thing. And gettin' fucked outta their minds.*

That's crazy, I'd said.

For a connoisseur, you don't know much. Where you been, boy? The desert?

Yeah, actually. The Sahara. But only for a day or so. I was headed for Tamraght. Got killer waves there.

Welcome home, he'd said, passing me the vaporizer. *Welcome to the new world.*

▪

You're a good kid, Beamer declared. It was a day or so later, and we were stoned, staring into the street. August sweltered, heat waves rising from the grates.

I mean it, he said. *I like you.*

Buddy-cop movie, through and through. The climactic moment, when the rookie kid's been shot and the old geezer has to admit he actually cares about the little snot-nosed asshole.

You ain't like the other residents. But fraternizing'll get me sacked. So you can chill out here with me so long as you keep a distance. And we can talk. But no eye contact, you dig? Don't even look in my direction. That is, unless you need a cab hailed. But from what I've seen, that won't be a problem. You ain't going nowhere fast. Want to smoke up?

▪

Now it's Sunday afternoon and I'm telling him about the Hamptons. How everyone went from fear to adoration of Todd Evergreen, how it screwed with my head. He listens, watching the Fifth Avenue scene unfold before him.

It's just like the movies. The real ones, from the '60s and '70s. Like every moment is a pickup shot from *Midnight Cowboy* or *Taxi Driver*, every person as clichéd as the character actor who played them. Cars race alongside stroller-wielding nannies, shopping-bag-laden tourists race to fill their insatiable hunger. Joggers rush by, headed nowhere in particular, the journey less important than the calorie burn.

"So, you finally got the hell outta here," says Beamer when I've finished. "Some big fancy party for some famous geek.

Not sure how that invite went down, but great. But here's what I wanna know: *Did you get your sorry ass laid?*"

"That wasn't the point."

"That's the point of everything. You're a cool guy, Phil. I'm serious now. Got the dreads, good communicator. A little Afro-Saxon wannabe for my taste, but the rich bitches dig that down-with-the-brothers shit. So why the fuck didn't you hook yourself up?"

"Purity or impurity depends on oneself, Beamer. No one can purify another."

"Enough with that Buddha shit, too. Pretty sure he never got laid either." He scans the street, stealthily removing the vaporizer from his pocket. He inhales from a cupped hand, so quick you wouldn't know unless he wanted you to.

"Here," he says, doing a low-armed pass-off. I'm a foot below him, leaning against the rails. "It ain't so complicated, Phil. Get some pussy, eat a big steak. Pay your rent and there you go. Life can be pretty okay."

I take the piece from his hand, eyes still focused in front of me. Lift it to my lips and suck in. Instantly, the hash oil aligns my chromosomes, vaporizing all the needless yearnings. The great equalizer, an odorless, clandestine revolution.

Life can be pretty okay.

"So, the party was a bust," says Beamer. "But there'll be others, right?"

Instead of answering, I inhale again, the railing seeming to flex and mold to my body. I lift my face to the sun and I imagine my tribe of brothers, the underground revolutionaries, those everyday guys who are firing up their THC at that very moment.

The dude at the cart, selling dirty-dishwater dogs and toking up between customers. The cabbie *puff-puff-passing* his vapo-pen to the Wall Street suit he's toting in the backseat. More likely, the other way around.

All of us in the light of day, yet existing on an alternate plane of mind expansion. Doorman and cashiers and CEOs and world leaders.

Maybe Trump himself, at this very moment, is blazing up in his office fifty-two floors above us. Dude's got a ruby-and-diamond doorway, according to rumor. I imagine him watching as the jewels seem to drip to the floor. Glittery lava.

I return the vaporizer with a slick, behind-the-back maneuver, like some CIA operative handing over secret intelligence documentation. From the corner of my eye, I see Beamer pocket the piece as stealthily as he removed it.

"Well, at least you got the hell out of here," he says. "Was starting to worry you had some mental thing, like those guys on TV who stay in their rooms for fifteen years. Sick fuckers." He stops suddenly. "There's 47C's weekly appointment." His gaze is fixed a block away. "Two thousand eight Royce, Phantom Coupé. Four hundred K, right there. Just sailed a red light. Driver still thinks he's in India."

He takes his time down the steps, meeting the vehicle as it pulls up at the curb.

I watch him open a car door and hail the bag boy for the suitcase. Pleasant Face intact, he helps a woman from the backseat. She's at least six feet two, and that's before the heels, the dress so short I get surprised-flashed. No panties, just like those dumb Hollywood chicks in the magazines.

Look away, I think, but my brain is on stoner time. She catches my gaze for a second and gives me a small smile. *That's okay,* the expression says. *Look all you want.*

Beamer escorts her to the door, then holds open the glass beneath the gold TRUMP TOWER sign. She giggles, slipping him cash and a smile before disappearing into Wonderland Trumpville.

"Wow," I say, when he returns. "I think I saw her cooch."

"Lucky for you. I've had more old ladies flash me than I care to remember. Open the town car and there it is, elderly bald poon-tang. And you know what they do? Say, 'Thank you so much, Beamer dear,' and then give me a wink. Now I'd take 47C's weekly over that any day."

"What kind of weekly was she?"

"The kind with a suitcase full of whips and latex. Goes by Mistress Damage. Big with the Wall Street guys. They spend all day beatin' people up, so they pay her to give a little back. Or call them 'little bitch' and watch them clean the toilet with a toothbrush."

"No fucking way. How you know?"

"She told me." From the corner of my eye, I see the almost-flicker of an almost-smile. "Took her to the movies once."

"You are an enigma, Beamer."

"*Bridget Jones*, man. Would I make that shit up? Few years back. Not a bad movie, though. Even got her some Milk Duds. Extralarge."

"Then she took you to her dungeon and smacked you around?"

"Somethin' like that," he says, and closes his mouth.

Game over, I think.

"Hey," I say, suddenly remembering my stock is low. "Can you get me more of that stuff? The dark green with the fluffy buds?"

"Agent Orange. Tomorrow. But you can wait. Looks like tonight you'll be covered."

I follow his gaze. A car has pulled up, the window rolled down.

"Bentley Continental limo," mutters Beamer with a low whistle. "Flying Spur, 2013."

"Hey!" says M.C. through a cloud of smoke. "Hurry up, man! Desy'll go double-bitch if we make her wait." He notices Beamer. "How ya doin', brother?" he says, all friendly.

"Fine, sir," says Beamer mechanically. "Thank you for asking, sir."

Miller's head disappears.

I reach for my backpack. "You know him?" I ask casually, messing with the zipper.

"No, not really. Just seen him around, maybe. With 42C."

"Annalise, yeah. His girlfriend. Probably former, but what can you do?" I sling the backpack over my shoulder. "Well, see you later, nigga."

"Sure thing, peckerwood."

"Never heard that one. You figured out how to Google search. Welcome to the New World."

Then I'm gone.

I'd have given him a handshake or fist bump good-bye, but he's not that kind of friend.

Weird, I think, getting in the back. For just a second, right after he called M.C. *sir*, Beamer's face went from Pleasant to Scary Mofo.

▪

Kif from the Rif!" says M.C. He slaps me across the back, all smiles. The limo is huge, or maybe it's just the dark that makes it feel that way.

"Like the Bentley? Borrowed it from my dad's collection. He won't notice. Wait! I forgot the sound track!"

He hits a remote, the dark interior vibrating to life.

"Relax, Bentley seats in the back," raps a voice. *"Lil' momma we rollin' . . . rollin' . . ."*

"Rodney!" M.C. says, knocking on the divider panel. "You hear my man LL Cool? Let's get this shit goin'!"

Immediately, we are in motion.

"The P-I-M-P, the pockets are filled deep . . . he hard to kill G, the God is real deep. . . ."

"You gotta love the original B-boys," M.C. says. "Fuckin' Lil Wayne and shit like that? They had nothing on the old-school bad boys." Then he perks up, like he just thought of something really important. "And you remember our friend, right?" Miller motions to the corner.

Who? Maybe it's the tinted windows and darkened interior, but whomever he's pointing at fades into the seat like a human chameleon.

I squint, eyes adjusting. *There he is.* Same hoodie, same sheepish smile.

"Hey," I say.

"Hey," says Todd Evergreen.

"We never met, but I know you. I mean, who doesn't?"

Todd nods. At least I think he does.

"I mean, the party was thrown for you. That's what I was saying." *Fuck, Phillip. Get your words right. Why are you nervous? You've had dinner with George-fucking-Clooney, and that was when you were twelve, for Christsakes. Who is Todd Evergreen, after all?*

"Fuck, that scene was *sick*," says Miller, stretching his legs out long. He's closer, so I can actually see him a little. "Annalise freaks and I think, 'Damn. Whole night is goin' *Titanic* on my ass.'" He grabs my wrist, startling me, then forces my hand open and drops something in my palm. "Chill."

A blunt.

"Light it up, Kif."

For all the babble, I think, *M.C.'s one hell of a host.*

I blaze up. The lighter clicks and, for a split second, the interior is illuminated.

Todd is watching me. Not a flicker of emotion on his face. Except the eyes, maybe. There's something there. What is it?

Curiosity, I think suddenly, and suck down smoke.

"Hard from the wars, he tough as a battle-ax . . . don't hate him 'cause he hot, God put him where he at . . ."

"And I'm like, 'Fuck this party. This party fucking sucks,'" says Miller. "And two seconds later, there's my man Todd. Bustin' in with that security douche, Old Man Hoff goin' batshit. And then . . . fucking it's on!" Miller grins at me, his teeth very white in the dark. "I mean, the music sucks, but the bitches are going crazy, Cristal flowing. Bottles and models, dude. Annalise drunk outta her mind and outta my hair. And, fuck, just like that, we got ourselves a blowout! The whole fucking place was bumpin'!"

For a second, I'm not sure what party he's talking about.

"Lil' momma we rollin' . . . we rollin' . . ."

■

If by *blowout* Miller meant slamming shots at the bar while pouting, then, yeah. If *bumpin'* translated to muttering obscenities under your breath and getting progressively more fucked-up, then we're on the same page.

And that was after the Annalise fight.

Fuck her, he kept saying. *I'm talkin' to Evergreen and then we're gettin' hella outta here.*

By the time he finally got a window of opportunity—the only two minutes Evergreen wasn't inundated by people asking if he'd *play doubles at my club* or *come for cocktail hour*—M.C. could barely stand up.

Wait, I said. But he was already gone. Striding over like a man on a mission. A death one, maybe.

M.C. talked excitedly, swaying a little, even spitting on the guy a bit. Evergreen listened politely, throwing in the occasional nod. The same conversation the guest of honor had been having all night; one that required no actual talking on his part.

Trade the word production *for* venture, I thought, *and the Hamptons are just like Hollywood.* The inhabitants so far up their asses they could check for proper kidney function.

Got his number, said Miller, holding up his phone proudly when he finally returned. *Dude fuckin' loved me.*

Good job, I said. *Delusional*, I was thinking.

Now I'm gonna text Rodney, he said, fumbling with the keypad on his phone. *Time to blow this shithole. Fuck! Why'd they make these keys so small? Here, you do it.*

As we left the tent, he'd slung an arm over my shoulder, more a move for balance than a sign of camaraderie. *My man Phil,* he slurred. *You asshole. Fuck you. I hate you. Seriously, you're the best, buddy. You're Kif from the Rif.*

Ten feet from the car. *Man, I'm busted,* Miller said, then lay down in the mud.

I nudged his ribs with the toe of my hiking boot. *Get up.*

Whatever, he said, then passed out cold.

Dolna kuchka! A loud, annoyed voice. I turned to see Rodney. *Don't worry,* he told me. *I got it.*

I watched as Rodney, with clinical precision, pulled the dead weight that was Miller Crawford III to his feet.

"Want my help?" I asked.

"Nah," said Rodney. "I got it." Only slightly stooped by the sagging body leaned on his left side, Rodney drag-carried Miller to the car and deposited him, snoring, in the backseat.

M.C. only woke up once the whole ride back. *Annalise,* he said, then looked me right in the eyes. *That fucking cunt. I really love her.*

Two seconds later the snoring resumed.

Which is why, when I'd gotten his text that afternoon, I'd been pretty surprised.

Well, I thought, putting on my shoes, *I guess delusion is in the eye of the beholder.*

▪

Maybe Evergreen did love him, not that you could tell in the dark. And Todd himself sure wasn't saying. We'd gone miles, and not a word from his corner.

Miller, on the other hand, was going by the sharing-is-caring model.

"So fuck her. It was over anyways. Besides, she's still in high school. A junior, even. What, I'm gonna go to prom? I got important shit goin' on." He puffs the joint, then holds it out to Todd.

Evergreen shakes his head. At least I think he does.

"Just wait till you meet Desy," he says, shoving it at me.

Like a bolt of electricity through him, a sudden burst of energy. He's leaning toward Todd, his words coming fast. "Wait till you hear her shit. You'll get it, man. The *potential.* We're workin' on her first single at this *very moment.*"

"Can't wait," says Todd.

"I mean, she's like that chick from the Rock Exchange, only poppier. That one with a million investors. You know who I mean? Short black hair, from Iraq. Sexy little Iraqi punk chick, fuck, wuz her name?"

"Naaz," says Todd. "And it was one point five million investors."

"Naaz! That's her. I like that one song. The *dah dee dah* one. 'Blue . . .' Blue something . . ."

"Blue Damascus," says Todd. "It's the capital of Syria."

"Exactly! Desy's a lot like her. Naaz."

"So Desy sings lyrical ballads contemplating genocide and the subjugation of women?" I couldn't help myself. It just came out.

Wait. *Did Todd Evergreen smile?*

I could be imagining it. All the dark and weed playing tricks on my mind. But I swear, just for a second . . .

"I wasn't talking about the lyrics, man," Miller says to me. "I was talking sex appeal. I'd bang that Naaz chick, for sure. And Desy's got the same vibe, only throw in a little crazy. Not in a bald-Britney-umbrella-stab way. More I'll-hold-this-knife-to-your-neck, but-I'm-just-messin'-with-you. Let's-fuck-instead! way. Sexy/Mental, that's her brand." He drums his fingers across his knees, excited. "So, for her first video, this is what I'm thinking: asylum chic. Like heroin chic, remember that? But we up the booty quotient. Junkies don't have booty, right? So . . . white walls, close-ups on medical instruments. Gleaming steel, intro beats. Drum goes *bum bum bum thud!* And there's Desy. You seein' this? Desdemona Goldberg—gotta work on the last name, little, you know, awkward on the tongue—her hair all messed up likes she's been rollin' in bed. Tight leather pants and—*wait for it*—a straitjacket. *A straitjacket.* But, like, a low-cut one that shows lots of titty."

Is he kidding?

"And heels. Six inches at least. Insta Psycho-Ward Hotness. And maybe throw in some sexy nurses with stethoscopes as backup."

He's not kidding.

Finished, he takes a gulp of air, leans back, and looks at Todd eagerly.

Nothing.

"But tasteful, too, know? Classy vibe. We'll get Spike Jonze to direct."

Silence.

Awkward, I think.

"What's the song?" The words burst out of my mouth, probably too loud.

"Still workin' that out. Got this great guy on it. Done some of Kanye's shit."

Did Todd fall asleep? Die?

Next to me, Miller is holding his breath.

That's when I understand: this whole thing is a pitch. The Bentley, the sound track, the weed. He wants Todd's approval, his potential investment. Why did it take me so long to see? If anyone should have known, it's me.

I mean, it's been part of my existence since the day I was born, as familiar as the surf and palm trees. There it is, on every patio of every four-star restaurant during lunch hour: one tool pitching his wares, the other deciding his fate. And my mother? She's the top decider, the queen of the Tinseltown ash heap.

My pilot script, says the gas-station attendant, then shoves a handful of pages at Mom after fueling up her eco-acceptable transport. *My demo reel,* says the bartender. *My movie,* says the film student after chasing us through the parking lot of Ralphs when second grade let out.

My website, my cross-media revolution.

I have the concept, they say. *The vision. I'm creating a movement.*

Your movement is redundant, I want to tell them. *Your movement can suck it.*

When I was six, my kindergarten teacher gave me her screenplay. *Just give it to your mom,* she said, then patted my head, gave me a cookie, and assigned me the coveted role of Wake-Up Fairy during nap time.

Shouldn't have been so proud, looking back now. I mean, can't they say Wake-Up *Genie* at the very least?

That moment, and so many others. One of the reasons I split LA in the first case, went as far abroad as my hiking boots could take me. I wanted to flee that insatiable American need, the drive to feed on the charred remains of what was once called *art*. The drive to create those remains by sucking any soul or dick in proximity.

So why am I here now? What does M.C. want from me? And does it even matter?

"I love it," I say. "That video fucking rocks, M.C."

From his corner, Todd gives a slight nod. This time, I know for sure. That's how hard I'm concentrating on him.

It isn't a yes nod, or a no one. Just a shift of the head in the up and down. Or a bump in the road.

Miller breaks into a smile. He's beaming enough to light up the dark.

I'm glad for him. After all, that's why I said it in the first place. Why I'd praised his video, even though it's idiotic fluff with no redeeming value whatsoever.

What it comes down to is this: one force is more powerful than the reprocessed, reproduced, recycled *concepts* in the dump-yard of our modern cultural existence—hope.

And that's what I'd saw, pure and unadulterated, on Miller's face.

Living without hope, said Buddha, *is burying oneself.* Plug in drowning, and you got me. Or almost.

He may demean women and have no discernible talent, but Miller's a good guy. And maybe—*just maybe*—a friend. So why take the thing he cares for most?

"Thanks, man," says Miller, still grinning. "But guess you guys can see for yourself in a few." He leans back and sighs, content. "But just so you know, Desy picked the place. So don't blame me, 'kay? Could be a strip club." He snorts. "Or the Four Seasons. With Desy, you never know. *Crazy bitch.*"

9
CHAPTER

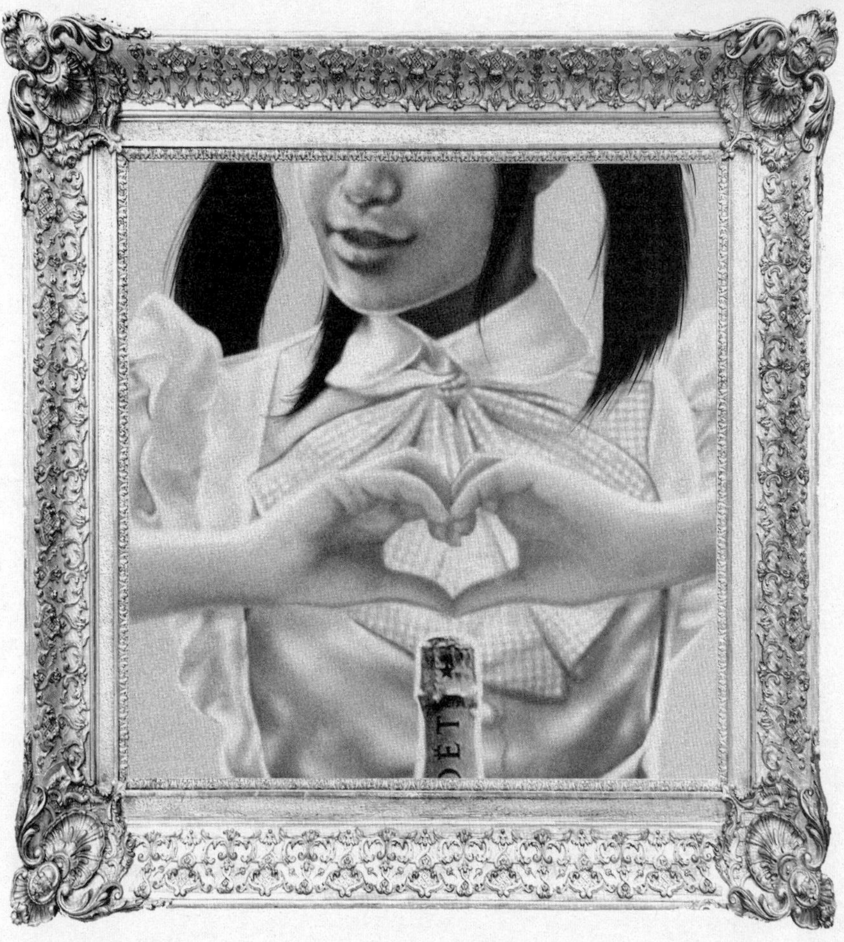

"Welcome Home, Masters!" @NaughtyKitty #BBparty #Moet by Anonymous

Desdemona Goldberg

I'm going to see Miller! That's the very first thing I think.

I smile, pull up the duvet, and clutch it under my chin. I smile to myself for a moment. Then I reach for the phone on my nightstand.

He didn't call. He didn't text.

I feel my heart dropping, my throat constricting. Panic attack, one therapist said, then offered all these ideas to make it stop. Yoga, meditation.

For me, there's only one thing that really works. I call it *crunching numbers*. When I told my therapist about it, she called it obsessive-compulsive behavior. I called her a dumb headshrinker bitch and never saw her again.

True, it's weird, but it calms me. And with the sudden pounding at my temples, I know today it's the only thing that will help.

I push the duvet off me (*crushed velvet in king size, $2,252; $830 for the matching set of sheets*). A yawn, then I swing my legs over the side (*antique French four-poster, $154,000*), get on my feet (*maroon angora carpeting at 450 square feet, $5,976)*, then off to the bathroom to brush my teeth (*Sonicare FlexCare with Dual Handles, $615; tube of Crest, $8.75*).

By the time I turn the faucet (*Kohler two-handle, $874*), I feel my heart rate slowing.

I've calmed down a bit, but the question remains. *Is Miller . . . using me?*

He's only called twice since that night in the bathroom and returned a mere one of my eight texts. And now he wants to meet up, yet he didn't call or text last night? Is this about my career or just doing me over the toilet again?

Not that I didn't enjoy it. I mean, the sex was *delish*. But first and foremost, I'm an artist. A hottie with a sick bod comes second.

I won't be anyone's potty-room slut.

Suddenly furious, I storm down the hall (*maroon angora carpeting, 726 square feet, $8,987*). "Magdalena?" I shriek. "I need you!"

Where could she be? I stomp into the kitchen (*Italian porcelain tile, $10,000, but I'd have to check*), and that's when I see the note.

Picking up a few things . . .

Painful scrawl, like a kid would do. And a little smiley face.

Too sweet. My heart could just burst in my chest.

Oh, Magdalena, I think, running my hand over the words.

It probably took *hours*. She's such a dear. Sweet little nanny, with her precious knitting needles and pants bought at the Spanish Woman Store.

Magdalena, that *precious gem.*

Has it really been eleven years? I mean, she was already *ancient* when she got here! But I don't care. I wouldn't trade her for every Swedish nanny on Central Park West. They would have left anyway, they always do. End up married to a golf pro or, like, Ethan Hawke.

Magdalena is mine for life.

FYI, the word *nanny* is mega-degrading. I mean, she's a maid, too! Not to mention, stand-in mom. Even, like, therapist. So what if her English sucks? She's like the shrinks in the movies who don't say a word. Let you stretch out on the couch and talk yourself silly. And even better, she can listen for *hours.*

And at this moment, we have loads to discuss, re: Miller. So where is she?

P.S. I *totes* forget private chef! *Mami* makes a mean guacamole.

▪

Before Magdalena, I'd been lost in a sea of flimsy nap-time cots. Buried alive under building blocks. I was Eloise, but instead of the Plaza I'd been taken hostage by a pre-K time-out Nazi.

Miss Muson had orthopedic shoes and hair coming out of her nose. On top of insulting my aesthetic sensibilities, she was a megabitch.

I was headed for big things, but those creativity-assassinating asstards at the Montague Preparatory Academy for Educational Excellence? What did they know of artistic gifts? I mean, the plaid jumpers alone! My little eye sockets ached.

To them, square blocks only fit in square holes. *Lits.*

Stop shoving that piece, Desy, said Miss Muson during Cognitive Play. *The block is* square, *do you understand? The hole is* round.

Got it, I said. Then shoved harder.

Desy, I mean it. Count this as a pre-warning.

Ummm-hmmm, I said. I could take direction. If the one giving it wasn't a totes imbecile, that is.

It won't fit, don't you understand? Stop. That. Shoving. Your aggression is scaring the others. It won't fit—

Because you won't let it! I'd shrieked, cutting her off. That was right before I threw it. In her stupid little face.

Pre-Warning got an upgrade.

I was always wrong. Every action I made, every question I answered. Even when I was right. Even when the answer was obvi.

What will you be when you grow up? Miss Muson asked a day later during Contemplation Hour.

I'd piped right up. *An It girl!*

That's not a job, Desy. That's a concept. She'd sighed. *Besides, I didn't see the Sharing Hand.*

It girls don't do Sharing Hands.

This is a another Pre-Warning, Desy.

Your Pre-Warning can kiss my ass, I said. *And when in the hell is Nutritional Enrichment Time. I'm fucking famished.*

▪

"*Find an environment more fitted to her unique needs,*" quoted Dad. *Your needs, Des.* Those were his words. I was in his office and he was pissed. The school meeting had tanked worse than his postapocalyptic *Oklahoma!* revival.

He wasn't angry at me, of course. *Never!*

And I said, put it to me straight. Fuck the rigmarole, I got a meeting. So he goes, "One more Warning, she's out." And I go, "What constitutes a warning? This I gotta hear!"

Dad kept talking. That was his thing, never shutting up. I'd seen him do it at Sardi's for a table of clients. Close the place and then keep going in the limo ride after. Grandpa was the same, I guess. Before running the show, he'd been "Joke-a-Second Goldberg," Vaudeville's Top Second Banana.

As for me, I'd heard enough.

C'mon, Des, said Dad. *Don't cry.*

Sure, Montague was yucksville, but what I hated even more was *rejection.*

I can't help it! I sobbed. *I despise it there!*

They said I was bad! I wailed.

Who gives a rat's ass what they say? So you bit someone? Big whoop.

She stole my LEGOs when I went to pee-pee! They were mine and she took them!

I know the type, said Dad.

She was a bitch!

They usually are. He'd sighed and leaned back. Over his head, the Tonys and Drama Desks sparkled on their build-in shelf.

I told you I didn't wanna go!

You don't need that crapola, he'd said. *And I sure as hell don't, what with this show. And you bet your bottom dollar I told that headmaster. I mean, I got time for this hoopla? Forty grand I'm paying those ninnies. Get off your ass and educate, that's what I said. And forget about those opening-night tickets for your silent auction! So here's the thing: forget that place.*

I'd stopped, looked up. I knew that voice: the no-more-fucking-around one. Just the week before, I'd heard it on a conference with Julie Taymor. *A puppet does not a plot point make,* he'd said, mega for reals. *Put the animals in little clothes or something. It's called theatricality, honey. Don't like it? Go back to that experimental shit. I'll even get you the venue. Know a great alley in the East Village.*

We'll get you a tutor or something, he said, all producer mode. *Or better yet, another nanny. Fuck this shortage bullshit, I'm not buying. We'll get a nanny/tutor combo, textbooks, the whole chasarigh. How's that sound?*

I looked up, smiling. *That's what I wanna see,* he said. *Know what I'd be doing if I'd followed the rules, honey bunch? Hocking* shmatas *in the garment district for four-fifty an hour. What does some teacher know, anyway? She put on six hits on Broadway? And forget the school BS, I never got a degree and look where that got me!*

He'd opened his arms wide, and I could see his point. Eleven-room co-ops didn't come easy, especially ones with Park Avenue views and wraparound balconies.

Forget them, Des. You come from Goldberg stock. And what are Goldbergs?

Legends.

You got it. He smiled big. No matter what I did, my reviews would always be raves. *You got the spark, baby. Just like your mom. Lit up a room, that crazy bird. Thank God you got your mind from my side, huh?*

I didn't care what he called her. Didn't even remember her face. Did herself in when I was two with a bad-review/sleeping-pill mixer.

At least it hadn't been in vain. She'd gotten the Tony nod years earlier.

Never met Gramps either, but you could still see the GOLDBERG'S REVUE sign on Forty-Seventh Street. Right between a tchotchke store and a Starbucks.

Burlesque, my dad said, *is women taking off their clothes. Only classy.*

I'd tried it myself. That had been Warning Three. No imagination, those people. Usually show-and-tell was such a yawn-fest, and the pasties had been totes adorable! I'd made them myself with Christmas tinsel.

You, Desdemona Goldberg, are the whole package, said Dad.

Overture, intermission, and curtain call included. And anyone who says different? Forget 'em.

Always good with a closing line, my father. A big finish.

I love you, Dad. I didn't have to act on that one.

In the end, we got a great nanny. To Magdalena, I was a *perfecto* ten. In fact, there was a shrine of me right next to her Our Lady of Guadalupe one.

And homeschooling was *da bomb!* Forget teachers, I learned more from the Powerpuff Girls than they'd ever teach me.

It was a fab few years. But ultimately, Page Six ended my homeschool staycation.

▪

Which bombshell Broadway heiress celebrated her graduation from rehab by giving a drunken lap dance to a notorious boy bander at a private New York club? Guess he left that famous purity ring at home. And if that wasn't enough, the wannabe actress/model/singer sex kitten was seen downing shots with the Beebe, loudly discussing her father's soon-to-premiere of a White Way revival and making several trips to the unisex bathroom to "freshen up." If that striptease on the bar was any indication, she was refreshed all right. Too bad she forgot to pay that $10,000 bar bill before the bouncer kicked her out. . . .

Well? Dad said when he finished, throwing the paper down on his desk. *What do you have to say?*

It was even better this time, and I'd heard it, like, forty zillion! They called me a *bombshell*! A *sex kitten*! It was like a dream come true.

That wasn't what Dad wanted to hear. I could see it on his face.

Lies, Dad, I'd responded. *I swear.*

Most of them, at least. Beebe? *I wish.*

But, hey, Dad, what do you always say? No press is bad—

Shut the hell up, Des.

I'd stared at him, shocked. How dare he? And how freakin' weird. Dad never got pissed with me. I mean, he hadn't even blinked at that underage-drinking thing. Even tried to positive-spin the mandatory wilderness rehab. *It'll be fun,* he'd said. *Just a little vacation, kiddo!*

And in the end, he was right. It hadn't been *that* horrif. I mean, I'd learned tons of new skills! How to BS a Therapy Powwow, for starters, and how to get liquor past a Rehab Ranger. Not to mention, the art of mirrorless lipstick application! Superhandy in packed nightclubs.

And life lesson numero uno? Where and how to get it on au naturel.

Behind a tree, doggy style. *Just FYI.*

Hard life lessons, to be sure. But I never made the same mistake twice! And just so you know, trees are for grip, not balance. Bark burns hurt like a bitch.

It'll fly by, that's what Dad had said. *You'll be back at Barneys in a jiff!*

So what the fuck was this? One little blind item and he goes all Alec Baldwin on my ass?

Then he'd given some yawn monologue about jeopardizing his rep, and think of my own rep, and the family name and some other BS horseshit. *How I needed to focus,* blah blah blah, *plan for my future,* obladi oblada, and *what the hell was I going to do with the rest of my life?*

The chance I'd waited for. That door finally swinging open.

I want to act, I said, straight-up *Chorus Line*–style. *And sing. I just want to perform, Dad! So maybe, I don't know, you'll give me a little part? In your new show? I swear that'll be the direction I need.*

Fat chance of that, he'd said. *You gotta earn your stripes.*

I had been totes offended. After all, there was more to me than Page Six. More than rumors and hype. Think you got me pegged? Just keep shoving. You'll never make me fit.

▪

Sometimes I was the square hole, sometimes the round.

The thing is, people would always try to put me in a box. The school psychologists, the clinicians. The wilderness ranger at Rehab One, the ex-navy SEAL at Rehab Two, the endless 'tards who charge $800 an hour just to repeat my sentences and up my dosage.

ADHD, they would say. *NIMH and ICD.* And just for the hell of it, why not throw in a little OCD?

But I defy labels, except the kind they put on Oscars. And trust me, there'll be plenty of those. I'll have a space ready right next to my Grammys.

Re: the pills. I'm cool with those. When I remember to take them. Which doesn't happen all that often.

And besides . . . I'm more interesting without them! Ask anyone. Ask my manager, Miller.

Miller, that adorable boy. *Such a little sweetie!*

▪

Uplifted by Magdelena's presh note, I turn on the coffee machine and do a little impromptu tap number on the kitchen floor while it drips. "Magdalena will be here soon," I sing. *Step-ball-change, shuffle-heel-turn.* "And I heart Miller Crawford the Third!" I fan-kick my way to the mug rack and grab one.

Miller appreciates my talent as well as my ass, I'm sure of it. He sees what I always have. A headliner, of course!

I'm on my way, I think. And Dad didn't even need to help! A grand jeté, though not so grand. Too bad that ballet teacher was a bitch. Still, I'm pretty good for half a class. Not quite Mila in *Black Swan*, but my tits are bigger. I'm probably better at cunnilingus, too.

A pirouette, and I knock into the sterling silver bread basket, catching it just in time.

Miller believes in me nearly as much as I do. *Star potential,* he says. *Sex appeal.*

I know all that, I say. Still, hearing it from a hottie like him is totes validating.

Today I'm seeing Miller! The thought re-goos my insides. *Hurry home, Magdalena. I want to tell you about your future son-in-law!*

Espresso safely in hand, I open the fridge and look for something to nosh. *Low fat*, I remind myself. *Gotta look fab. Remember, Miller's going to make you a star!*

Then that little voice in my head: *Unless he's using you, that is.*

A surge of anger, and I slam the fridge door *(KitchenAid Architect, $9,246)*.

That bar *was* pretty out of the way. Not to mention gross. *Legendary,* Miller had called it. *Punk.*

Legendary does not include bottle service, I guess. And bathroom attendants? *Not* punk.

That part was okay, though. I mean, who wants some lady with a bowl of Blow Pops listening to you fuck?

A romantic adventure, that's what I'd thought. I mean, why else go to the Lower East Side?

But now I see the truth. How could I have been so blind?

That jerk was hiding me! Seething, I grab an apple out of

the Tiffany fruit bowl *(sterling silver in palm pattern, $1,995).*

I hate you, Miller Crawford III. And where the fuck is Magdalena?

I have to get out of here. My head is spinning, the kitchen walls closing in.

Get dressed first, I tell myself. *Looking good is the best revenge.*

Besides, I can't be late. I'm meeting Miller, after all! Sure, I hate him, but I still want to do him, too. But why does he have to be so cruel?

I storm back to my room in a tizzy (*rare antique Turkish prayer rug, $45,000*). I rush into the closet and press the remote. I watch the clothes spin by me (*customized walk-in revolving rack, $5,499; $1,634 installation fee*). A gift from Dad for my eighteenth, made by the head of tech for *The Lion King*.

I pick the first thing that screams *Fuck me*.

Feeling superpissed, I remove my nightie (*vintage Halston slip, $243*) and dress (*formfitting Prada bodycon with built-in uplift corset, $3,400*), I put a little something on my face (*NARS, base and concealer, $235; Lancôme Teint Idole powder foundation with SPF15, #3, $54; Vincent Longo Le Plus mascara, $32.50; M•A•C Ruby Woo, $22; Dior eye shadow, three shades, $42.75; Too Faced highlight illuminator, $34; fake eyelashes and glue from CVS, $3*) and spritz on the perfume (*Chanel No. 5, 6.5 ounces, $473*) and go for I-don't-care effortless with the hair (*Hermès scarf tied Jackie O style, $1,445*). Semisatisfied with what I see in the trifold, I grab my bag (*Versace calfskin satchel, $4,399*), slip on my shoes (*platforms, designer unknown, $4, Sal Army sales rack. I just love vintage!*), and head out the door.

Fuck Miller, I think. *I'm going to be a pop star. And if he apologizes, maybe I'll let him come along for the ride.*

Okay, I'll admit it: I'm not the easiest girl in the world. I want everything at once, and I want it now, and there's never enough time. Minutes slip through my fingers, entire days go poof before my eyes.

Time is a bitch on Adderall.

Sometimes my heart is on speed dial, my pulse fast-forward, my brain vomiting images like an MTV reality show. *Is it too late?* I think. *Did I miss my cue? Hurry up, little girl, or they'll leave you behind!*

Then Miller, like a shot of calm. A dose of okay no doctor could write.

From moment one. Eyes lock, tightrope gone. Cray-cray, especially since I was dancing on a bar. And swinging my bra in circles over my head.

Stripper? *Puhleese.* Hogs and Heifers, not Bob's Peep. I mean, I already had six others hanging on the wall. One right next to Julia Roberts's!

FYI: she's a 34B.

The song ended, and there was his hand. Reaching out to help me down.

Sure, he looked like another Ivy League prep. Not my peeps for sure. But I saw something else. Underneath that Brooks Brothers? A secret freak. A flame just waiting to burst.

And what did Miller see? The free-spirit sex-kitten of Central Park West? Holly Golightly with dirty talk and a knife in her boot?

Who gave a flip either way? What mattered was I'd sucked him in.

As for me? I was a goner when my feet hit the floor. When he'd smiled and said, *Damn, you one sexy bitch.*

So romantic I could die.

And now he treats me like some secret fat girl he's fucking? Some booty call?

Huffily, I stomp down the hallway, stopping for a sec to look at the Picasso. *It's not straight,* I think (*Sotheby's auction, $2.8 million*).

As I walk toward the living room, I realize the time has come, beginning the mental tally. Not healthy? I've turned coping into a game! What could be more healthy than that? *I know way more than any dumb headshrinker.*

I tick off the last number just as the door opens. *Magdalena!*

I squeal with joy, rushing into her arms.

"A new record! Can you believe it? Just an hour and a half, Magdalena, and I touched just under *four point five mil!* A rough estimate, but how ridic is that!"

The Picasso was what did it.

"Bonita chica," she says, then pats down my hair with her wrinkly hand.

"I love you, Magdalena." I say, then touch the diamond earrings I'd bought for her for Mother's Day (*$14,000*).

Grinning, I add them to the tally. Even though I'm happy now.

Enough of that, I think. No more numbers. *This,* I decide, *is going to be fa ab day.*

▪

Two hours later and from a corner banquette I'm watching Miller squirm. "Welcome home, Master," says the waitress as he enters the restaurant. "We happy to serve you!" She gives a few giddy bounces, her pigtails swinging, the petticoats bob-bing right along. Her poufy skirt is a little pink cloud, the apron tied in a crisp bow. And on her head—*too much for words!*—the most adorable fluffy, pink cat ears in the entire world.

So precious I could eat her alive!

Two other guys enter behind him. A pretty one with dreads who must be this Phillip guy Miller has been talking about. The big-time producer's son. Hello, connection! And the other—*could that really be him?*—Todd Evergreen.

"Oh! I mean *Masters*. Welcome home, Masters!" She smiles, giggles, and then modestly covers her mouth. "Tee-hee!" Not a laugh, but the word. *Tee-hee.*

She's classic French Maid, but with a twist. Or is *twisted* what I'm looking for?

This was the best idea *ever*. I could have been a social director or publicist. The head of a branding firm, even one of those promotion chicks.

Or maybe just a Maid Café girl myself. I mean, I'm not Asian, but who cares? I have *range*. Maybe I'll be a movie producer. For my own vehicles. Content control is key, BTW.

But first, my pop album! And there is my manager, who, at this very moment, is being harassed by an Asian manga French Maid. OMFG, I could LOL till I puke!

"You follow me, Masters?" she says in a high-pitched squeak. Wonder if the voice is real? She's nineteen, at least. Then again, you can never quite tell with those Asian chicks.

Miller stares at her with pinched eyebrows. "What the hell is this? I'm totally confused."

He looks bewildered. Or maybe just stoned.

Hilarious. I dig my phone out of my bag and snap a picture, perfectly timed with another *tee-hee.*

Time to rescue him, I suppose. The poor dear, so *adorably* confounded.

"Darling!" I yell. "Right over here!"

Relief all over. He heads for my table with his boys in tow.

I quickly post the shot of Miller—his mouth gaping, totally perplexed—to Instagram long before he arrives. *Crop. Walden . . . no, Lo-Fi. Done and done!* My anonymous album, of course. Miller insists we stay on the DL till I launch. Then it'll be official. My stardom *and* hot manager-boyfriend!

He throws himself onto the furry, pink chair, smacks his hands across the doilied-up table, and says, "Where are we, Desy? This place is wiggin' me out. I mean, whassup with the . . . pink?"

Over our heads, the chandelier goes *jiggle-jiggle*, sending off rosy glimmers of light.

He's *such* an asshole.

I turn from him with a pout. "We're not talking." I check texts on my iPhone 5 with a diamond monogram and try not to think eighteen thousand.

"What did I do now?"

"It's what you didn't do, M.C." I stare into the pink horizon. "No 'Hello,' no 'Nice to see you.' You *sit* down, just like *that*. Not even the bittiest kiss to my cheek."

"Baby." He stands and comes around the table. "How could I be so cruel? Especially when you're my *everything*."

A peck to my cheek and I turn in his direction. Not the whole way, but a little.

He smiles in that way he has, making my insides go to goo. "I forgive you!" I chirp. "Now you can sit!"

He does.

A sip of pink lemonade from a stripy straw, while letting my eyes circle the table. Then I dab my lips with a lacy napkin and turn to Miller. "Introduce me to your friends!"

"Aight. Well, this is Phillip and this is—"

"*The* Todd Evergreen!" The words just burst out. They have a habit of doing that.

"And Naughty Little Kitty," squeaks a voice. "You like my furry ears?"

The three of us look around, confused. Then we realize the voice is coming from the floor.

The Maid is on her knees, holding an order pad in her clasped hands.

"Aren't you just *darling*!" I say.

"Meow!" She pretends to claw the air in front of her. "You like kitties?"

"I suppose." Instantly, she's on her feet and bouncing off.

"What the fuck?" asks Miller. "What is this place?"

"A Maid Café, of course. The first in New York! So fresh *Time Out* hasn't even done a review yet!"

He looks at me blankly.

"Anime fetish dining. Sexy little girls with big eyes? Manga, silly! What do they teach you at Columbia? It's all the rage in Japan!" I sigh, then grace him with a tiny smile. "You must get out more, M.C. Really. You know literally nothing of the real world."

"I present you!" says Naughty Kitty, having returned. In her arms, the tiniest kitten I've ever seen. A real one.

"No," I blurt. "I'm allergic."

In truth, I'm not. I just *abhor* animals. They just seem *unsanitary*. I mean, who licks themselves clean? "You no want baby cat?" says Naughty Little Kitty, obviously unnerved, the kitten going *mew-mew* in her arms.

"I'll take it," says Todd Evergreen, reaching for the gross little furball. He holds it out, staring at its face. "Kinda looks like Iggy Pop."

The kitten goes *mew-mew* and crawls up his hoodie sleeve.

"Iggy who?" I say.

"Tee-hee," says Naughty Kitty.

"That is no longer adorable," I tell her. "So do not do it again."

▪

This is not going well. My fab day is going *hiss-hiss* like a deflating balloon.

Miller is acting weird, Phillip just smiling from stonerville. And as for Todd Evergreen, well, he hasn't said a single word since taking that damn cat.

Iggy Pop has a personality, at least. *Mew-mew,* it says, peeking out from the neck of Todd's hoodie. Little upstager.

"Twinkle twinkle," says Naughty Kitty with jazz hands to the face. "Chocolate disco, sunny rainbows, bark-bark-doggy-*woof*!" She puts her hands to her ears. The fluffy, pink ones, I mean. *Here comes the big finish,* I think. Head bob to one side. "Meow! Meow!" Head bob the other way. "Meoooooow!" Dramatic hand wave over table, then reaches into apron pocket. "Now Naughty Kitty say . . . your food is yummy!"

A cloud of pink confetti falls.

A little bow from Naughty Kitty. "Masters happy? More confetti, maybe?"

"No," say the guys in unison. A bit aggressively, I might add.

"And you, Princess Desy?"

"No, thank you very much, Naughty! But I just love what you did to my omelet!"

I look down at the cat face, the whiskers little red ketchup stripes. *Too presh!*

"Thank you, Princess Desy! And I like you sooooooo verrrrrrryyyyyy much! And later we play Jenga?"

"Absolutely. Though I'm a Candy Land girl myself!"

"Will you hold my hand on Gumdrop Alley? And can I be the blue gingerbread man?"

"Done and done, you adorable thing!"

"Yay!" she squeals, then pounces away, happy as can be. I turn to the boys. "Isn't this fun?"

Silence.

Debbie Downers, I think. I glare at Miller. *This was your idea,* I think. Get Evergreen's advice, win him over.

Stage this right and he might invest, he'd said. *But not obvious, right? Just ask some questions and shit. Get career advice, yaknowwhatimean?*

Of course I did. But how could I perform to this crowd? Worse than a blue-haired Sunday matinee.

I turn to Todd Evergreen, who pushes his rice omelet around on the plate as the kitten bats the strings from the neck of his hoodie.

Scene-stealing brat. "Todd, I've heard loads about you, darling! 'He's an absolute genie,' that's what they say. Wait, I meant *genius. Genie*, *genius*, same thing really, don't you agree?"

"Sure. I guess."

"Your work is *fabu*, and I mean that sincerely. Don't you agree, M.C.? Isn't the Rock Exchange just too much for words?"

"You'll find some," says Miller, giving his little troublemaker smile. Darling!

God, how could I ever be mad with him? I mean, he's just *cute as a bug.*

Not to mention, his cock is *huge.*

A big, throaty laugh. A Des signature one. "Todd Evergreen this, Todd Evergreen that. And here you are . . . a real live boy!"

"Okay, Desy," says Miller. "Down a notch."

I loathe Miller Crawford III. And I was being nice. His cock isn't really *that* big.

"Silly," I say. "Todd, you must tell me all about yourself. The absolute works! But first, we need a pick-me-up. Let's get the fuck out of here."

"I'm game," says Todd.

Finally, it speaks.

▪

We hit up the Boom Boom Room. Once the boys get tipsy and a bit loosened up, I can finally get to topics that really matter. Mainly, *me.*

"So I wanted to perform. I mean, *duh*! Do you believe in destiny?"

"Well," says Phillip. "It depends how you define—"

"That was rhetorical, darling!" I say, then tug one of his dreadlocks. "Aren't you too much?"

He gives a sheepish grin. *I must really love Miller,* I think, wiping my hand on the cocktail napkin in my lap. *Let's talk unsanitary.*

"So anyways, I say, 'Dad, put me in your show.' And mind you, I'm only four! Just teensy-tiny, pigtails and all. 'Just a wee part,' that's what I say. And he goes, 'There are no little-girl parts in *Hair*, Des.' And I say—*this is too much!*—'Then write me one!'"

Miller downs his shot and makes a face. "Can we get some more shots up in here? Where's that waitress?"

"Just a sec, sweetkins," I say, giving him a don't-interrupt-I'm-in-charm-mode look. I turn back to Phillip and Todd. "And FYI, the cast gets naked, you know? Butt. Dingalings and bouncing tatas everywhere! But never mind that . . . Dad couldn't stop me if he tried! Come opening night, I just threw off all my clothes, ran up the aisle, and joined the Tribe!"

"You got naked?" asks Miller.

"Well, of course, boo! That's what they do in *Hair*!" An act earlier, but I don't mention that part. I've always been a renegade.

Then I hear something. Could it be?

Did Todd Evergreen just chuckle under his breath?

One thing about me? I can take a cue. "Want to see? Don't worry, I'll keep my clothes on. Maybe." Before they can answer, I'm on my feet. *"Let the sunshine in,"* I sing out, clear and rich. My hair swings, my hips gyrate, I spin with my arms overhead, belly-dance style. *"Let the sunshine in!"*

I stop suddenly. One stanza, that's enough.

A few claps from patrons. Stunned by my artistry, I figure.

"Wow," says Todd.

Gasping for breath, I give a very low, graceful curtsy. *Leave 'em wantin' more,* just like I say.

I feel a surge of adrenaline. "Let's go."

"C'mon, baby," says Miller, lifting the half-empty bottle of Cristal. "With a two-G minimum, we oughta get our money's worth, you think?"

"I got it," I say, throwing Dad's Black Card on the table. "Now, let's roll. These people are *yawn*."

A little blow in the car—*a Bentley, how delish!*—and we make a pit stop at Provocateur.

Patrón for the boys, a Buttery Nipple for me. Evergreen does a pass, just like with the coke.

What is he, a monk or something?

Another round. Crown Royal for Phillip and Miller, a Dirty Pussy for me.

"Eww," I tell them, wrinkling my nose, "whiskey is ick! Though I did a thousand-dollar shot once. In Beverly Hills, with the Saudi sheikh."

"Muslims don't drink," says Phillip.

"Silly! Not that kind of sheikh."

"What other kind is there?"

"The kind on reality shows! *Sheikh It Up*? You ever see?"

Phillip bursts out laughing. "You're a trip, Desdemona."

"And you, Phillip, are adorableness!"

"You know what Buddha said about laughter?"

"I haven't the faintest."

"'When you know how perfect everything is, you'll . . .' Wait. Something about laughing at the moon. Damn, that was some killer coke!"

"You are too much!" I say.

"No, you are!"

Evergreen watches us with a faint smile. *That's okay,* I think. *You can bask in my light.*

"Mew-mew," says Iggy, peeking out of his pocket.

"Hey, kitty cat," says Todd.

Zip it, I tell it with my eyes. "Let's go." I reach for my bag. "This place is so done."

▪

The 40/40 for pineapple martinis, but the good table is gone. Kirsten Dunst and her entourage, each one more raggedy than the next. That jeans-with-holes-sweater-sack-messy-hair-hipster-thing is *so* yesterday. Not to mention fugly!

So why is everyone looking at her?

"C'mon," I say, already standing. "Let's bounce!"

More lines in the car. *Fun!* Cielo is all hair gel and muscle shirts. Totes Bridge and Tunnel. "I don't do Jersey Sausage Fests," I say, refusing to get out of the Bent. "But I know this great place!"

"How tanked are you?" asks Miller ten minutes later. "This place is great?" We are in the back of one of those greasy kebab places, between Pac-Man and a photo booth.

"You'll eat those words," I say, lifting the pay phone.

"Better than eating here. Whadda they serve? Rat?"

I roll my eyes and press two.

"Password?" says a voice.

Wait. *What was it?* "Rumplestiltskin? Beer pong?"

"No dice," says the voice.

"Supercalifra—"

"Nope."

Phooey! Guess I can't annoy my way in. Okay, one last try. Just a shot in the dark: "Todd Evergreen."

"Wrong again. But I like that dude, so come on in."

Next to us, the photo booth buzzes.

"C'mon," I say, pushing aside the curtain. The boys look at me, eyes wide. "Sillies! There's a secret door in here! What's a secret club without one?"

▪

I'm at the intersection of totally trashed and having a blast. Could go either way.

But not for Miller, I guess. "This isn't working," he says, his breath all warm on my neck.

Goose. Bumps.

True, the place is dead. Secret bars are better in theory. Though the décor is scrumptious! Long, polished bar and hanging lamps. Lights so sexy low I could jump him right here.

BTW, I lied about his cock. It's *gargantuan.*

Next to us, Phillip and Todd are chatting. Meaning Phillip is babbling new age BS and Todd's petting Mew-Mew the Spotlight Hog.

"I need your help, baby," Miller whispers. "I need that star power." Just the sound of his voice makes me *tingle.* On every inch.

For a moment, I stare at his perfectly scrummy face. The curl of his upper lip, that little freckle by his ear. In this light, his eyes are deep blue pools. I'm going to dive in headfirst and take a swim.

I reach for his hand.

How'd I get so lucky? One day, nothing. The next, Mr. Everything comes striding in.

I want to eat him alive. Devour every yummy inch.

I'd die for this man, I think. I'd give him a kidney. I love him so much I'd even waive the prenup.

Of course I won't say that to him. At least not yet.

In that moment, it's just Miller and me, heads nearly touching. Just us two on an island.

"We need a show, that's what I'm thinking. He sees you live, that's all it'll take. He'll be buggin' to invest. Poppin' bands at us left and right."

"Poppin' bands? How ghettolicious! What about an open mike?"

"Too small. Think bigger, baby."

Your cock?

"Desy. Focus."

"I'm listening, sweets!" *Wow,* I think, *that coke was awesomeness.* Glad I tried that new delivery service. What was that guy's name? Teamster? Beman? Maybe just one more itsy-bitsy line? We could slip away, lickety-split. The bathroom again? Or will that make it "our place"?

"Des! Did you hear what I said? I want it to be *your* show. You headlining."

Now he's got my attention.

"But I need your help." He leans in close, his voice all hushy excited. "To make this happen, Evergreen's gotta trust us. He's gotta love us. He's gotta have the best fucking night ever."

"I know just the place!" With a fingertip, I draw a heart in Miller's palm. "And as for Evergreen, don't worry your pretty face."

I let go of his hand, tweak his nose, and reach for my purse. "Trust me, babykins. Todd Evergreen will have *the time of his life.*"

■

"Do it," I say. "I'm not asking, Todd."

We are back in the Bent, on our way to fabulousness.

Todd looks from my face to my tits and back, his eyebrows

lifted. Behind me, Miller and Phillip have stopped breathing.

"That's right, this is the real deal. *Afterschool Special* shit. *You're not leaving this car till you snort coke off my tits."*

"Des—"

"Shut it, Miller." I've got to concentrate. "I'm working the peer pressure here, okay?"

Evergreen just looks at me. Not a smidge of emotion.

He's cute, I guess. In a totally nondescript kind of way.

"Snort it off my tits, Evergreen. I mean it." I lift them up for easier access, making sure not to mess up the white line.

"Why not?" he says with a shrug, then bows his head.

No nips, by the way—just cleave. I mean, *I'm not a whore.*

Still, it was a lot of boobage. And a shitload of coke.

"Good, boy!" I tell him with a giggle. "And OMG, wait till you see this place, Toddy. Divine! But first"—I turn and lift the girls—"it's Phillip's turn!"

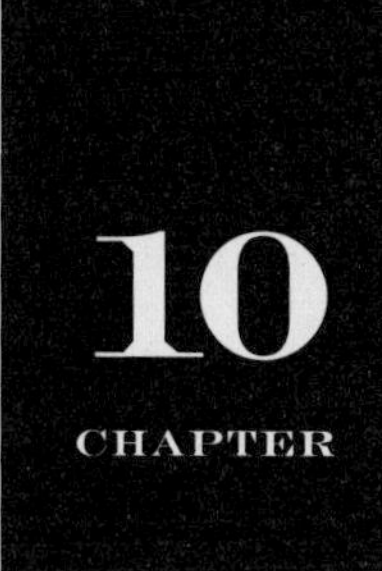

Champagne fountain.
#bestdayofmylife by Anonymous

M.C.

She's bananas, but she's got my back. And, yeah, she can act the bustdown ho, but sometimes you just *want* a nasty bitch.

And that shit with the tits? I nearly blew my wad right there.

But I'll give it to the girl, she got this thing crankin'. Even if I gotta wear a fuckin' parka.

"Minus five degrees Celsius," the waitress tells Evergreen. Since that crap in front with the cat, the staff won't back the fuck off him. Felines is bitch candy, swear to God. *Oohs and aahs*, the desk girls making a little bed in the coatroom. *We'll watch the sweetie, don't you worry!* And I'm, like, *A drink, maybe?* And now the furry-hat server, also on his ass.

I may be a VIP, but he's *VIP with a Cat.*

Now he's getting a full rundown of the place. "One hundred percent imported Swedish ice!" says Fur Hat. "All shipped here in cube form!"

Is that, like, better than the shit in my freezer somehow?

"Three hundred pounds each, isn't that wild?" she says.

Ice queen for reals, I think. *Evergreen must be bored outta his mind.* I give him a sideways glance.

Wait. Did he nod?

Maybe it was that shot. Or second line. Or third.

Evergreen can get his party on. Who knew?

And damn, Des has great tits. Now I'm warming up. In the crotch area, at least.

I lift my drink. The one I finally got. *After* Cat Boy, I might add.

I almost drop the glass but catch it just in time.

Fucking mittens.

I gotta admit, Des was right about this place. *IceCapade!* she said when we pulled up. *It'll blow your mind!*

Have fun with that, said Rodney, giving me a look. *I'll stay right here in case you want to leave, sir.*

That's M.C., you fuck.

Don't freeze your balls off, M.C. Then he laughed.

And he was right, that sarcastic asswipe. Even with the parka, it's hella cold. And the venue itself? Like some whacked-out Antarctica drug trip. Everything ice, from floor to domed ceiling. *Meant to replicate being inside a whale's belly,* according to Hat Girl.

Wait. Was that just the LED? For a second, I thought . . . Evergreen smiled. He did. This time for sure.

Desy came through! By the end of tonight, the Todster will be my best bud. And investing in Des? A total no-brainer.

I mean, she's an easy sell. The moves, the ass. A Jewish Beyoncé. Okay, not the voice. But good enough, with a studio fix. And we'll change the last name to Gold. Desy Gold. D-Gold. That's even better. Nutso Des, that goddess money machine. Shit, I love that schizo freak!

But where the fuck is she? It doesn't take forty-five minutes to pee. Even in girl time.

I scope out the crowd, but the place is too packed. Everyone in puffy coats, neon LEDs changing colors through chunks of ice. Red-orange to purple-blue, then back.

Branding genius, this place. Or else some jacked-up hallucination. Am I that fucked-up?

Now Hat's moved on to cell pics. Mr. Whiskers, her cat. "He's six," she tells Todd. "How long have you had Iggy?"

"Eight hours."

She cackles like he's a Seth Rogen vehicle.

Enough of this piddly bullshit, I think. "Have you seen that chick? The one who was with us?" I cut in.

"There are lots of chicks here," says Hat.

"She's wearing—"

"A parka?"

Sarcastic bitch.

"Never mind." I turn to Phillip and Evergreen. "Going on a mission, guys. Be right back."

"Don't freeze your balls off," says Phillip.

"Yeah," I say. "Already covered that."

I feel a lot better on my feet. Push my way through the human marshmallows, checking faces. *This is going great. Des is a champ.*

I still feel kinda shitty, but better than I have the past two weeks. Since the moment Annalise went batshit, to be specific. And, yeah, showing up to her party late was bad, and stoned even worse. But bad enough to ignore my calls? *Calls*, not texts. That's how much this matters to me. How much this has fucked with my head.

At the center of the room, a gathered crowd. *Crowd equals Desy,* I think, and push ahead.

Annalise will get over it, I tell myself. But until she does, I gotta focus on something. So I'm going balls to the wall with this Des thing. And Des herself? A nice little distraction. Not wifey material, but a good side dish.

"Excuse me," I say, trying to get through. Everyone's packed in, like puffy fucktards. This fat guy won't move, his back to me. Watching some sort of show, I guess. "Dude, do you mind?"

"Hiiiiiii!" A hand on my arm. *Finally.*

I turn, but no Des. A girl I've never seen. "Do I know you?" she asks.

Do you know a better line?

She smiles, her face going purple-blue to yellow-pink.

Cute, I think. But not now. I got an act to sell, a label to launch. Now I just got to find the product to place. "Nah, don't think we've—"

"No, I do know you!" she says. No, *squeals.* Why do girls do that? "The Hamptons, right?"

"I mean, I've been there, but don't remember meeting—"

"Noooooo!" she squeals. *Again.* "The Hoff thing! We totally had a conversation. You don't remember? You asked who that guy was—"

"Listen, I really gotta—"

Her hand in my face. With a card. "Holiday Publicity. I'm April Holiday."

It sounds like a porn name.

"I know, I know. Sounds like a porn name, right? But I swear I'm not. Got clients in music, fashion. Working with a royal right now! The guy you asked about at the party, actually! The one with the girl on his lap."

Now I remember. Wish I didn't.

That dude was a royal? Now I hate that pussy mofo even more.

"He's your client?"

"Yes. Christian. He's great." *A great big fucking douche,* I think. *Who had my drunk girlfriend on his lap.* "He's launching a jewelry line! I was there helping him find investors. Brrrrrr! It's freaking cold in here."

"I guess." I take the card. "Well, it was nice—"

"And you're a music guy, right?"

I just stare at her. *How'd she know?*

"It's my job! I know *everything*!" She giggles. Seriously, she's kinda cute. I move in closer, just for a sec. Total freak, but I can't help it, I'm kind of into that. I've always dug a train wreck. I mean, just look at Des. And who knows? Maybe she's got contacts or something.

"Like what?" I say, leaning in. "What do you know?"

"Well, your name is Miller. Miller Crawford. Of Crawford Artillery." She throws up her arms. "Don't shoot, 'kay?"

Never heard that one before.

I fight the urge to roll my eyes. *Whatever.* Why am I wasting my time? "Yeah, well. You could have read that in the *Times*, the *Journal* . . . seen the deb escort pictures."

"Ooooh! Is that a challenge, mister?"

No, I think. *Abso-fucking-lutely not.*

"I'm up for it!"

Shit.

She moves a little closer. "You're launching a label. Scouting for talent." Voice low, let's-fuck eyes.

But the whole thing feels less sex and more creep. Weird, too. I keep that shit on the DL. Is this some *Fatal Attraction* thing?

"And you socialize with Gerald Hoff," she continues, almost licking her lips. "You know, *Miller*, I'd looooove to meet him. His new editor, actually. Cordelia Derby? She's doing a launch party for *The Set*, and I want to get Christian's stuff featured. Like, *so bad*."

Oh, I get it. *I* got the contacts here, not her. Only I don't. I have no fucking idea what she's talking about. Or even care. "You got me wrong," I say, backing up. "I don't even know what that is."

"*The Set*? His new magazine?"

I shake my head. Who reads magazines? Unless *BuzzFeed* counts? "Look, I gotta—"

"No, wait." she says, grabbing my arm "Seriously, this is a big deal to me." Now her voice is different. Deeper or something. She stares at me, all intense. Demon possession, maybe? Or just straight-up mental? Am I gonna get Lindsay Lohan'd here? I glance over my shoulder. *Move, fat guy!* I think. *What could be so freaking fascinating?*

"Just . . ." She sighs. "Look. Miller. Total transparency, okay? I could use some help. I mean, you're in . . . these circles. And they're kind of hard to break into, you know? I could get to Angelina Jolie faster than Hoff. I've called every department at Hoff Media, like, twice. But no go. Left, like, forty-five messages with his secretary alone."

Tough shit. She think *that's* bad? Mr. Media King's said five words total to me. In two years. And I'm fucking his daughter.

Was.

"Look. I was just messing around, okay?" I got on my calmest, crazy-ho-tamer voice. The one that works on Des, at least most of the time. "I wasn't at that party, okay? I must look like that guy or something. I was just f-ing with you. Don't know any Gerald Hoff either. So I'm sorry about that. But, keep, like, chasing the dream or whatever."

There, I think, turning around.

"You do!" she says. "You *do* know Gerald Hoff!"

Damn. She's crazy loud. People around us stop to stare.

She scowls at me. Hands on hips, face all red-orange with anger. "I thought you were cool. But you're just another lying, entitled rich kid."

"Hey, lower your voice, okay?"

She snorts. "Don't know Gerald Hoff?" she yells. "You're dating his daughter, for christsakes!"

A scream. Like, ear-piercing.

But it didn't come from April not-a-porn-star Holiday.

The fat guy shuffles away. Scared, probably. Finally, I see what he'd been staring at this whole time.

Right behind, the center of the action. A huge chunk of ice, covered in fur. A girl sprawled across, like a queen. Cleopatra, allowing for admiring subjects. Who are mostly a bunch of gays. Who are now glaring. *At me.*

I mean she *was* sprawled. Now she stands in the center of the slab, staring at me. Eyes blazing.

D-Gold herself.

A shiver up my spine. And not ice-related.

"You have a motherfucking girlfriend?" she shrieks.

08/02 12:17

Are you ready for tonight?

Can't wait!

08/02 12:19

I made reservations for 8.30 pm. Is that good?

Better than chocolate ice cream with sprinkles!!!

08/02 12:20

You are adorable.

Cordelia Derby

"You been prayin', sweet pea?"

"Of course, Mama. Every day."

I'm in my new office, talking on my fancy, new hands-free and skimming through the rack. *No, no, no, maybe. Wait, changed my mind . . . no.*

"And you ain't takin' the subway, right? They got rats with diseases—"

"No, Mama, of course not! They got me a car service."

"Well, that's all fine and good. But you're still carryin' the Mace, right?"

"Of course! It's cute as can be. Those little pink Swarovski crystals on the canister . . . you think of everything!"

No . . . no . . . maybe . . .

"You promise, Cordelia? Don't be fibbin' to me, now."

I hold back a sigh. Jesus says respect thy elders, but sometimes she just pesters the living daylights out of me.

"Well?"

"Yes. I promise." *Wait a sec . . . what's this?* I pull it out quick as can be. "Yes!" I shout.

"Good Lord! I heard you the first time, sister!"

"Oh, no. Sorry, Mama. I just found the best piece. The sweetest little chiffon jumpsuit, and the color . . . *gorgeous*. Remember those raspberries I used to pick by the lake? That shade. The ripe ones, I mean. Sort of mauvy—"

"Listen to you, missy! Sounding all big city. Now, us little town folk? We just say *purple*."

"That's funny," I tease. "Especially from a lady with a closet full of Versace."

"Yes," she says, voice serious. "We sure are blessed."

"We sure are. Especially since—" I stop myself just in time.

"Since what?"

"Since I got this chance." *Hold your horses, girl.* Though this secret's bursting at my seams. It's the awfulest, most wonderful thing!

"*Blessed.* Just remember that, Margaret Cordelia. And the Mace. You know, I read about these hooligans they got up there, knock you out in broad daylight and take your kidney—"

"Don't you worry, Mama. I'll keep mine, thank you very much. If any hooligans mess with me, I'll kick 'em where the light don't shine." I giggle at the thought. "They won't be walkin' when I'm through!" *Whoopsy.* "That came out wrong, Mama." I feel the tears rising.

"I know, sweet pea." I sniffle. "Now don't you dare, little girl. Buck up, you hear? Why'd you go to that big old city in the first place? C'mon, tell me."

"A fresh start."

"Exactly. We got to put the past behind us, you hear?"

"Yes, ma'am."

"Besides, there's no crying in business. You be sweet as pie but never weak. Ain't that right?"

"Yes," I say softly.

"And you got a magazine to launch, don't you now?"

"Yes."

"Then go forth and be the light Jesus intended you to be, sweet pea."

"Amen. Love you, Mama."

"Bye, sweet pea."

I hang up the phone, blow my nose, and remind myself of the facts: *It's all happening, everything I could ever want!*

And the magazine? That's only the half of it!

See, you can turn lemons to lemonade! Or, since I'm a hoity-toity magazine editor now, lemons to Lemon Drop martinis.

I head on over to the calendar on the wall, the one I put up next to the styleboards and rough page layouts. I count down the days.

Only two weeks until the launch party for The Set! *And two hundred million things to do!*

Quick as a lightning bug, I run through the list in my head: *Printer check-in, header redo. Finalize shoot wardrobe, call the photographer about locale. Cloisters permit? Mitzi update: advertising. Art director consult, sales-team review. Sponsor contacts?*

Mental note: Papa's Christian Business Leadership buddies. The CEO ones who owe him favors, especially.

Lord Almighty, I think, *this'll be quite a feat. Thank goodness I have Jimmy!*

I dial him up on my fancy new headphones. The ones he gave me, that darling!

"Miss Cordelia?"

"Jimmy, could you come on in here? I'm fit to be tied. There's just so much to do, I'm fixin' to have a Wintour-esque conniption fit!"

"Be there in seconds, sweetums! And, missy, don't you worry 'bout a thing. Shall I bring one of mama's little helpers along with the double skim latte?"

"Oh, bless you, you sweet thing!"

"Besides, you ain't got reason to fret. Know why?"

"Why?"

"You got me."

Jimmy had been a dream. The rest of *The Set* team, unfortunately, hadn't been nearly as hospitable. If the new leadership hadn't gotten them worked up enough, pushing up the first-issue release surely did the trick. *It won't be possible,* said Janette, the creative director, her face going red and splotchy. Adult acne, the poor dear. *That's less than a month! And we're still in the conceptual phase.*

I have faith in your abilities, I told her, and true to my word, she's been just peaches in her brand-new editorial-assistant position!

It had only taken a day or so to understand. Mama had been right all those years. *A powerful woman takes control, but knows her charm is stronger than her yell. There'll be jealousy and fretting over the piddliest of things, but just wear your smile as a weapon. And your panty hose, of course. Even on Fridays! Ladies don't do dress-down days.*

All these years, she'd made it look easy. But that kind of carefree took work, sure as can be. Especially for a girl such as myself, who, like Papa had been saying since I was a lil' bit, had natural sweetness running through the veins.

That's why, no matter the in-house shenanigans, I always made sure to bring cupcakes for staff meetings!

And Jimmy? A secret weapon and saving grace. I knew Jesus had my back the day his résumé showed up in my inbox.

Allison, my previous assistant, had always wanted to be a full-time mother. It took a little pushing, but she'd admitted as much! *Follow your heart,* I'd told her, *and remember Hoff Media offers a terribly generous severance package! Perhaps you and little Lillian will take an educational trip? I heard the Grand Canyon is lovely this time of year.*

"And did I mention? We got Deuce de la Deuce!"

"The party planner! Oh, you are too much!"

I beam at Jimmy, who's posed with legal pad across my maroon love seat, the one that perfectly matches his tie. *Did he plan that?* I wonder with a smile. After all, he did pick the piece himself! A *business expense*, he'd explained. *How can you make great art when your interior designer is OfficeMax?*

"Deuce de la Deuce! I mean, the man is impossible to get," Jimmy said in a faux whisper, "but—and I'm not naming names—I have connections!"

"How in the world?"

"Let's just say Dolly Parton—meaning the one who plays her during the Saturday late show, Max—has a *muy importante* cousin!"

"Deuce de la Deuce?"

"No, silly! Deuce's little twink boyfriend!"

We both giggle with excitement. *Note to self: Is Twink that homosexual Teletubby? Must be some drag-queen slang. Google ASAP.*

"He'll be here on Thursday, and he's already scouting venues!"

"You are a godsend, Jimmy! And thanks for that little booster. I feel so much better."

"Those are practically coffee in this industry. Oh! I forgot. The copyeditor on *Social Bitches* sent back a rough edit—"

"*Social B's!* With four little stars after the *B*!" I say, trying to look angry, but he just laughs. "It's the suggestion of the word, you know that! But . . . I just don't know, Jimmy. Do we even need to suggest such a thing?"

"I've told you before, Miss Derby, B's are the next big thing! And if anyone should know, it's me. I play Cher after all! Only every second Friday, but you should just see me rip into those queens in the audience! I once punched one square in the nose during 'If I Could Turn Back Time.' He wouldn't stop taunting me, but that sure shut him up quick!"

"You are too much! I'm just fretting, of course. Remember, I want sophistication and hipness!"

"Of course! 'Old-fashioned class with a modern, sexified edge.' I helped you write that mission statement, don't you forget! Tagline: 'What happens if Donna Reed marries a billionaire, gets a high-end makeover, and learns the arts of twerking and vajazzling?'"

"That one is new! Love it! And you know I think you're a dream. It's just . . . Social B's? What will my papa think?"

"That you're the hottest thing in the fashion game."

"Well, might not do it for him, but I suppose this is about more than his opinion—"

"This is about revolution."

"Yes, of course," I say. "But honestly, hon, you must tell me. Is this whole approach just too . . . over-the-top?"

He leans forward, face suddenly all serious. "I would never steer you wrong, Cordy. I adore you too much for that! And this is going to be fresh, I promise. The freshest thing to ever hit the high-end-magazine scene. This is Blanche DuBois in Betsey Johnson and garters, Taylor Swift in Oscar de la Renta, minus the stalking—"

"Sookie Stackhouse in vintage Chanel without the white trash and bloodsucking?"

"Exactly! And Paula Deen without the fat, racist thing! That one was a joke, honey. But we got it, you think?"

"We surely do." I can't help but smile. This friendship is spit-shine new, and near about the last thing I ever expected. But it's also a big old blessing!

Now don't get me wrong, I've never had anything but affection for the gays. I mean, I think those two on *Modern Family* are cute as can be, and I can't rave enough about Dwayne, my personal shopper at the Dallas Bergdorf. *Visionary!* But Jimmy is my first official friend of light-in-the-loafers persuasion.

Why had I been so worried?

I smile at him, hardly believing what I've been missing. Handsome, wicked funny, and smart as a whip to boot. And to top it all off? A hometown boy. Well, Oklahoma. But close enough.

If I was his type, who knows? We might just have a thing.

That is, if I wasn't in love!

"Mmmmmm-hmmmmm," he says, looking at me with raised eyebrows. "Someone's got a date tonight, don't they?"

"How'd you know?"

"You got it all over you, hon. And then there's the new shoes . . . *fierce*!"

"You are the sweetest thing!"

"Miu Miu?" I nod. "I just love the little crystals on the heel! And with that adorable patent leather in front . . . sweet *and* sassy. Or business and pleasure—"

"Are you saying I got the shoe version of a mullet?"

"Shut your mouth!" he says. "But a mullet can be hot. I once did a guy with a mullet! Closeted farm boy who came to OKC on the weekends. Put away the tractor, put on the white jeans . . . and big city, there he was!"

I try not to look shocked.

"Don't look so shocked!"

"Oh, it's not . . ." I try to think fast. "It's just . . . white jeans?"

"I know, I know. Slim pickin's, what can I say? Well, hopefully your mystery man has better taste . . . ?"

"He does. And stop fishin'."

"Okay, okay," he says, rising. "But we call it Okie noodlin' where I'm from." He gives a little sigh. "Now you know I'm here, don't you, darling? If you ever need to talk."

I smile. It's a nice thought, laying your soul bare. And maybe I just will, who knows? But for now, I like having a secret. A delicious one at that!

He rises, smiling. "Well, back to the fashion grindstone, I suppose. Need to check in with Art guys about your Friday. But have fun tonight, Miss Southern Belle!"

"I will, sweets!" I blow him a kiss.

He stops suddenly at the door, hand to forehead. "Oh! I almost forgot. You got a call during your two o'clock facial. M . . . something. Wait." He flips a page. "M.C. Wouldn't give a last name. Says you met in the Hamptons?"

"Oh! Of course. Yes." *Miller,* I think. I'd made a habit of learning everything I could about Hoff Media, especially the important players. And ex-boyfriends of the heiress sure counted, even ones who got drunk as a skunk at Hamptons garden parties. Miller Crawford III. *Why in the world would he be calling me?*

"Said he's got a proposition," chirps Jimmy, then winks. "Now who is this man exactly?"

"I barely know him myself! Just someone I met in passing."

"Well, that happens once you hit the big time, don't it,

girl? I'll leave the number right here. And soon as you find out the deal, Miss Derby . . . you *must* tell me!"

"You can count on it, sweet thing!"

▪

A few hours later, and I'm in some alternate world. The lights are low, enormous leather chairs here and there. Couples lean toward each other, their faces lit up by love and candlelight, though maybe I'm just imagining the love part. Funny how I've been doing that these days!

"Romantic, isn't it?" says the maître d'. "In fact, Bacall and Bogart got engaged here!"

The tablecloths are checkered, just like at the barbecue picnics we used to throw at the ranch. But other than that, this place ain't like nothing I ever seen in Texas.

The ceiling is crammed with a whole dang universe, boxing gloves and baseball helmets, toy dump trucks and signed *Vanity Fair* articles. "That model airplane was a gift from JFK," the maître d' says, pointing. "Your first time at the 21 Club, I'm assuming?"

"Yes." I cringe. Caught gape-mouthed like some hick tourist! My mama raised me better than that.

"That's why I took you the long way," he says, then whispers, "and because you're pretty!"

"Thank you," I say, hardly offended. For one, he's old. Forty at least! And for two, well, I do look pretty fetching. After all, it's the first lesson I learned in junior cotillion training, even before table manners or the fox-trot. *Clothe yourselves therefore, as God's own chosen ones,* Miss Longmire had said. *Colossians 3:12–14.*

Does Jesus want you showin' off your belly, havin' SLUT *bedazzled across your rear end?* she'd added. *No, of course not. He died for your sins, so least you can do is look classy for him!*

Miss Longmire, bless her old-maid soul, had been our Sunday-school teacher as well. And she'd be pleased as punch, God rest her dead and buried self, with my new Alice and Olivia cocktail dress. The pale yellow is a dream, hugging me in all the right places, the silk going *swish-swish* against my skin with every step. The girls aren't quite on display, but the fabric is so airy I feel pretty much naked.

"Well, thank you for the tour!" I say, as we turn a corner and he holds a door open for me.

A few steps down, and I get the willies. Beneath is a small room with a few creepy doors, one a gleaming steel. "Wait, where are we going?" I ask, remembering that man with the cute little dog and no pecker who made dresses out of women. *What movie was that?* One of the kids in Youth Brigade got a copy, and not an *Edited for Christian Viewing* one, either.

To this day, I wish we'd gone with *Kung Fu Panda.*

"This is the where they kept the liquor during Prohibition," says the maître d'. "Over the years, it's housed the private collections of Richard Nixon, Sophia Loren, and Elizabeth Taylor."

That's just hunky-dory, I think. *But are you planning on skinning me?*

"Penélope Cruz is in this room," he whispers as we pass a door. "But yours is even bigger." We pass another entrance, and he stretches out his arm, motioning for me to go ahead in.

I must look nervous.

"A private room," he says reassuringly. "Very exclusive. Someone, young lady, must like you a great deal."

A few steps in, and my eyes adjust. And there he is, rising in the darkness to greet me. "Christian!" I squeal, and go running into his arms.

Just like a movie, only one that doesn't scare the bejesus out of you. The kind that makes you just plain glad to be alive!

Tonight, I decide suddenly, *I'll take the plunge. I'll let him touch my chest.*

I like him so much, I might even take off the bra!

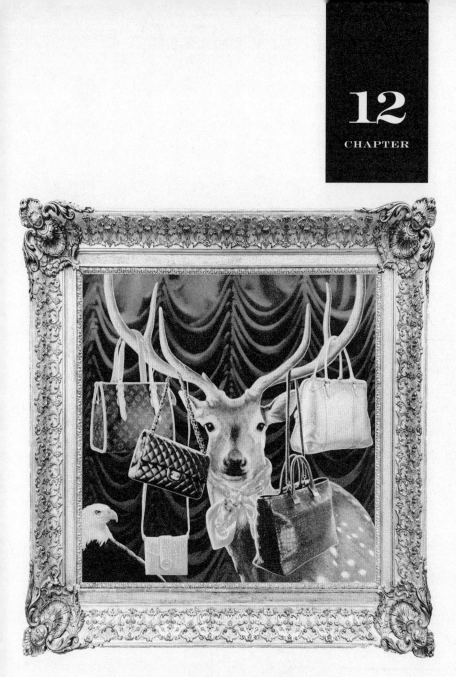

Hold my purse, deer?! #Vuitton #Chanel #Birkin #Balenciaga #taxidermy by Anonymous

Christian Rixen

"I have never seen hands this small," I say, making slow, languid circles on her palm. "But the rest of you is miniature as well, I suppose."

"You make me sound like a dwarf, Christian Rixen of Hirschenborg! Pardon me, *little person*."

"Enchanting, how you say my whole name when you are annoy—"

"Don't change the subject, mister! I'm not so little. Five feet five!"

"*Diminutive* is a better word, perhaps."

"Only because you're so dang tall!" She purses her lips and pouts, yet we both know the anger is a façade. In no time, she is giggling once more. "I was little back in the day. Daddy used to say, 'You're no bigger than a tater bug.' But I grew, thank goodness."

"A tater bug?"

"A bug that lives in potatoes, goober!"

"Goober?"

"Stop teasing me!" she squeaks. "It hurts my feelings!"

I look at her pityingly, though we know this to be an untruth. She finds the subtle mockery an aphrodisiac.

Never, in my lifetime, has a woman required such tremendous effort.

In Denmark, the women came to me. Lined up, awaiting the opportunity to . . . what is it that a tiger does? *Pounce.*

Take the most beautiful girl in the room, the one who spent the evening knocking potential suitors to their knees. I should only have to wait, if I so chose, for her to sift through the *kæmpe nar* debris and present herself, ready and willing, for my disposal.

As for dates, they are as foreign to me as Cordelia's Jesus. I'm accustomed to, perhaps, a series of questions during the drunken half hour prior to the inevitable exit. *Where do you study? Your musical taste? Long-term plans for the future? Ready to fuck?*

The interview is necessary as, come dawn, you must decide: a future together or pull a *hindbærsnitte,* saying, *Shall I fetch breakfast?,* and shoving a flat, sprinkled pastry in her mailbox before you run.

I, of course, would never debase myself in such a manner; I would send a servant instead.

"I want to put you in my pocket and carry you around," I tell her. "Is this a strange thing to say?"

"Yes." Another laugh, equally as charming.

"Have some more wine." I'm already pouring from the newly uncorked bottle the sommelier just delivered, holding it out to me as though presenting a firstborn child. As well he should at forty thousand kroner a bottle!

"No, I couldn't," she says.

"You could. And this one is special, acquired just for you. Château Margaux."

"Sounds fancy."

"It is." I lift my glass, though she simply peers at her own, face concentrated, as though facing down a cunning, fearsome opponent.

"Just a taste."

"I don't . . ." She halts at my expression. One, I am sure, that appears both hopeful and pleading. "Just this once," she says, lifting the glassful with the solemnity of Communion wine. "After all, Jesus drank it, right?"

Once again, I am surprised by her lack of irony, her vigorous reverence for a fossilized dogma. Along with the vast majority of my Danish countrymen, I find religion a lovely, if rather antiquated, series of rituals. Christmas trees are nice, but the deep contemplation of a child savior born thousands of years ago? Rather tiresome.

Her face conflicted, the rim touches her lips.

I am fascinated by her convictions, which I find both enthralling and infuriating in equal measure.

She sips.

Sådan!

"It's good." She smiles.

"As well it should be. Nineteen ninety-four, an excellent year."

"The one I was born in!"

"Indeed," I say, hiding my surprise. Six years is a sliver of time, but still I ponder the question: Is this not, as the Americans say, the paradigm for robbing the cradle?

"Don't worry, Christie!" she says, as though reading my mind. "Eighteen is legal. You won't get arrested!"

"How could I worry in the presence of such loveliness?" I say, a quick recoup. "And besides, they rarely arrest those of royal descent."

"Oh," she says, gazing off abstractly for a moment, her eyelashes appearing to flutter independently of her body. "Well, I guess you can't believe everything you read on Danish Google."

I reach for my wine and swallow, in the next ten seconds, what I estimate to be $250 worth.

▪

For approximately six months, I lived as the average man.

An average man of extraordinary abilities, perhaps, but also one who fetched his own coffee in the morning, obtained from an ordinary local smorgasbord. The average student in transit to class, I would push through the still-drunk throngs seeking nourishment after their drunken evening escapades, offer up a *god morgen* to the harried waif behind the counter, and stir in two cubes of sugar. With my very own hand.

I had never been so happy.

At the Jewelry Academy of Copenhagen, I was learning the secret language of precious minerals, their dispersion and fracture and placement within the refractive index. I had come to understand some compounds were far older than a title and far more enduring than the sacredness of royal ceremonies.

Beauty born of this earth, not bequeathed upon it.

Rubies, for instance. And diamonds.

In cutting a diamond, my instructor Emil informed us early on, *the most time will be spent in evaluation of the rough stone. A delicate, thorough scientific process that takes into account directional hardness, gemological context, crystallographic plane orientation . . .*

He'd circled the room, allowing each of us to hold the raw materials. Five small, unremarkable rocks in my cupped palm, gray and rough as those I had found on the beach in Hornbæk as a child, identical to those I aimed at the unsuspecting local boys who called me "pussy rich boy" and refused to let me join in their football games.

You must consider many possible outcomes, use science and the eye, determine what facets will enhance the luster, fully disperse the white light. . . . Ultimately, you decide which flaws to remove and which to keep.

These little nothings in my hand. Little nothings that, once cut, could transform beyond imagination.

I had been jealous of those diamonds. For being allowed flaws in the first place.

Nothing is harder than a diamond. To cut one, you must use another. Most students preferred the saw, the phosphor-bronze blade edged in diamond dust. A tedious yet reliable process with a determined outcome.

I preferred the hammer. One well-calculated blow could achieve perfection. The risk being that a minuscule miscalculation might destroy the stone itself. To do this correctly, cutters were trained for years, even lifetimes.

I was willing to put in the time.

If any knew of my royal status in Copenhagen, they did not let on. Or perhaps they simply pretended not to, sensing this to be my wish. I had convinced my father to relieve me of servants. I knew this would be my one chance and opted to try real life on for size, to see if it fit my measurement. As for my tailored uniforms of the past, I traded them for jeans and button-down shirts. Shirts bought at the mall and paid for out of my own wallet. An H&M one at that.

Whatever they knew, my classmates treated me as an equal. By day we discussed stone setting and burnishing techniques and learned to manipulate metal, curving it at will. I would roll up my sleeves just like the others, burn my fingers right along with them.

Through each new design, and inevitable misstep, we began to define our singular visions, our unique aesthetic approaches.

During long beer-fueled evenings—yes, *beer*—we debated tradition versus the avant-garde, innovative usage of material versus mastery of technique. *Can we not have both?* I would ask, to which the others would roll their eyes and moan, *Oh, Christian, you're a broken record!*

True, piped up Ina one day, *Christian's opinions may be repetitive as hell. But I think we can all agree his work is stunning.*

My classmates had simply nodded, as though this fact had long ago been agreed upon.

For once, I was stunned into silence. She was one of the most talented students in the school—I was awed by her color arrangement and use of gemstones—as well as the most intelligent.

Now get me another beer, Christian, she had added. *I will need it to endure more of your jabbering.*

I was no longer that young man entrapped on the family estate, the one whose only recourse had been coke-fueled yacht getaways with idiotic heiresses. There were no more champagne-bath parties in Monaco, whole afternoons wasted on spraying thong-clad girls with bubbles.

That part had not been so bad, to tell the truth.

But this was better. And I still partied, but I did it like every other young man in Copenhagen, avoiding those places my ilk frequented. I opted for the nonprivate of establishments, taking on the routine of the everyday citizen: hit the bar around midnight, get trashed by three, and exit, young woman in tow, no later than five.

And no matter the adventure, I was never late to class in the morning. Not ever.

Sometimes I would even forgo the pussy, staking out the early-morning dens of outcasts. I would smoke with whores, play darts with bikers, and otherwise stumble about with the ne'er-do-wells of Copenhagen.

My partner in these escapades was Jais, a rough-and-tumble kid from the wrong side of Jutland, whose use of natural pearls was both twisted and innovative. *Is there a right side of Jutland?* I often queried. *Fuck off, rich boy* was the standard response.

Jais was the only soul to whom I offered up full disclosure, slurring the truth during one 7:00 a.m. round of beers at Spunk in the red-light district. *My father is a count,* I had said.

No shit, he had responded. *You hold your beer bottle like a prissy girl. Well, in that case, next round's on you, Your Highness!*

If too inebriated to make it back to the dorms, he would crash in my expansive apartment, the one loaned to me by my father and stationed in the center of Copenhagen. *Do not vomit on that,* I would tell him, motioning to the settee he had sprawled across. *It was a gift from Queen Margrethe.*

A fuckin' ugly-as-shit gift, he would say, then snore.

Jais was the one who took me to Christiania. *I can't believe you've never been,* he said, to which I responded, *I do not get out much.*

In truth, I had avoided the place. My scene had been more five-star-club hopping in Ibiza than squatter community built on an abandoned military compound. At some point, those hippies crashing on the grounds had taken root, the government giving them residency. And now they'd grown into lawyers and politicians, their acreage lush and untouchable, and the government horrified to have given away such valuable land in the center of city. And even within Christiania itself there was exclusivity. I cringed at being designated to Pusher Street with all the other outsiders.

I had been an outsider long enough.

Do not bring a camera, I had oft heard it said, *or they'll kick your ass right out of there.* Not to mention, the raids were frequent, the government shutdown attempts regular. The land was valuable, everyone knew that, and Danish officials resented this freak settlement. As for me? I had no idea what I had been missing.

Jais knew this place well, had been escaping to it since childhood. *Obviously,* I responded. *You're from Jutland.*

As if you'd go anywhere you could get your hands dirty, he had said.

There was plenty of dirt in Christiania, as I soon learned. And I wanted to see every bit.

The hidden skate park, where some American World Cup champion was crashing with three girlfriends and one sleeping bag. *Yo,* said one of his entourage, offering a joint and stories of living on the beach in Malibu. *After this, I'm off to Morocco. Hear they got killer waves out there.*

What is in this? I had said, holding up the joint. *I can barely see your face.*

Eternal salvation, my friend. Enlightenment.

I smirked. *Americans,* I thought.

There was the ancient, grizzled man who opened his decrepit shack, revealing a pristine rare-car collection. *A million kroner worth,* I had muttered. *More,* he said through his yellowed beard.

There were the cafés, each a new universe, the inhabitants living in their chess games and books, their dramatic entanglements and massive spliffs. They bathed in the communal showers, bedded down in makeshift communal dwellings. Their new families lived in enormous gravity-defying tree houses, cinder-block sheds, and reclaimed artillery stockades under the ground.

We even went beyond the regulated confines. The progeny of Christiania, barefoot and shirtless, following us warily with their eyes. They were the grandchildren and great-grandchildren of those hippie founders, and while the tourism helped fund the massive community's legal bills, we were far from their kind. No one lived in Christiania without an invitation or legacy, and their parents were intent on keeping it that way.

I was more like those kids than they could have fathomed.

Yet Jais waltzed right in, and no one dared ask him to stop.

Jais showed me twisting pathways and ornate mansions, the surprising structures that rose unexpectedly from the brush. We saw Hans Christian Andersen–like fairy-tale houses of glass and chrome, mammoth concrete cubes hidden in the trees. *Enough of this,* he said after an hour. *Let's go to Pusher Street and get fucked-up.*

Because this, as most Danish citizens were well aware, was the main purpose of this mystical dwelling. For interlopers and tourists, at least.

▪

Not again, said Jais a few hours later. *Another raid.*

I followed his gaze to the flock of police assembled at the entrance to Christiania. They were halting every person who exited.

We had been on our way out, still passing the hash pipe. The hash itself had been transported, scored from one of the Iranian Mafia–run carts lining the street, painstakingly weighed and offered up in a yellow gift bag.

Shall we turn around? I asked, every nerve on edge.

No. They're already inside, most likely.

I started to hyperventilate.

Chill, Your Highness, said Jais. *They always do this. They'll ask some questions, write you a ticket. And Pusher Street will be up and running again by morning.*

What about the pipe?

Let me finish it off. He grabbed for it.

He was right about the ticket. My name, my documents, a few questions, and a slap on the wrist. But what Jais had not expected? The photographer using the cops as a cover. *Stop,* I had said to the flashes. *I thought there were no cameras in Christiania!*

Get the hell out of here, the cop told him. But by then it had been too late.

By the next morning, my cover was blown, my picture in every newspaper. The Count was furious and refused to pay my tuition. *This is what you do with your chance?* he had sneered. *Well, there will be no further vanity endeavors, Christian. Time for you to grow up.*

I would not have returned to my intership, even having been given the choice. It would not have been the same. I had not changed, but my fellow classmates had. My one attempt had led to them eyeing me warily, muttering *fraud* under their breath.

My father showed a bit of mercy, not having me removed from the family home immediately. I made good use of the month before I was officially summoned back to the castle, hitting all the right spots with all the right women. *I am starting a jewelry line,* I would tell them, so drunk I would occasionally even slobber on them as I spoke.

Tell me all about it! they would say. *And you must describe the castle!*

Spit on their clothing, vomit on my own, they never seemed to mind, willingly posing for the press that now regularly trailed me. *Might as well give them a show,* I would say, then do something to bring more shame upon my legacy.

Handsome Royal Heir Out on the Town! said the headlines. *The No-Account Count Strikes Again!*

When my father offered America, I knew it was my last chance. *A place to be reborn,* I had thought. *To meld tradition and avant-garde. To create something entirely new.* Only the raw materials would not only be diamonds this time. They would be me.

▪

I had not found myself," I say with finality.

"Oh, Christian," she says.

The story I have told is founded in truth, though I omitted key details and embellished others. In America, I have heard, they call this spin. Yet I am careful. Cordelia has seen the pictures, of this I am sure. The one where I am passed out in the car, or the one where I scream at the photographer, my face enraged. That candid shot where I stumble from the club, shirt untucked, model on my arm. Or *under* my arm, as she was holding me up.

These portraits, I believe, are not an adequate rendition, as they are of someone I do not know. A jester, a hammered buffoon. Someone who had lost his path—his art—and has now crossed the ocean to find it again.

Cordelia listens carefully, eyes growing wider, her wine disappearing with each absentminded sip. I refill the glass, my speech never missing a beat.

Danish women are known for their toughness, their power. They run corporations and believe in equality, if not superiority, to their male counterparts. They can fuck and not grow attached and, if unsatisfied with your performance, state their annoyance clearly.

Not that I know from experience. Except, perhaps, for that time with the Spanish pop star in Costa Brava. But in that case, the coke was to blame.

A Danish woman would never respond in this manner—at one point, Cordelia's eyes even fill with tears—allowing her emotions to be on such blatant display.

In the end of this story, I follow my own path, one that takes me two thousand miles on a private charter. I land here—at this very table, in fact—but those demons continue to haunt me.

"Oh, Christian," she says again, reaching for my hand. "That's just not fair!"

In that moment, I realize the truth: it is exactly what I have told her. Especially the overbearing-father part.

"You deserve better," she says.

Is she for real? I wonder, once again running my thumb in slow circles against the back of her hand. Do I admire her naïveté or simply feel sorry for her? That open heart, like an unbound wound, waiting to be broken. That wanting of the best in people, which is destined to lead her to disappointment.

Perhaps, on some level, I am jealous. Or simply thankful.

"And that is why I am here, in America. To bring my art to the world, to make contacts and launch my brand." I move up her bare flesh, drawing a steady line, the pressure of my thumb light, the hairs on her arms rising. "Or perhaps"—I have begun to wonder myself—"I came to meet you."

A pause as she takes this in. *Why am I nervous?*

"You're giving me goose bumps!" she finally says. "Do you have those in Denmark?"

"No. And we do not have rainbows, either."

"*Oh, you!* I was talking about the word *goose bumps*, you know that!"

"Ah, yes. *Gåsehud*. The literal translation is 'gooseflesh.'"

"That's so pretty! Not the dead-goose part, of course, but the Danish. I love hearing you speak that language!"

"And I love watching you hear." Now I am tickling the inside of her elbow. "Unfortunately, I cannot stay in America forever. In fact, I worry I must leave sooner than later."

"Why?" she says, her worry palpable.

"I only have limited time, and a limited budget. My trust fund will not be available for years. I came to seek investors and be noticed, which is why I was in the Hamptons, in fact. But it seems America has not taken the . . . what is that saying? Not caught the fish?"

"Taken the bait."

Now I am running my nails lightly along the curve of her shoulder, my hand moving toward her face.

"I will not let that happen."

"You," I say, her chin in my hand, "cannot stop what is inevitable."

She peers up at me.

I sigh, pulling away. "Well, I suppose we should finish off this wine."

Her expression tells me everything.

In that moment, I know. It has taken four encounters—excuse me, *dates*—but she has finally cracked the drawbridge.

I'm sure of it. By later tonight, I'll be inside the castle.

■

"Well?"

"I have to be—"

"Why are you whispering?"

"She is in the next room."

"She's still there? Good sign."

"Indeed. And there's more—"

"Tell me. *I'm dying!*"

"She wants to feature my pieces in the magazine. A whole spread!"

April Holiday shrieks so loudly I must hold the phone from my ear.

"You did it, buddy! Now you're gonna *blow up*!"

"Yes, yes. But the launch party is in two weeks, so she says we need to schedule the shoot immediately. I said I would have my manager contact—"

"I'll reach out first thing, get the whole DL on this party shindig—"

"Wait until she leaves here, at least. April, hold on a moment, will you please?"

Balthazar is staring at me. I am clad only in boxers, the sleep still in my eyes. "Sir, will you take breakfast in the parlor?"

"That's fine."

"And the young lady?"

"Why not?"

A pause, a curt nod. Before he exits, I see a flash of disdain.

"Who was that?" asks April. "The girl?"

"The butler."

"The butler! You are a riot, I swear! Well, this is great, Christian. Wasn't I right about calling her?"

"I suppose so."

"I mean, I'd pretty much given up on Hoff Media, and staking out the daughter's boyfriend? What a nightmare! That moron. Took three hours of surveillance to get him alone."

"Yes," I say, voice still low. "But I shall have to—"

"But he'll get his, don't you worry! That's what anonymous tips are all about. Even better when you got the visuals! And right now is the *perfect* time. I mean, no press is bad press, right?"

I have no idea what she is talking about, nor do I care. "April," I say, exasperated, "I must go. She might wake at any moment."

"Just one more question, okay? So how *was* the little Southern belle?"

I pause for a moment. "A virgin."

"No!" Again, I am holding away the phone. "Are you fucking with me?"

"I am afraid not. I have the ruined sheets to prove it. Listen, I really—"

"Gotta go. Gotcha. But don't forget about that check. I mentioned it last week, remember? Made out to Your Fifteen Minutes LLC?"

"Your fifteen minutes?"

"Oh, Christian. The personal paparazzi staffing service? And FYI, buddy—the head honcho—is überpissed. Says his actors got roughed up by Hoff's goons. He's like, they're trained professionals, April. Some of them are, like, SAG—"

"Fine, fine," says Christian. "But see to it we get the negatives. I should like to see the images they shot."

"Images!" She cackles. "There was no film in those cameras, you silly royal! Just flashing bulbs."

"Oh," I say. "Rather a waste of money."

"You never know. Might have impressed that little Southern virgin." April snorts. "Lucky you make rings, huh? She's probably already got the Vera Wang picked out."

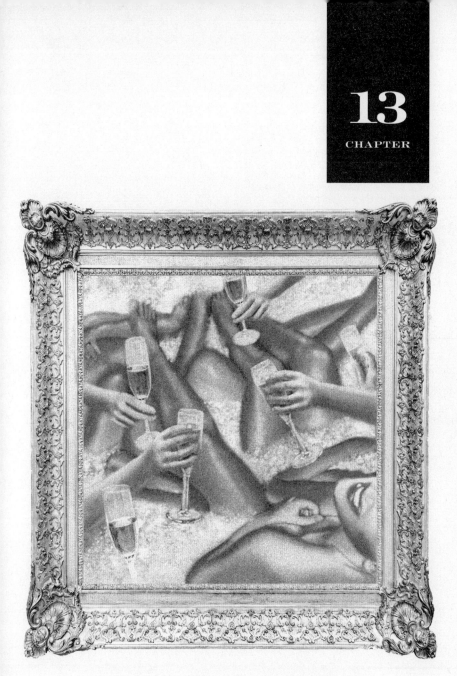

Models and Bottles #champagne #hottub #wilhelmina #getwet by Anonymous

M.C.

"Have you ever seen anything more precious?"

"I guess not," I say.

"I mean, just look how little they are!" Cordelia holds a tiny sandwich between two fingers, all dainty.

"Yeah. Gotta eat a lot to fill up, though. Hey, is that the cucumber?"

"No, the truffled quail egg. Here." She takes one from the tray. "This is what you want."

I stare down at my plate. "I don't remember the last time a woman served me. Besides, like, Rosita. Our cook."

"Well, I never! That's just plain strange."

"Bourgeois is what it is," mutters the burly guy to her left. He reaches out with his grubby hand, grabs a salmon, and stuffs the whole thing in his face. Then goes back to brooding, the poser.

"But really, aren't they just something else?" says Cordelia, as though nothing has happened.

Are we still talking about sandwiches?

"I just love the Plaza," she says, staring up. "Charming, don't you think?"

"Sure," I say. *When you're looking up. Like, into the stained glass and palm trees.* That way, you don't see all the pretentious robot pricks around you. *Did I mention Eurotrash?* Them, too. And don't forget about the asstard to my right, staring off into space. What kind of name is Deuce de la Deuce anyway?

Douche is more like it. "My mom used to take me here. When I was a kid."

"Did you love it?"

"When she went to the bathroom, I guess. I'd drink her sherry."

"You must have gotten quite the whupping!"

Whupping? Is she for real? "Nah, she never noticed. Just ordered another one. Kinda a hobby for her. That and committees."

"Junior League?"

"Yeah. Daughters of the American Revolution, Westport Women's, Save Our Tots . . . a ton of others. I can't remember them all. But the meetings were all about drinking, I'm pretty sure."

"So you were a little troublemaker?"

"Nah. Just talked too much. I mean, to the wrong people. Well, not wrong, just NOKD. That's what she'd call them. 'Not our kind, dear.'" *Be quiet, you fucktard.* "See? I still can't shut the hell up."

"Try harder," says Brood-ster.

For the second time since arriving, Deuce de la Deuce has risen from the dead. Showed a flicker of interest. First in the food, and now in being an dick to me. And we've only been here twenty minutes. The other ninteen and a half, he's just sat there. Staring. With a scowl.

Dude thinks he's James Dean. Like, a really ugly version, maybe. Dean with a potbelly and 'stache. A 'stache with *curled* ends.

Waxed, curled ends.

I'm not fucking around. You can't make that shit up.

Heard of a dress code? I think. *Heard of business casual, you fuck?*

I didn't want to wear the blazer either, but that's what you do. It's the Plaza, right? The place has chandeliers. And here's jack-off in a Harley jacket and biker boots, pouting like a little bitch. A little bitch with a fucking *waxed 'stache.*

Deuce de la Deuce: *classy motherfucker.*

"I don't do small talk, you get that?" he booms, like reading my mind. He reaches for a scone and shoves the whole sucker in. "I am here to make art."

He glares at me with crumbs in his beard.

Cordelia doesn't even flinch. "We sure do!" she says with a big smile. "Aren't I lucky? A true artiste to guide us! Yessiree, we should be discussing our forthcoming party!"

Yessiree? Is that even a real word? I thought it was some shit they made up for cowboy movies.

"This is not a party," says Deuce. "This is a Happening. An Event." He leans in close, breathing through his nose like a bull. "This is a transformative arena in which the spectators will be . . . transported."

"Like *The Hunger Games,*" I say.

He narrows his eyes at me.

Not that we didn't see this attitude coming. *He's the tiniest bit difficult,* Cordelia had said on the phone. *But really, all bark and no bite. People are just* dying *to work with him! And if anyone knows about temperamental artists, I'm sure it's you, Mr. Manager!*

Mr. Manager. I liked the sound of it.

And she was right. I do know about temperamental artists. Or *artist,* singular.

Time to get real, M.C. At this point, you haven't got shit.

Where is the little songbird? Cordelia had asked when I arrived for tea.

"She's got a recording session," I had lied. *But she sends her hi. She's totally pumped!*

It isn't like I could tell her the truth. What would I say? *Thanks for the gig, I can't wait. And PS, the performer is MIA.*

Ten texts, six messages, five e-mails, two pokes, one Google chat request, and a dozen roses. And still jack shit.

After that IceCapade thing, I knew I had to act fast. That's how pissed she'd been. To turn it around, I needed a miracle. Or a stage. For Des.

Sure, April not-a-porn-star Holiday had been a pain in my ass, but I had to give her props for the heads-up.

And when I'd asked, Cordelia had said yes. I'd been shocked as fuck! I mean, I'd barely even got my pitch out.

Desy sounds like a delight! she'd said. *I'll get Jimmy on to schedule her this very instant!*

Delight? Not quite accurate. But still, this was big. And Des would forgive everything before I even got the words out. I mean, she lived for this shit. She was gonna be center stage.

By text four, and response zero, I'd started to worry. *Time to amp them up,* I'd thought.

And I did, each one worse than the last. And the response was silence.

Begging, pleading, sucking up. Not a freaking word. Dead air.

Now the show is in less than a week, and I'm at a production meeting at the Plaza, eating fucking finger sandwiches and shitting my pants at the same time. The reason? *There's. No. Fucking. Act.*

This is bad. Really bad.

At least it can't get worse.

"So tell me what this . . . entertainment presentation requires," sneers Douche.

Guess it can.

"Yeah," I say, looking from his fugly mug to Cordelia's big white smile and thinking, *Wow, you really fucked yourself on this one, didn't ya, M.C.? This is one for the history books. This is failure on an epic scale. Even more epic than Columbia. And your GPA last semester was 1.3.*

Lucky Dad endowned that new fellowship. Worst I'd gotten was a very-disappointed-hope-you-will-exert-more-energy-toward-your-academic-success letter.

I rolled a big, fat doobie on it.

"We just need a stage," I say, racking my brain. "A good sound system. But really, uh, Deuce, I want it to, like, adhere to your vision. Cordelia says your vision is, like, y'know . . . transcendental."

Wow, Miller. You really pulled that one out of your ass.

"Exactly!" he booms. *Douche Rises, Part Three*. "You get it! You get me. I knew you would, I just sensed."

"Yeah. Totally."

He's leaning forward now, all up in my grill. Those little waxed curls taunting me.

Don't tug the 'stache. Don't tug the 'stache.

"You must tell me *your* vision," he says. "Lay yourself bare. This is what Cordelia has done."

I shoot her a look, eyebrows raised.

Her eyes get wide. "Oh! No, not like that!" She giggles, blushing. "I just told him what matters to me! And he won't let me see the result until day of, can you believe it? That's faith, pure and simple. And, lordy, I must have a lot of it!" She beams at him and he takes it, like she's the UV to his tanning bed.

"Helps that Deuce has quite the reputation. I mean, everyone in the free world is rarin' to hire him! Booked up for months—"

"Years," says Douche.

"—years! Bless my assistant Jimmy for pulling those strings! So don't you worry, M.C. Just tell him what you got pictured. What you care about. For instance, I said faith. The Bible, of course—"

"Archetypes are wondrous," says the Douche to himself.

"And nature! The sun, the beach—"

"Nature as the driving force, both to destroy and renew."

What the fuck is he talking about?

"I mean, *especially* the beach! That was pretty much every Kappa event I ever planned! The Life's a Beach Luau, the Jimmy Buffett Clambake Bonanza. Even the charity events! Limbo for Lupus. Oh, my gosh, we had the cutest little hula-girl costumes for that!"

For a moment, I'm distracted, picturing her with coconut-shell boobs and a grass skirt.

"A vision!" Douche smacks his giant palms on the table. People turn to stare. He moves in close. "Images," he whispers. "Just give me that."

Fuck. *Think, Miller.*

Don't tug the 'stache. Don't tug the 'stache.

Get your shit together. Images. How hard is that?

"Maids," I blurt. "Asian maids. But not, like, the clean-your-house kind. Hot girls. Aprons and short, puffed-out skirts. Pink ones. Everything pink . . . the lights, the chandeliers, the kittens—"

"Do we need a permit for that?" Cordelia types a note in her phone.

"Strike the kittens. Candy instead. Lollipops. That's it.

They're dancing and sucking lollipops—" I have no idea what I'm saying. Just that it's getting me kind of hot. "And it's like, this wonderland. The manga, fetish . . . carnival. That's it. A big carnival! Like Disney World dipped in pink . . . and on acid."

I realize they're staring at me. What the fuck was that? A lollipop carnival? What kind of homo am I?

The Douche nods his head. Up and down, real slow. "Genius."

Madonna starts singing. *"Living in a material world . . . I am a material . . ."*

"My phone!" says Cordelia, breaking the spell. Checks the caller ID. "His home number? He never calls from . . ." She smiles at us. "I have to take this. But it'll be quick, I promise! 'Kay?"

The spell is broken. Cordelia speaks quietly, eyes wide and intense, and Deuce de la Deuce is back in the food. He digs through the tray of little cakes with dirty fingernails. "What are you talking about?" she says, obviously upset. She turns to us. "Let me just run outside, boys. Won't take me but a lil' ole second! But that idea, M.C.? *Divine*. This is going to be the best party—excuse me, *happening*—in the history of New York City!"

Then I'm alone. With the Douche.

"Candy," he mutters. He leans back, staring intensely at a white-frosted cake square he's got between thumb and first finger. "The sweet, dismissible inevitable."

He pops it in his mouth.

Crumbs. Everywhere.

■

Three texts, two e-mails, and one phone message. All within the next few hours.

Nope.

But 6:00 a.m. the next morning? *Riiiiiiiiiinnnnnggggggg* . . .

"Miller, you lovebug, where have you been?"

Bitches are crazy, yo.

14

CHAPTER

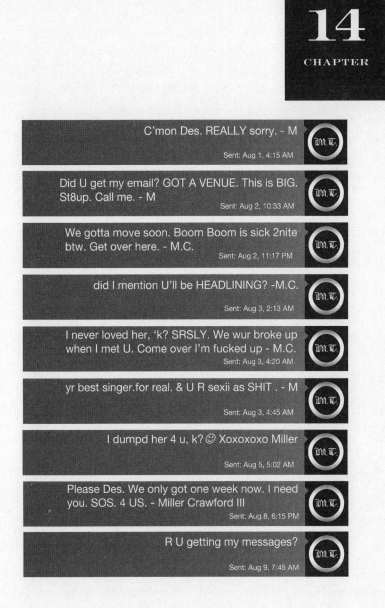

C'mon Des. REALLY sorry. - M

Sent: Aug 1, 4:15 AM

Did U get my email? GOT A VENUE. This is BIG. St8up. Call me. - M

Sent: Aug 2, 10:33 AM

We gotta move soon. Boom Boom is sick 2nite btw. Get over here. - M.C.

Sent: Aug 2, 11:17 PM

did I mention U'll be HEADLINING? -M.C.

Sent: Aug 3, 2:13 AM

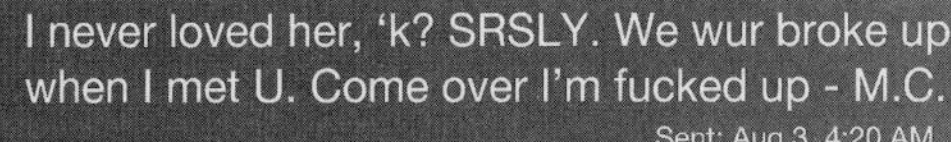

I never loved her, 'k? SRSLY. We wur broke up when I met U. Come over I'm fucked up - M.C.

Sent: Aug 3, 4:20 AM

yr best singer.for real. & U R sexii as SHIT . - M

Sent: Aug 3, 4:45 AM

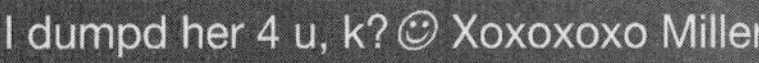

I dumpd her 4 u, k? ☺ Xoxoxoxo Miller

Sent: Aug 5, 5:02 AM

Please Des. We only got one week now. I need you. SOS. 4 US. - Miller Crawford III

Sent: Aug 8, 6:15 PM

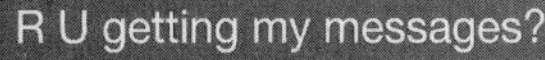

R U getting my messages?

Sent: Aug 9, 7:45 AM

Desdemona Goldberg

"Me?" he says. "I've texted you, like, a million times—"

"No, I don't think so. But forget all that! Aren't you just dying? Isn't it the most fab thing in the entire world?"

"What are you talking about?" he says, his voice all adorable sleepiness. "What time is it?"

"I have no idea. I've been up for eons, darling! Calling everyone I know. Have you ever seen anything so marvelous?"

"What are you talking—"

"I mean, you can't buy this kind of press! I'm just beside myself with happ—"

"Desy!" he yells. "Stop talking for a second, okay?"

Asshole, I think, pinching my lips closed.

A long time passes. Practically eternity.

"Are you there?"

"You said to stop talking—"

"I know what I said," he groans, like some mean, old, grumpy bear.

"You yelled in my ear, Miller. And that's my *tool. As an artist.*"

"I think you mean your voice, Des."

"Whatever. But isn't it exciting! Who do you think the source was? Someone at IceCapade, I suppose—"

"Slow down, baby. Okay? Just for a sec. I need to ask you something, okay?"

He called me *baby. Oh, Miller.* He's just so scrumptious! "Sure, lovey!"

"So this thing you're so excited about . . . was it, like, something you saw on TV?"

This makes me laugh. Hysterically. "No, darling," I say, wiping away the tears. "It was that article. That blog in the *Ogler*! About you, me . . . oh, *just everything*!" There is a silence. "Well, I'm sure you're as thrilled as I am! But first things first. We have much to do before the launch party!"

More silence.

"Okay then! I'm coming over in fifteen minutes. Shall I bring croissants? No, wait . . . I'll bring cronuts! They're all the rage."

I hang up before he can answer.

I send him the link, then race around, gathering my things. He texts back, *What the fuck?* Less excited than I had hoped. but I know why he's *really* upset.

Article, smarticle. He's just missed me, of course!

I know I'd been a meanie, making him suffer like that. But *a girlfriend*? And a dried-up, pruney one at that. I mean, I know all about Miss Annalise Hoff. I practically have a PhD in Facebook Investigations, after all.

Stalking? Please. My natural curiosity is one of my best qualities! It's part of my glow, my effervescence. It just bursts right out of me like champagne bubbles! And from what I've seen of her tagged photos, all that's bursting out of Annalise Hoff is *uptight, frigid bitch*.

Miller doesn't love her—that much is clear. And of course I'll forgive him! He just needed to suffer a bit first.

Besides, I think, packing up my Birkin, *I was busy!* The second I got his news—*what a cutie he is with those adorable texts!*—I went full throttle. The new hair, the stylist, that weekend detox in Nevada. Those algae shakes were totes ick, but I dropped seven and a half pounds! *So* worth it.

I'm going to be everywhere, I'd thought. And being in the public eye? That's no joke.

But the question remains . . . am I ready for Pop Stardom?

AYFKM? I've been ready since the day I was born.

One last check of the bag. *Have I got everything? Advil, Adderall, La Mer, face wipes. Tiara, deodorant, mascara* . . . wait! What about money? *Infinite, Palladium, Ultima; check, check, check. AmEx Gold and MasterCard Black.* And just in case, two thousand in cash!

The show is in less than a week, after all. I know from his many texts and phone messages. And I've already started rehearsing with my backup girls! Who knows what the next few days will bring? But one thing I can promise for sure? It'll be a whirlwind!

With that thought in mind, I head for the door. And the second my hand touches the knob, I realize.

I've been so busy, I hadn't crunched numbers one time! Life is too wonderful!

I'm really growing up.

▪

It isn't until I'm on the street that I see the headlines at a newsstand.

Todd Evergreen? Really?

Well, it just goes to show you. You can't trust anyone.

All the more reason to believe in yourself!

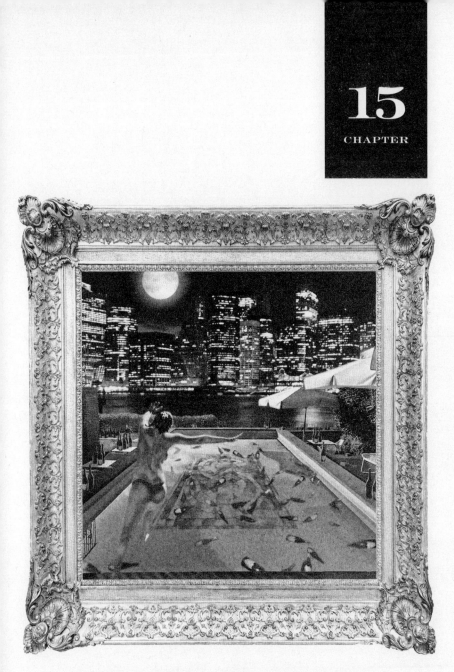

On top of the world! I own this city. #BBparty #skinnydip #domperignon #pool @Desdemona_Goldberg by Anonymous

Annalise Hoff

"Daddy?" A blurry-eyed glance at the clock: 9:00 a.m. Slept through the alarm again!

Of course, lately, I haven't been setting it at all.

His private line, his breath labored. I sit up so fast there is a rush to my head. "Are you okay, Daddy? Is it a heart attack?"

"What? No. This isn't something Sloan-fucking-Kettering can fix!"

"What's going on, Daddy? This is about Evergreen, isn't it?"

I had been waiting for this call. Since the Hamptons thing, Daddy and I have barely talked. I thought he must still be angry. Until the stories started coming. All those headlines, on every newsstand, all calling Evergreen a fraud.

Just wait it out, I told myself. *Daddy will come to you.*

Now he has.

"You spend time with the Kid, I take it?"

"The kid?"

"Evergreen. And good for you, Annalise, for sloughing off that dead weight—"

"Dead weight?"

"Look, honey. I don't have the time to bullshit. But if that boy of yours has been traipsing around town with him—"

"What boy?"

"Stop asking questions!" he bellows.

I shut my mouth tight.

"That Miles or Milltwat or whoever the hell he is—"

"Miller," I say softly.

"—if that Miller socializes with Evergreen, you must have, too." *What could he possibly be talking about?*

He must mean at the party, I think. That horrific Hamptons debacle. My inebriated ex-boyfriend throwing himself on the guest of honor, giving me one of a thousand more reasons to despise him.

"Of course, Daddy," I lie. "And all this has been a terrible shock. Evergreen seemed like such a lovely young man!"

"Yeah, lovely like a SARS outbreak. Now I got all these Rock Exchange artists joining the lawsuit. Said they were promised fifty-fifty, but the paperwork was sketchy. Copyright infringement, the whole la-di-da. Got the board breathing down my neck, and too late to stop this thing from going public. This could be a huge loss, Annalise."

"Oh, Daddy! I am so sorry. But what was that about Miller—"

"—legal team running in circles," he says, ignoring me. "They're saying no comment. Saying they don't know how this shit got out there. Probably some of those wannabe rock stars milking their fifteen minutes. 'Suck it up,' that's what the lawyers say. 'Let 'em get their ducks in a row.'" He is talking so fast I can barely keep up. "But the bad press? *That'll be a monster.*"

Something in his voice scares me. Furious is the average Tuesday, but this is furious unhinged, King Lear in act 3. "Know what the press is gonna say, Annalise? Look at Hoff Media, screwin' over these poor, starving artists, capitalizing on their talent, their fucking little heartfelt songs, their bullshit coffee-shop guitar-playing whiny fucking—"

"Daddy, no one would ever believe—"

"Like hell they won't! Wake up, honey. Big, bad Gerald Hoff, King of Media, stealing dreams. Forget eat me alive, they'll skewer and kebab me first."

"Oh, Daddy."

"But you know what really gets me?" he says, the pain in his voice ripping my insides to shreds. "The Kid."

"Evergreen?"

"That little fuck. Got a feeling he knew this was in the works. Why he sold so quick, I'll betcha. How the Christ did I miss this? How the fuck did I get played by . . . *a kid*?"

"Oh, Daddy. You've been so nice to him!"

"And know what nice gets you? *A big pile of dog shit.*" A pause, and his breath begins to steady. "I gotta nip this one in the bud, honey."

Just like that, he puts the hurt in a folder and files it away. Now the plan of action goes into effect.

"This story is just getting bigger, you can count on it. Think the press is bad now? Just wait until the court papers go official. So I need to divert attention. Put focus back on Mr. Internet Hero, show he's a fuckin' fraud. Turn the press on him, just like they did to that Assange character. *But I got nothing*, Annalise. That's why I need you."

I knew it, I think, going on full alert. I knew I would get another chance to prove myself. And this one makes that soiree I planned for him—*nuclear implosion would be more apt*—look like a little blip.

"Are you with me, honey?"

This is my father's reputation, I think. *This is our family name.*

This is a second chance. To take it all back.

"You bet, Daddy."

"That's what I like to hear. I got a secret weapon, that's what I was thinking. An ace up my sleeve. I got access. I got the smartest little girl in the world, Annalise Hoff." I eat up every word he says. "And the legal team? They can fuck themselves with that laying low BS, 'cause my little girl's got more guts than all of 'em. You're a Hoff, after all. Am I right?"

"Absolutely."

"Get something on the Kid. A drug problem, a DUI. I'd settle for unpaid parking tickets at this point. Gimme a place to start, and my media team'll run with it. We'll castrate that little fuck."

Forget the morning inspiration, I tell myself, rising from the bed, marching to the curtains, and letting in the new day. From here on out, it's all about me.

"You up to the challenge, Annalise?"

"On it, Daddy."

"That's my girl."

"Just one little thing. What you said about Miller and Evergreen—"

"Yeah, I'm just glad you got rid of that excess baggage."

"Excess baggage," I repeat.

"I wouldn't have known, but my people sent it along, trying to keep me in the loop. One of them recognized Evergreen from the party. His hood, at least. Usually, I avoid that shit like the plague, right? Fuckin' *Ogler*. That crap is as bad as Page Six."

I do not fully hear the rest. *A conference call in fifteen,* I think. A *Gotta go*, maybe a *Love you* or *Buck up* or *Swing for the fence, kid.*

A dial tone.

My hand, clenched around my crystal iPhone case, is clammy. I swallow, trying to dislodge my heart from my throat.

Twenty-two seconds and a Google search is all it takes.

It is all there, the write-up not even blind. And if the paragraph were not devastating enough, the accompanying snapshot does the trick.

I imagine how it appears to a perfect stranger:

Champagne bottle on ice. A block of it, to be exact. Four individuals, all young and wearing parkas.

Young Man One, slightly slumped. The hood pulled up from the neck of his jacket obscures his face. The other, dreadlocked and glassy-eyed, stares off into space.

Next to them, a Handsome Young Man, his arm wrapped around the shoulder of a Whore.

Her tongue in his mouth. His in hers.

As for the post itself? Even worse. I've shoved down three Xanax by the second paragraph.

BROADWAY LEGACY HEATS UP ICE BAR WITH ARTILLERY HEIR—BY STAFF

In an *Ogler* Exclusive, sources tell us that Desdemona Goldberg, daughter of Broadway-legend billionaire Hymen, showed her drama queen roots at IceCapade last Tuesday. The object of affection? None other than Miller Crawford III, son and sole heir to the Crawford Artillery dynasty.

Accompanying Crawford and notorious party girl Goldberg were an as-yet-unidentified young man (tips can be sent to insider@ogler.com) and Phillip Atwater, son of notorious Hollywood heavyweight/female-equality advocate Phyllis. Judging by his "Who gives a f***?" reaction, we guess Phillip is on board with the PDA. Besides these guys were all about being equal . . . *equally slutty*, that is!

"They were pretty much doing it, right there," the source, who also provided the candid shot, tells *Ogler*. "At one point, she was straddling him and, like, dry humping for the whole place to see! I mean, they were *totally* wasted. Like, *sloppy* drunk." But the lovefest, we're told, came to a quick end when Goldberg got wind that Crawford was taken. And his longtime girlfriend? None other than heiress Annalise Hoff.

Yeah, *that Hoff.*

In a CW teen-drama-worthy twist, *Ogler* has learned that Mr. Guns is (*was?*) managing Goldberg's music career. As of this week, he'd gotten the okay for her single debut to drop at . . . *wait for it* . . . Gerald Hoff's new magazine launch!

How juicy is that? Cheating on Hoff's daughter, and using his magazine to launch his recently dumped side dish?

"It's gonna be a big deal," says our source. "All these fashion people, these amazeballs designers, this *sick* up-and-coming European jeweler—a royal!—everyone is talking about. It'll be a *scene*!"

Ogler would put bets on that!

In the end, *Ogler* thinks this public falling-out was for the best. The Rifle Heir might have *jumped the gun*, but judging by the "bathroom visits" and "like, ten rounds of shots," this romance was destined for a, ahem, *premature discharge* either way!

More to come. . . .

FILED UNDER: *Lifestyles of the Rich and Vomitrocious; Trust-Fund Crybabies; Rich Kids*

They can go to hell, I seethe, pulling up a contact on my phone. And there will be hell to pay as well, they can count on it.

Miller, of course, and the Slut. And most of all? *Todd Evergreen.*

But first on the list? That lazy, good-for-nothing informant. What do I pay him for anyway?

He picks up on the first ring. "You saw the article, I guess. Listen, I had no idea—*someone*—had called the office. But I was still working her for info. How was I supposed to know Miller was your ex? And a manager? He just said M.C. when he left that message. I mean, we hadn't settled on music for the launch party, let alone considered live performances!"

"This is completely unsatisfactory," I blurt. "I thought you were up to the task."

"I'm not a mind reader, okay? I'm an actor. And a pretty good one. I mean, she thinks I'm Southern, Annalise. And gay! Do you understand how hard that is to pull off? I've got a wife and two kids. I'm from Queens."

"Britton, I hired you for a reason, and that was not to hone your craft," I say.

"This hasn't been an easy role to pull off, either. And I went to Juilliard—"

"I do not give a rat's ass where you went!" I bellow. "I paid you to do a job!"

Calm down, Annalise. You're losing it.

I hear him sigh. "Well, there is something . . ."

"Go on," I say, forcing my voice to stay level, my teeth to unclench.

"She's got some demons. I mean, I sensed right away. Must be all that character analysis in school. And then last week she was crying to her mom on the phone. I listened on tap. You need to reimburse me for the headset, by the way."

"And?"

"Something happened. In Texas. That's why she came here. 'A fresh start,' those were the words her mother used."

"Is that it?"

"Yes, but there's something there. Something big."

"Find out what," I snap. "And, Britton? That launch party needs to be a *disaster*."

"No problem there. I got Deuce de la Deuce on it."

"Deuce de la Deuce?"

"The party planner. Aka Brian Hernando, this weirdo director from my class at Juilliard. He's freaking out. Says this is the ultimate environmental theater. 'I won't just play Deuce de la Deuce, I'll be him.' This dude's so experimental, he once did a whole show starring an egg. And Cordelia? Bought the whole thing right away. Seriously, she was in like Flynn!"

"So it will be—how shall I put it?—a less than tasteful affair?"

"Are you kidding? A total freakfest, I'll bet."

This is the only good news I have heard all day.

After I hang up, I feel a tad better. Probably just the Zannies, but at this point, I will take what I can get.

I will take all this hurt, this embarrassment, and mentally transform it, I tell myself. I imagine sharpening it into a point, molding it into something far more useful. A hate bullet.

I will kill them, I think. And that is the thought that sets me over the edge.

Tears, snot, heaving sobs. Throwing shit against the wall. Not heirlooms, of course, but stuff that I know will shatter on impact.

I scream and carry on and stumble about. I am a Lifetime movie, I am that extra in the psycho-ward flick banging her head against the bars. Jodi Arias? That bitch is a Girl Scout compared to me.

I hate them! Every last one! Not just Miller, though he is up there on the list. That whorish slut, that hack at *Ogler*. Candace and Renata and that fucking lunatic bitch who grew me in her uterus! That redneck atrocity who elbowed me in the gut, and even Daddy for letting her.

And more than anything? *Todd Evergreen.*

When he showed up, everything just went crumbling.

Wait a second! I stop suddenly. Stand in the center of my own debris, frozen, tear-soaked clumps of hair stuck to my cheeks.

I forgot someone. Miller, Evergreen, the Slut . . . and *Phillip?*

How could he? I was so nice to him. I actually liked him, believe it or not. And that almost never happens.

I need to talk to him, I think. *Now.*

My life is in ruins, and the least he can do is tell me how it happened.

You have to take stock of artillery, after all. Before you aim the weapon.

16 CHAPTER

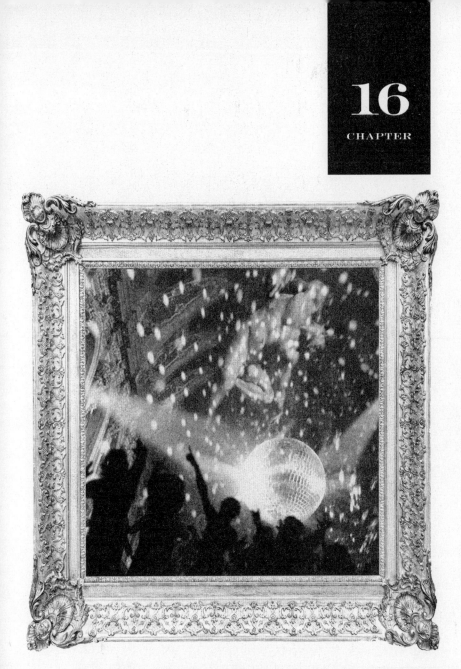

Sistine Rave! #BBparty #mirrorball #drugs by Anonymous

PHILLIP ATWATER

"I thought you were my friend."

The buzzer is startling enough—no one comes here besides food-delivery guys—but what stands before me induces astonishment in the purest form. Annalise Hoff, face without makeup, looking like a devastated twelve-year-old girl.

"What have I done to you, exactly?" she spits. "To bring on such blatant, horrific disregard for me?"

The fury is an illusion. Playacting. Beneath the layers, I see her truth: someone has ripped her heart from her chest, gutting her from the inside out.

And while the timing is a surprise, the arrival was destined.

No one saves us but ourselves, according to Buddha. *We ourselves must walk the path.*

I have paved this one myself, waiting patiently for the ground to dry. Trudged the miles, no end in sight. And now that I have finally reached the end, all I can say?

"Um . . . are you okay?"

"Do I look okay?" she hisses, then storms right past me.

"Who lives like this?" she shrieks, pacing the wood floor of my bare living room. "You do not have a thing."

"I don't need anything." *Or didn't,* I think.

"That's just naïve."

"That's just the truth. Look at Gandhi, look at Buddha. The greatness was not in what they carried, but what they carried inside—"

"I am sick as fuck of your new age bullshit!" she yells, her tiny figure suddenly much bigger than the room itself.

Behind her, through the curtainless floor-to-ceiling windows, Manhattan spreads out, a glimmering universe of steel and chrome. "Everyone *needs* things, Phillip," she says. "You're an imbecile to think otherwise."

"They need people, too," I say calmly. "Isn't that why you came here?"

"Do not flatter yourself. I certainly do not need people like *you.*"

"Don't say that, Annalise. I'm your friend. I really am."

"You knew." She takes a few steps toward me. "You knew he was cheating on me. Admit it!"

I should have been more prepared, foresaw this encounter when Miller texted the link this morning. *Can U fuckin believe this shit?* he had written.

This shit was destined, I had longed to write back.

Instead, I wrote *Wow.*

"I admit it. He was cheating. In your own bed, in fact."

She opens her lips to speak, but nothing comes out. She just stands there, mouth hanging open and tangled in her own web of fear.

"Beamer—the doorman—told me. He saw Miller himself. Says he comes when you are away for the weekend. You gave him a key?"

I see the answer on her face.

"He doesn't bring Desy here. At least Beamer doesn't remember someone like her. Just random hookups, I guess. But lots of them."

I do not want to cause her pain, I want her to hurt less. *Three things cannot be long hidden: the sun, the moon, and the truth.*

When she finally speaks, her voice is a whisper. "Why didn't you . . . tell me?"

"I just found out. Besides, you would have discovered soon enough on your own. You're smarter than him, Annalise. You know that. And since we're being honest: *he doesn't matter*. And we *both* know that."

She stares at me, the sunbeams making a halo in her hair.

"He is . . . *was* . . . my boyfriend!

"He was a prop. Like the expensive flowers at your party, the ones they shoot with chemicals to keep so perfect. Like those silly drinks on those fake-silver trays. *Pretty*, I guess, but also *pretty much worthless*."

"Those trays were sterling, you asshole!" Then she narrows her eyes. She laughs to herself, like someone just told the least funny joke in the world. One about mass suicide or nuclear holocaust or something. "Oh. Now I understand. *You're in love with me*. That's it, I suppose. Well, Phillip, let me just set you straight: *I will never, ever, fuck you*. The very thought of it makes me want to *vomit all over the floor*."

"Thank Christ for that!"

But instead of relief, she hears something else. Repulsion, I suppose, for her very existence.

In that moment, the spark hisses to a flame. I put up my hands as if to say *Wait*, but I am too late.

She is coming at me. Screaming. "I'm not good enough for you, you lying bastard?"

Then she's pummeling me with her little fists, trying to scratch the truth right off my face with her perfectly manicured nails.

Within seconds, I have her restrained, an arm pinned to each side. A variation of the kung fu choke hold taught to me by a former monk/hippie wanderer on a Moroccan ashram. Only this one is less choke hold and more backward hug.

I know I am not hurting her, so the struggling is okay. *I'm still strong,* I think, a little cockily, even though I haven't surfed in forever.

"You are a fucking moron," she yells. "I hate you and Miller!"

After thirty seconds, I start to get uneasy. "Please stop," I plead. "It won't do any good, don't you see?"

She finally gives up, her body going limp. Now she just cries.

This time, it's my heart being ripped out. My insides gutted.

I lower her to the floor. Sit beside her and let her sob it out. A tentative arm around her shoulder, and within moments it's my shirt that is wet.

"Why is everyone such a fake?" she bawls into my shoulder. "Why even try? They just disappoint you in the end." An awkward hug, but only awkward for me. She just kind of collapses against me, sobbing on my chest.

"'Pain is inevitable,'" I say, stroking the back of her head like I do for Ye-Nay when she bumps her head or loses her stuffed unicorn. "'Suffering is optional.'"

"And you are the worst fake of all," she says, the words muffled on my chest.

"That's true."

"You make no sense." She pulls away. She stares at me, not unkindly, through the tear puddles in her eyes. "*Who are you,* Phillip Atwater?"

I sigh. "Your half brother."

■

I know the stages of grief. Add a few lines of coke and some barbed wire, and you've got the Stages of Annalise.

First, there's Disbelief:

How do I know this is a real DNA test? Which testing facility? Is that even certified, or some place you heard about during, like, a Judge Judy *commercial break?*

You bet *I will call that doctor. You can count on it.*

And where would you get my DNA in the first place? The Hamptons? Which glass? A champagne one? Highball? . . . Okay, which drink then? The one with the edible pansy garnish? . . . A purple flower, you imbecile.

And if you cannot remember which one, why should I believe you in the first place?

Then, Anger:

You are obviously a compulsive liar. A deluded pothead. Is this some sort of acid flashback? Besides, it makes no sense. Utterly irrational. What year was that again?

When she worked at William Morris? No. Not possible. My father was already big-time, why would he lower himself for some development girl on some B-list films?

Besides, your mother is a dyke. What are you, a nutcase?

Bargaining:

Okay, it was the nineties, I will give you that. And, yes, maybe Daddy was having his crazy years. Masters of the Universe *stuff, probably doing everything in sight. Even lesbos. And maybe they were partying and—yuck—had sex. But let's keep our heads about us, Phillip. The odds are highly unlikely.*

After all, he would have told me.

Depression:

You mean, he just signed it? Just gave away all his rights? So your mother really is as convincing as they say. Well. Isn't that just the sweetest story I ever heard! Knock up some lesbian and let her bully you into walking. Just fills you with hope for humanity.

So Daddy is a liar, too. Everyone in the entire world is a liar, and I swear to God, I hate every single moron who ever existed.

A psycho mother was not enough, I suppose. Now I have father who's been keeping a second family *secret for—what?—my entire fucking life? And—added bonus!—some pothead pseudo-hippie kid shows up out of nowhere, waltzes right in, and says, "Oh, hi, nice to meet you. I live next door. And PS . . ."*

And finally, Acceptance:

You are my half brother. Phillip Atwater is my half brother.

▪

Hours later, and we lay in the darkened room, our backs on the bare, polished wood. In front of us, the New York sky is growing darker.

"What are we? Some twisted second-tier *Gossip Girl* episode?"

"Never seen it."

"God, Phillip." She reaches for the whiskey. "You really need to get out more. See the real world. And I am not talking about the *third* kind. Places with news coverage, cable access. What is this stuff by the way? Really excellent."

"Wild Turkey," I say, laughing. "Maybe you're the one who needs a dose of real life."

"Shut up. Look at the sunset."

Above us, the skyline is dripping orange and red.

"Beautiful," I say.

"Perhaps a little gaudy for my taste, but nice, I suppose."

We do not bother to toast, just as we haven't with all the

other shots. Besides, you can't click rinsed-out McDonald's soda cups.

Maybe she's right. I really should buy some stuff.

"So you came here for me," she says for the fifth time.

"Yes," I answer for the fifth time.

"And your mother? She just approved that?"

"Approved? *Blackmailed* is a better word." I sigh, remembering her anger, then her stunned silence. "She sent a PI to come get me, even froze my bank account, but I refused to come home. Until she told me the truth. I never bought that whole sperm-bank thing, not for a second. She's way too picky for that. If she was going to have a baby daddy, he would have to be top tier. I'm talking high-quality jizz here. Genius stuff. I'm talking—"

"Daddy."

"Exactly." I sigh. "I mean, she may be one of the best liars in Hollywood—she's a producer, after all—but I know the way she thinks." The whiskey is making the words come faster and more honest. Or maybe it isn't the Wild Turkey at all. Maybe it's just Annalise. "Don't get me wrong, she loves my sisters and brother, but I've got something she loves even more. *Her own genes.*"

"You have siblings?"

"Adopted. Dahnay is the oldest, he's from Ethiopia."

"An ethnic baby, how very hip. It is all the rage on the Upper East Side, you know, though Asian girls are the offspring of choice. Six Asian-Jewish fusions in my class alone! Jing Yi Wasserman ran against me for class prefect." She giggles. "She lost, of course."

"Oh yeah?"

"Have you not heard? Everything I do is perfect, Phillip. I am utterly flawless."

"No shit. That must be exhausting."

"Amen to that." She reaches for the bottle. "But, if we must engage in this abhorrent bonding ritual; I will tell you this: *I was always a tad jealous of those girls.* My mother could barely stand the sight of me, and theirs wanted them more than anything. Same reason your mother wanted you back."

"She wanted to own me. There's a difference."

"No," she says with a sigh. "There really isn't."

Outside, the sun has officially set, replaced by the gray dusk.

"So how did you blackmail her?"

"I said, 'If you don't tell me who he is, I'll never come back.' And losing me? That would have been worse than losing a movie property to Harvey Weinstein. Like, a potential Oscar sweeper."

"So she told you about Daddy."

"Yes. And I about shit my pants. So I said, 'Okay, I'll come back'—this was later, of course, after I'd done some research on you—'but only to New York. The Trump Tower.' And it just so happened, an apartment was open on your floor. I mean, I came for *you*. But getting on your floor was a nice surprise."

"Why would she say yes to that? It isn't a cheap place to just hole up."

"I threatened to go to the press."

A pause.

"You know what I just realized?" she says. "We are a great deal alike."

"Do you think we look it?"

"Maybe. Except I wash my hair."

"Dreads aren't dirty."

"Maybe not, but they are a debacle nonetheless. And no brother of mine—" She stops suddenly, the word just hanging there.

I am drunk, I think. *I am drunk with my sister.*

Then one more word. This one just as powerful.

"Why?"

I know what she is asking. Why I came here in the first place. I just don't know the answer to that one.

"A crisis of faith? A search for self?" I say, pouring two more shots. "Maybe I just wanted a dad."

Like mirror reflections, we lift our heads, down the shots, and go back to our positions on the floor. "Will he like me?"

"Well, he will certainly be surprised." Then: "Yes, I think he will. He might even love you." We smile at each other in the dark. "You, Phillip Atwater Hoff, will be everything Todd Evergreen was not."

And then she tells me the rest.

▪

What do you say when your long-lost half sister, the one you just met but feel like you've known for a lifetime, begs for your help?

You say yes.

You say it despite the sketchy motives, the nonsensical reasoning. You say it even though you know it probably won't work. She's manipulating you, playing on your affection, and you both know it. But still, you say it.

Yes.

In the end, it is the clichés that get you.

For the family name. For me. For your sister.

It goes against everything Buddha ever said, pretty much

shits on all four of the Noble Truths. And forget not straying from the Path of Righteousness; this route is bad karma just waiting to happen.

The thing is, Buddha is great and all. But blood? That's even more powerful.

Yes. That's what you say. *Yes, I'll help.*

"What I need is information," she tells me, now so drunk the words are slurred. "Dirt. Daddy can't find a thing, and his people are the best. Todd Evergreen must be hiding something, I know it. But how can we find out?"

"We can't. But I might know someone who can."

"When can we meet him? Does he take checks?"

"Cash only." I pull myself to my feet and offer her a hand. "And just follow me."

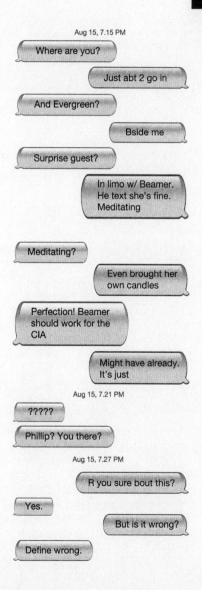

Aug 15, 7.15 PM

Where are you?

Just abt 2 go in

And Evergreen?

Bside me

Surprise guest?

In limo w/ Beamer. He text she's fine. Meditating

Meditating?

Even brought her own candles

Perfection! Beamer should work for the CIA

Might have already. It's just

Aug 15, 7.21 PM

?????

Phillip? You there?

Aug 15, 7.27 PM

R you sure bout this?

Yes.

But is it wrong?

Define wrong.

Cordelia Derby

"Have you ever seen anything so wonderful in your whole life?" Jimmy doesn't say a word, just stands there with his chin about hanging to the floor. "Deuce, you are an absolute genius! Don't you think so, Jimmy?"

"It's simply . . . unbelievable!" Jimmy finally says.

"Unbelievable?" says Deuce. "Is that all you can think of?"

"I'm just . . . overwhelmed."

"'Overwhelmed,' he says. Well, isn't that nice?" Deuce's face has turned all red. "You never believed in my talent, did you, Britton? Just like the rest of them. I'll always just be a joke to you, won't I?"

Before Jimmy can answer, Deuce has stormed off, his big old boots making no sound across the sand.

"What in the world was that? And why did he call you Britton?"

"Artists, darling," say Jimmy, who looks suddenly nervous. "You know they're all a little crazy!"

"But he acted like he knew you."

"Well, we have socialized. I know his twink, after all." A twink—I recall the Urban Dictionary entry—is an effeminate, young gay man. Not a Teletubby at all!

So why does Jimmy look all shook up?

As of late, everything's been ruffling my feathers.

This is your night, I remind myself. *Don't go letting anything ruin it!*

Then again, as my granddaddy used to say, *That's easier said than did, pumpkin pie.*

But, oh, my Lord, how fabulous is this scene!

"This is *to die*," says Jimmy as though reading my mind. "But where are the magazines?"

"Delivery will be here in a jiff!"

"Can't believe I haven't seen the final version, missy! And with a last-minute reshoot even. You wouldn't even let your good friend Jimmy see the proofs? Lordy me."

"I wanted it to be a surprise!"

"You silly girl, keeping secrets from me!"

"Every girl should have a little mystery, don't you think?"

"Well, I suppose so. And speaking of mystery, when's that man of yours arriving?"

"Should be anytime," I say, a chill running through my body. So much for being a good judge of character. I couldn't have been more wrong about that lying, son-of-a—

Focus on the work, Cordelia, I think. *Focus on what matters. Mr. Christian Rixen will be dealt with in good time.*

"I can't wait! And as for this"—Jimmy opens his arms wide—"utter perfection, my dear! And I'm not just talking the set. I mean, I'd part the Red Sea myself for that Alexander Wang. You look simply divine, Miss Cordelia Derby."

"Why thank you," I say with a tiny smile.

"And by tomorrow, *The Set* will be all New York can talk about. They'll go absolute goo-goo!"

"Hey," interrupts a rail-thin girl in even smaller swimwear. "Where do you want the bikini babes?"

"Behind there, dear." Jimmy points to one of the enormous glass façades rising to our right and left, each one at least forty feet high! The Plasticine-sealed constructions rise, the swirly, whirly paint job in the prettiest shades of blue.

Lucky we were able to snag an airport hangar, I think, giving myself kudos for sweet-talking the facility manager. Between these risers is a long strip of sand, where umbrellas and tiki lamps and tables are being arranged.

"What are they?" the girl asks.

"Just wait until they turn on the water pumps," he says. "Then you'll see for yourself."

"Gotcha." She jogs away. Next to us, two of the Teamsters watch her pass, chins to floor. She's a sight for sore eyes, with her enormous chest and gold lamé string bikini. Everything must be larger-than-life, that's what I wanted. Even the people!

"Excuse me! Boys!" says Jimmy, snapping at the Teamsters. "Those umbrellas won't put themselves up!"

They exchange a look, shoving stakes in the sand with renewed force.

There's a sudden screech. "Oh my!" I say, covering my ears.

"Just the soundman adjusting the levels," says Jimmy. "Don't worry your pretty little ears! Just want to make sure we can hear once those pumps get going!"

"Oh, I'm calm as a cucumber."

For a moment, we stand there, watching everyone scurry about. Stocking glasses under thatched huts, pushing carts of supplies, and generally buzzing around like busy little bees. Even the littlest conversations seem bigger than life, magnified by the enormous dome hundreds of feet over our head.

"And you need not worry about planes, you hear?" says Jimmy, following my gaze upward. "They haven't had them here for years!"

"You're the one who seems nervous."

"I know! And you're just fine and dandy, aren't you? It's weird."

That's what happens, I think, *when you hit the bottom. When you're so cried out the well has pretty much dried on up.*

Something strange comes over you. The most peculiar sense of calm.

Nothing can touch me now, I think, watching the wonder that I helped create. *And not ever again.*

And that part of me that's gone? Well, I sure as heck can't get it back. So I'll just have to take something that matters away from him.

In the end, I made an executive decision, just like a good editor does.

I'd take his dreams.

Tonight will be a success of biblical proportions, I'm sure of that. At least, for me.

"Where is my dressing room!" shrieks a voice. "And what's with all the sand?" I turn, and there is M.C., a sheepish smile on his face. And next to him? Five little Oriental girls—whoopsy, *Asian-Americans!*—whispering to each other and giggling.

But they aren't the cuckoo part.

Crazy as a loon. I know the second I see her.

"You must be Desy," I say, extending my hand. "Sure is a pleasure to make your aquaintance!"

M.C.

"Just relax, Des!"

"Relax? Are you insane?"

"Miss Desy is upset!" says Naughty Kitty, straddling a pipe, her legs swinging.

"You're gonna fall, Naughty Kitty," I say.

"Naughty Ahi!" says Desy. "Can't you remember anything?"

"Tee-hee," Ahi says, swinging her legs more.

"I told you that's a no-no, Ahi!" yells Desy. Behind her, Ika and Uni are working on her hair. "Lift that higher," Desy tells the girl holding a mirror in front of her.

The girl heaves it up, giving me the eye. *What's her name?* She makes a kissy face at me.

"I want you gone, Ebi!" screams Desy.

Ebi. That's right.

"Noooooooo!" whine the other girls.

Ebi stumbles backward, the mirror tipping dangerously in her hands.

"Don't break that!" I say. "It was a fucking nightmare getting it in here."

"Language!" says Des. "Not around the girls!"

Giggle giggle.

Mirror up, back to the hair.

I had to rip that thing from the bathroom wall, demolition-style. *Can't you get ready in here?* I'd asked Desy.

This bathroom is too small! she said. *I need space to prepare!*

Lucky for me, there'd been bolt cutters in the toolshed. *This* toolshed. It hadn't been easy to get that mirror off the bathroom wall, either.

This is not a dressing room! Des had wailed.

Yeah, I'd said. *But let's play pretend.*

Pretend you're not a fucking crazy bitch. Pretend this is not going to be an epic-fucking-failure.

Now she's driving me half-crazy and still only half-dressed. Outside, the guests are loud. Ten minutes ago, only a few voices. And now a roar.

And have I mentioned the show? A time bomb waiting to happen. *So what do you think?* Desy had asked after the first run-through at that studio in Manhattan. *I've been working on it since your first text message!*

I'm not sure, I'd said.

You better be sure, M.C., she'd hissed. *It's this or no show at all.*

But . . . sushi?

Oh, silly! Everyone adores sushi, don't you know that? It's like Katy Perry and the candy, only über more sophisticated!

Now, watching Des, I pretty much want to kill myself.

"This will not do!" says Des, and for a second I think she's woken the fuck up. "I look like the Jolly Green Giant! Take the shiso out this very instant!" Ika and Uni begin to pluck the leaves from her hair. All two thousand of them.

"Don't you, like, want to run the choreography?" I ask.

"Please, I know what I'm doing. I'm a professional, M.C." Then, literally two seconds later: "M.C.! I swear to God I can't remember the words!"

"There are only four lines, Des. And *you wrote them.*"

"I wrote them so I wouldn't *have* to remember them!"

Shit-balls-fuck-piss-I'm-gonna-strangle-this-skitzo-bitch . . .

Cordelia's assistant Jimmy arrives, holding a tray of shot glasses. *Saved!*

"Thank God," I mutter, handing one to Desy.

"Not that one!" he squeals, grabbing it from me. So fast he spills some on me. "This one is special." He hands over an identical shot. "For our star!"

"Whatever," I say, reaching for one of the others. "Drink up, Des. For the nerves."

Mine is long gone before hers.

"Aren't you a darling!" says Des. "Don't you just think of everything!"

"That's my job, sweets!" Jimmy says.

"No, Ahi!" Des says, slapping away the tiny hand creeping across the tray. "No shot for you, dear. I need my girls focused!"

Naughty Kitty—shit, *Ahi*—sits cross-legged on the floor. Sulking.

"And by the way," says Jim, "you sounded *fierce* up there!"

Not sure what sound check *he* heard. Ours involved no singing, just Des bitching on the stage for twenty minutes. *I can't hear myself! The track is too loud! The backup sushi can't do choreography for the life of them!*

Giggle giggle.

Shut up, shrieked Desy.

Now I watch her down the shot. Can she pull this together? If not, any hope I had for investors will pretty much implode. And considering the rumors, Evergreen's probably outta the picture.

Wonder if he'll even show? Fuck, Hoff must be pissed.

At least it'll take his mind off me. Since that *Ogler* BS, I'm on high alert. Watching my back for a jumping from the Hoff Media Mafia.

And what about Annalise?

If I weren't so freaked out about seeing them, I'd probably be out there right now. Instead of trapped in here with Ahi, Ebi, Ika, Uni . . . and Psycho Bitch from Hell.

"Where the fuck is my tail!" shrieks Des, digging frantically in her bag. "Why don't I have a wardrobe person? I mean, what kind of moron manager are you, M.C.?"

The kind who's about to get ass-raped by the Society Page.

Giggle giggle.

Christian Rixen

"What is this, Cordelia?"

"Oh? You don't like it, sweet pea? I thought it was just downright clever—"

"Clever? This is ludicrous!"

I sense the eyes upon us, the bikini-clad harlots restocking trays of magazines. To our left, the water pumps roar, my temples grinding right along with their machinery.

"Might we discuss this somewhere less chaotic?"

"Well, I surely don't see where, Christian. I got about five hundred people needing my attention out there!"

"Well, I am in need of your attention as well!" She raises her eyebrows at my rather brash delivery, and yet, in this moment, I could not care less. "What happened, Cordelia? These are not the images we decided upon!"

"Which ones were those?" she asks innocently.

"Are you playing a game with me?" I slap the rolled-up monstrosity of a publication against my palm. "The Cloisters courtyard? Gothic arches and models in Oscar de la Renta?" I flip through the pages with shaky hands. "I have it on good authority you were there, as you were next to me the whole time. You even chose the group-shot locale, under the coat of arms!"

"Oh, yes. Of course! Completely slipped my mind—"

"If that is so"—I hold up the first, and most offensive, of several half dozen barbarous pages—"then what, may I ask, is this?"

"That, I may answer, is a directorial choice."

"'The Princess Plays the Pauper: Christian Rixen of Hirschborg's Royal Jewels Redefine the Recessionista Regality?'"

"Ain't it something?"

"This person is wearing a garbage bag with my Majesty brooch!"

"That *model*, Christian!"

"But these are homeless people!"

"Well, yes. But the most attractive ones we could find!"

"And what of this one? With the empty paper cup? What is she *doing*?"

"She's soliciting quarters! And don't those earrings look just darling against her cardboard box?"

"What have you done to me?"

Breathtaking indeed. I cannot seem to catch my own, her smiling face spinning right along with the water pumps.

"I know it's a tad edgier, Christian. But I'm sure it'll make you the toast of the town!'

"Toast," I say, seizing my forehead, the magazine dropping to the floor. "I shall be ruined."

"Oh, don't be such a party pooper!" she says, as though from the end of a tunnel. "I'm sure your folks back home'll be just pleased as punch! The duchess 'specially."

"The duchess?" I search frantically for something to hold me up.

"Your fiancée, silly! Balthazar—what a dignified man!—told me all about her. Called me from your apartment, in fact. We had the best heart-to-heart. What a lovely man! *So* polite."

I reach like a blind man for her shoulder, but she steps aside with a little sigh, sending me headfirst into the wall of rushing water. "I was never going to marry the slutty duchess!" I shriek.

"Well, isn't that a shame? I'm sure she's sweet as pie. But, oh my, Christian, just look at you! Wet as a dog. And that suit was lovely. Armani, I'm guessing?"

Annalise Hoff

What do you think?" asks Britton. "Was this what you were looking for?"

I calmly replace the pages in the manila envelope. "This is exemplary work. You have done a fine job."

What he cannot see is my racing heart, my insides doing a happy jig. This is so much more than I could have hoped for! The girl has uncouth all over her, practically wears it like a Herve bandage dress from two seasons ago.

"Yeah, well, it wasn't so easy. Had a friend at the Dallas Rep dig up the report. Said it was research for his role on a teen drama, but the local police weren't as friendly as you'd think. Guess that 'Southern manners' stuff is a bunch of bullshit. But the records weren't closed, so they had to fork it over."

"And the transcripts are accurate?"

"Sure thing. Those sorority girls couldn't wait to talk smack. Did the phone interviews myself! Well, not with any Kappa girls, they were scared—"

"I can see why."

"—but the others gave me all sorts of dirt. Hey, I could have been a journalist, you think? Maybe I could play one on *Law and Order* or something, I should have my agent look into that—"

"Britton!" I bark. "Do you want that bonus or not?"

He nods vigorously. "Then how should we get this information, shall we say, in circulation?"

"Done. I got the assistants on it. Hate the boss as much as

you do. Lots of them used to have editorial positions before she demoted them."

"Excellent." I smile. "Really stellar work. And as for the party itself?"

From our darkened spot in the abandoned lot, we gaze at the enormous aircraft hangar forty feet away.

"How terribly déclassé," I say.

"Well, a scene for sure. Last count, five hundred people."

"And the décor?"

"Well, it's something, that's for sure. I guess you could say over-the-top."

"I would expect nothing less."

"But actually kind of cool." Then he catches sight of my expression. "For a theme park, I mean."

"And the performer? Is she holding up?"

"Halfway, maybe, after that drink I brought her."

"Only half a dose, just as I ordered?"

"Sure thing."

"Good, otherwise she would be incapacitated. We need her coherent enough to make a spectacle, after all."

"No worries about that! Last I saw, Miller was trying to restrain her. Saying she couldn't go on in that state—"

"She must!"

"Yeah, that's what she was saying. Screaming, actually. Right before she bit him." The smile spreads despite myself. "Still, I better hurry. Call the cue before Animal Control gets a heads-up."

"Just wait four and a half minutes. First, I have a text to send."

He nods. "And, Annalise? I like that dress. You look pretty."

"I know. Far too much for this monstrosity."

"Maybe sometime we could—"

"No," I say. "We couldn't. Go."

I watch him jog through the dark, already reaching for my phone.

Where are you? I write.

When we have finished our exchange, he sends a smiley face. I smile right back, having meant every word.

A glance into the lighted compact, a coat of Lip Addict, and a lift to the hem of my black silk Carolina Herrera slip dress; I am ready.

I take long, confident strides toward what is only right.

Phillip Atwater

"Whoa." Though I consider myself an articulate person, that's about all I've got.

"I'm with you," says Evergreen.

Two minutes earlier, we were in a cab, our driver asking if we were lunatics. "There's nothin' out here. What, you two on drugs or something?"

I laughed. For once, I wasn't.

When he'd seen the limos lining the hangar, he'd shrugged. "Rich freaks," he'd muttered under his breath. "What, the Four Seasons ain't good enough?"

A Launch of Biblical Proportions, says the program, *a Magazine to Part the Social Seas!*

To our left and right, monster waterfalls gush, their white-foaming tops just curling in. And the walkway between? A beach that would put Malibu to shame.

The whole effect is overwhelming and trippy as hell. Like the sea has actually parted, two enormous waves split in half. And everyone is right there in the middle, on the ocean floor, sipping mixed drinks and mingling.

The only thing missing is Moses himself.

Girls in thong bikinis offer cocktails to black-tied men, their dates wearing ball gowns that leave trails behind them in the sand. There are tropical plants and thatched huts, hula dancers gyrating between lit tiki torches. Female guests recline across bamboo chairs, sipping from coconut shells, while jacked-up male models fan them with banana leaves. If it weren't for some strategically placed greenery, the dudes would be straight-up naked.

Everyone seems naked, to tell the truth. Like their minds are so blown they've forgotten who they are, laughing too loud and drinking too much, the uptight fat cats flirting with girls in grass skirts, the buttoned-up matrons unrolling their stockings and putting bare feet to sand.

"Ladies and gentleman," says an ominous miked voice. "Please migrate to the front, as our presentation is about to begin."

"Want to go?" I ask Evergreen, too nervous to even look him in the face. Not that he would look at me back. Whatever the *Times* says about the mess with the Rock Exchange, he's still Todd Evergreen, distant and emotionless as the sand beneath our feet.

What if he doesn't want to go? I'd asked Annalise earlier that week.

Then you will convince him, she said. *That is your gift, Phillip. Unassuming, nonthreatening. Others are happy to have you along on the ride.*

Was that a compliment?

I suppose.

She might be new to half sister, but she'd always be half bitch. For some reason, that thought comforted me.

Besides, she'd been right. All it had taken was one text.

Want 2 go 2 Set launch w/me?

Sure, he replied. *Why not?*

And even now, with everyone talking lawsuit and devalued Rock Exchange stocks, he doesn't seem to care. He doesn't seem *anything*. He fades into the background, just like always, as if the hoodie were part-time invisibility cloak.

Todd Evergreen is gone even when he's here.

Of course, not many know his face. And those who do can barely remember five minutes later. Ditto one single real fact about him.

Except for Annalise and me, that is. And Beamer.

But in half an hour, everything will be different.

Beamer had agreed to come up after his shift, as long as *you get your drunk asses off my front steps before I get sacked.* When he finally showed up around 2:00 a.m., he'd stared out the window and listened. Heard the whole sordid tale, Annalise wringing her hands as she spoke, with me chiming in with *I still don't believe it* and her shooting shut-up-Phillip-let-me-finish looks.

Like I said, eternal half bitch.

Once she was done, there'd been silence—five minutes, at least—before Beamer had turned with a smile. *Well, I've heard some crazy shit in my time, but those is some real fucked-up white-people problems.*

Then he'd pulled the vaporizer from his pocket and taken a long, contemplative inhale. Put it away and looked me straight in the eyes. *So what do you want me to do?*

Get some info on him, I'd said.

What makes you think I got that kinda access?

I know you got a PI liscense, you got, what did you call them? High-level Italian business associates?

If I could—and I'm not saying I can—it's a pretty big risk.

Yeah, I'd said. But you'll do it, right?

He'd stared at me for a long time.

Aight, he'd finally said. *I'll get the DL you need. But just this once. And only 'cause I like you.*

Of course, the envelope of bills from Annalise hadn't hurt either.

Besides, I'm all about family. And 'bout time you was socializing with someone besides me. Get your ass off my lobby steps. Shit, maybe sis here will turn you into a human being. You really need some furniture, boy.

I could not agree more, said Annalise, her smile lighting me from the inside out.

Now I scan the crowd, spotting her near the stage. To her left, the hulking, annoyed-looking man she calls Daddy.

My dad.

She catches my eyes, mouthing one word. *Ready?*

Before I can nod, the lights have gone down.

"Ladies and gentleman," says that ominous voice, "*The Set* is proud to present . . . Editor in Chief Cordelia Derby!"

Applause, a spotlight rising. At the center of the light is the girl from the party, the Southern one with big blue eyes and that huge smile. "Welcome, y'all! I just couldn't be more thrilled you made it to the official launch of the newest, freshest addition to the high-end magazine market . . . *The Set*!" More applause, totally polite. But underneath, I sense something else.

Almost immediately, the whispers have begun to rise.

"When we set out to create this magazine—and let me just say, my team is the best in the whole dang universe!—we asked ourselves one question: 'Now what in the world can you give the most sophisticated people on earth—New Yorkers, of course!—that they haven't seen a million times before? . . ."

Her voice is confident, but the murmurs are, too. I hear them coming from every side.

Did you read the police report? I've got a copy in my purse . . . someone left a pile in the ladies' room . . .

. . . saw the document with my very own eyes. A big stack of them by the coat check . . .

. . . yes, Margaret Cordelia Derby. Arrested. Can you believe it? All there, in black and white . . .

. . . true, I hated every last one of my Theta sisters. But run one over? A bit extreme, you think? . . .

. . . yes, right in the Kappa parking lot! Claims she didn't see her, but from what I hear, that girl is vicious! Practically fired half the staff her first day at The Set *. . .*

". . . for that debutante just as comfortable in pearls as she is in hiking boots," says Cordelia, sensing the unease, her smile a little more forced at the edges. "The new breed of society lady, whether throwing a formal dinner or kicking back with some wings at a Super Bowl shindig, she's . . ."

. . . No, the girl survived. Will have a limp for the rest of her life, though, poor dear. . . .

. . . just community service. Her father is rather important. . . .

. . . between her and that Evergreen, Hoff isn't quite the judge of character you would have hoped . . .

I glance at Todd, who seems to have retreated even further beneath his hood. Onstage, Cordelia Derby, unfortunately, has nowhere to hide.

Yes, all because she beat her for sorority vice president. Can. You. Imagine?

"Whether rock climbing at the newest fitness club or out clubbing, she's . . . um . . . oh, Lord, where was I?"

Her voice is no longer confident, her smile officially gone. She gives an awkward giggle, like fingernails across a chalkboard. "Well! I'm just awfully sorry! I suppose I just . . . got overexcited. I should have practiced more."

"The speech or the driving?" says a voice from a darkened crowd.

Silence. The really fucking awful kind.

Onstage, Cordelia does not breathe. Then, just like that, she lifts her chin high and smiles. The biggest, most painful one I've ever seen. "And now for the hottest musical debut in town," she says, voice clear and confident. Only, if you look hard enough, you can see the slight shake to her knees, the quiver of her bottom lip.

"*The Set* is excited to present Miss Desdemona Gold and the Sashimi Girls!"

"Goldberg!" screams a voice from offstage. "I told you, M.C.! You motherfucking moron!"

That's when everything gets really crazy.

Hey, boys, don't you want a piece of me. . . .

Hey, boys, don't you want a piece of me. . . .

I've been on some pretty whacked-out trips. That time I ate it on that Cloud Nine reef, blacked out for three minutes flat, and woke to the Filipino boys saying, "We thought you were dead, Amboy!"

There was that 'shroom trip in Amsterdam, when I was convinced God was speaking through my left hand; that orgy I had in Eastern Europe with one $20 hotel room, a bottle of absinthe, and three pairs of DD Romanian breasts.

But nothing quite compares to this: four little Asian girls dressed as sushi and dancing on chopstick-shaped stilts.

My phone vibrates in my pocket with a text: *Countdown time. Get ready!*

Onstage, the strobe lights are flashing pink and yellow, the bass so loud it vibrates my teeth. The girls, sandwiched between big white mattress pads—*are they going for rice?*—lift and lower their long wooden legs in freaky-ass choreography. One by one, they *wobble-step* to the center, chant their introductions, and freeze.

"They call me Ahi! I'm extraspicy." Freeze.

"Ebi . . . and you can shrimp me!"

"I am Ika, you widdle squiddy."

"Uni . . . strip-search this urchin!"

A beep on my phone. *Three minutes,* reads the text.

Wait, I got 2 c this.

It has to be now! 2 min 45.

In unison, the girls unfreeze, reaching for the belts—seaweed?—and drop the white padding to reveal shiny, skin-tight, silver-lamé bodysuits.

"Don'tcha wanna . . . wasabi me? Don'tcha wanna . . . wasabi me, boys?"

"This can't get more insane," mutters Evergreen.

As if to prove him wrong, with a quick light change, the girls awkwardly clomp backward in the sudden wash of blue. The music makes a clunky transition from booming to ethereal, the thumping becoming wind chimes, the grinding morphing into gentle tinkling.

A figure leaps on the stage, the lights go to full, and there's Desy in a string bikini and four-foot shrimp tail whirling in circles.

Music explodes.

Desy spins full force, hair and tail whipping, and the audience gasps.

She is breathtaking.

For exactly four seconds.

She trips on a pink fin, stumbles, and flies full force backward.

Chopsticks fall like dominoes.

"Noooooooo!" shriek the sushi, toppling to the floor with earsplitting thuds, high-pitched wails rising from the silver-lamé tangle of limbs.

30 seconds . . . almost there.

Desy does not hesitate, rises from the ashes like a shrimp-tailed phoenix. A few unsteady steps, blood gushing from a cut over her eye, and right back to the frantic dancing. If you can call it that. She seems unsteady, flinging herself across the stage, body moving independently of brain, singing her heart out as she barrels into equipment.

"You're my soy boy!" she sing-shrieks. "Eat me raw! Oh, my soy boy . . ."

Now! GO PHILLIP!

"Eat me raw, raw, raw!"

I turn to Evergreen. "Be right back."

I race toward the hangar entrance, not thinking about sushi or silver lamé or Desy at all. Just picturing Todd's face, open and unquestioning, that instant before I took off.

"You're my soy boy . . . eat me raw! You're my soy boy . . . eat me raw, raw, raw!"

Desdemona Goldberg

I sing like an angel, explode like a firecracker, leap so graceful it'll make your mama's dead mama cry in her coffin!

I outtwerk Miley, outheadline Gaga; grind Shakira to pepper, hip-pop Rihanna to hell and back! My voice so pitch-perfect it ruptures your eardrum, I crawl like the pussycat Beyoncé wishes she could be. . . .

I'm on fire! I'm electric!

I'm Audrey in *Funny Face*, only with bigger tits. . . . I'm Katy Perry with class, eating disorder Ke$ha, only richer!

I whirl like a banshee, my spin shooting stardust! I twirl you dizzy, then slice air before you vomit! Every single eye exactly where it should be . . . everyone in the room wanting to watch/be/fuck/adore me!

"Des, hold up!"

I will not be stopped, not by haters or players, doubters or soul-sucking, dry-cunted ex-girlfriends—

If only I wasn't so dizzy. Is the room spinning, or am I?

And where is that voice coming from?

"I mean it! Desy! Fucking stop!"

Miller. Onstage, coming right at me! I fake out his left, then slip under his right arm.

"There's no more fucking music!" he says, just catching me from behind.

"Noooooo!" I scream, but he's already got me over his

shoulder. I pound his back, shriek, kick the air by his face . . . try to bite and only get his shirt in my mouth!

Blood! Wait, it's mine . . . who does he think he is? I'm Desdemona Goldberg, doesn't he know that?

The audience watches me exit, mouths hanging open. I'm the biggest fucking star they've ever fucking seen!

But who is that crazy looking bitch Phillip's shoving on the stage?

Could my understudy really be a hundred years old with frizzy hair to her ass cheeks!

Totes ridic, I think, right before I pass out. Don't these people understand the magnitude of my talent?

Todd Evergreen

No. No way. It can't be.

"Wasn't that extraordinary!" she says, watching Desy's exit. Someone lifts a mike stand from below. Annalise? "One, two," she says. *Tap tap.* "Three, four." A laugh. "I've never used one of these thing, you'll have to excuse me!"

I lean in, squint my eyes. Robes? I can't tell. But that hair . . . No. Not possible. It can't be.

"My brothers and sisters, I have traveled a great many roads to be here with you. . . ."

Oh my God.

"Those both of the physical and celestial plane. . . ."

Oh my fucking God. Now the arms.

"Let us outstretch our arms. . . ."

The light.

"Let us welcome the light. . . ."

The heart.

"Open your hearts, my brothers and sisters . . . as we are one planetary family in eco cosmic light!"

Dead silence. Arms drop, hands clasped. A beatific smile to the stunned minions.

This can't be happening.

I look to my left, my right. Everyone watching the robed woman, eyes wide. Entranced. Oh my fucking God. . . .

"And thank you to my benefactors, for bringing me here today. As I mentioned, I have traveled a great distance to join you in the celebration of my seedling, this glorious root that was born of my uterian soil . . ."

No! Fuckfuckfuck . . .

"My son, Yum Caax Evergreen . . . or as you know him, Todd!"

FUCKFUCKFUCKFUCKFUCK . . .

"Toddy? My little acorn? Where are you?" A squint. "Could we lift the lights?"

By the time they rise, I'm long gone.

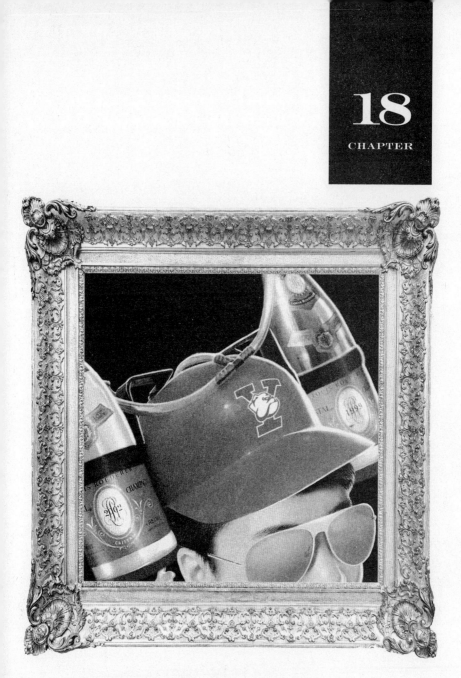

Magna Cum #cristal #champagnehat #yalie #skullandboned by Anonymous

Phillip Atwater

"That's it?"

"That's it," I say. "Lights up, Evergreen's gone, and then? *Nothing.*"

Beamer and I go quiet for a while, watching New York pass us by. *I've been standing in this same spot,* I think, *every day for the past two weeks.*

Even the homeless guy on the bench across from us has more important shit to do, feeding the pigeons from an old loaf of bread. At first they swarmed him, but now the ranks come clear, Alpha Pidge taking the lead while the others circle the edges and loathe him.

Annalise is getting ready to go back to school and M.C. won't answer texts. And as for Todd Evergreen?

"No one has heard from him since."

"Can't blame the guy myself," says Beamer. "With all that press? I'd have hightailed my ass right outta town, too."

I have to agree, having read the articles myself.

Every last one.

The *Daily News*, the *Post*. Every morning first thing, I'd buy them at the bodega, stuffing them in my backpack before someone could see.

Well, I'd think, *at least it gets me out of the apartment.*

Back at Trump World, I'd spread them across the wood floor, then walk around for a half hour, feeling guilty. The ritual always ended the same: belly to the wood, reading each word twice.

Following the *Times*'s piece, the headlines hadn't been so bad, just a series of unanswered questions: *Golden Boy Tarnished?*; *Possible Rock Exchange Lawsuit;* and *Rock Exchange Music Investment Stock: Could Go Either Way, Say Experts.*

Then came the Hoff Media fallout rumors:

Master of Media and Boy Genius on the Outs.

Hoff Claims Got Cyber-Punked: Evergreen Is a Fraud, Say Sources.

But immediately following *The Set* launch, it went to a whole new level. Word of his mom's walk-on spread quickly, followed by character attacks:

Evergreen Tied to Eco-Cult: "Children Eat Bark for Dinner," Says Source.

Rock Exchange Founder's Secret Commune Past: Goat Blood Rituals to Appease "Goddess Nature."

Drugs, Sex, and Granola: Ex-Member Describes Life in the Evergreen Cult, Adding "Yum Caax (Todd) Was Weird Even as a Kid."

Then came those leaked Rock Exchange contracts—no rights, no intellectual property, Todd gets everything, the artist left to rot—which led to a flurry of industry attacks:

Evergreen Stole Our Music and Got Rich: Band Faces Eviction, Rock Exchanger Living High on the Hog.

Jay Z Boycotts Rock Exchange and Kanye's Coming for You, Evergreen: "Don't F—with the Artists," He Threatens, "or They'll F—You Right Back."

By the time the documents were deemed fake, the damage had already been done, retractions mere two-liners printed after notices of subway delays and obits.

As of last Thursday, Assange still hadn't taken his copy down.

In the end, even Evergreen's own had turned, the Anonymous crew posting one of their creepy YouTube videos and influential tech sites calling his "innovation less than innovative" ("like a second-tier Spotify," said one). The bloggers had been even worse ("Suck my dick, Evergreen! Fight the Man? You are him"), and with the release of that picture, the gossips put in their two cents as well ("Nice hoodie, Evergreen," said *Ogler*. "What are you, fourteen?").

And, yes, I knew all that for fact. Soon as the papers were done, I'd move right on to the Web check.

If anything was clear, besides my guilt-ridden soul, it was this: give me a few more weeks and I'd be that *Beautiful Mind* guy.

Two weeks after *The Set* launch and not much had changed, except for the new couch, and that was Annalise's doing. I still stuck to the floor, unless she came over, at which time I'd make a big show of reclining like some middle-aged suburbanite after a long day in the office.

I knew you would like it, she'd say with authority. *Already feeling like home, isn't it, Phillip!*

I didn't tell her the truth: that my life felt like purgatory. And the calls from my mother hadn't helped the cause, either.

Not that I ever picked up.

The messages made demands, then pleaded. Bribed with the offer of my own place in the Hills, and resorted to putting my brother on. *Mom wants me to tell you,* went the monotone-voiced message, *that she thinks we need you. If you want to know what I think . . .*

Before he could finish, Mom would be yelling. Click, dial tone, and moving on.

This is what had become of my life in Trump Tower: a wood floor, a black Swedish sofa, a bong, my guilt, and headlines.

Oh, and Beamer.

"It's pretty jacked-up," I tell him, still watching the pigeons. "After the magazine release, everything kind of exploded. Evergreen might have disappeared, but he's still on every fucking tabloid."

"But that was the plan, right? What Hoff wanted?"

"I guess. And Annalise sure did." I look at the homeless man, the loaf nearly gone. "And you know me, man. I just follow the orders. Don't want to get bitch-slapped by my half sister."

"She ain't so bad," Beamer says.

"I know. Actually, she's pretty great."

"Besides, I get what she wanted. To protect your dads. Ain't nothing wrong with that."

My dads. It sounds so completely wrong.

I feel Beamer waiting for me to give something, but I have nothing. To Gerald Hoff, I still don't exist. *You will have to tell him someday,* says Annalise. *He will be glad to know you, Phillip. I swear it.*

Someday, I'll repeat. Then change the subject as quickly as possible.

"Did you see that shit on *Good Morning America*?" asks Beamer. "They was interviewing Evergreen's mom." Like forty-five times, maybe. I found the clip on Hulu. "Now that's one crazy white lady. I mean, I heard of tree huggers, but shit. That lady *literally* hugged a tree."

And called it her best friend.

"Nice woman, though," says Beamer. "Can't blame a bitch

for being nuts. That's chemical imbalance right there. I got a cousin who takes Prozac for that shit."

I sigh and watch Alpha Pidge chow down on his mountain of carbs. Once in a while, he'll let another dude in, but just for a taste. Soon as he does, he's chased off almost as quickly.

"Lady was pretty tore up on the way back," says Beamer. "Good thing you got her off that stage so quick."

I don't remember the details, just knowing I had no choice. The lights came up, roar of voices, and everyone looking around.

Evergreen was gone. I just knew it.

Toddy? His mother kept saying into the mike. *Toddy, are you here?*

Somehow, in the chaos, I'd beckoned her off the stage, grabbed her hand, and gotten us the hell out of there.

"She cried the whole ride to LaGuardia," says Beamer. "But what can you do? If those fat cats had a chance to sink their claws in, she wouldn't have been so love-my-fellow-man, you can bet your ass on that."

"Yeah, well, she didn't seem so great during the interview either."

"That Matt Lauer can throw down, that's for sure. Did you see how he ripped Chris Brown a new asshole?"

"Yeah, but he deserved it. The question is . . . did she?" Or even more, I think, did Evergreen?

"Feelin' guilty, cracker?"

"Maybe a little."

"What about everyone else? They all tore up, too? How 'bout that little whacked-out singer?"

"No one knows."

"M.C.?"

"MIA."

"That chick who ran over her sorority sister?"

"Haven't heard a thing."

"For taking her vice president spot," Beamer says, giving a low whistle. "That's some ghetto shit if I ever heard it."

I'd read the first issue of *The Set*, though, back-to-back. For what it was, I was kind of impressed. And that homeless jewelry thing was *sick*.

"And what about Sissy?"

"She's okay, I guess. Not around much. Got some school shit—"

"School ain't even started."

"I know, but she's like that. SAT course today. Or student council pre-term meeting. Or field hockey. Future Women Leaders of Whatever the Fuck . . . who gives a damn, y'know?"

"Well then, white boy," he says, reaching into his pocket for the vaporizer, "I guess it's just you and me."

I smile to myself.

That's when I get the text.

Hope to see you there.—T.E.

I click the attached image, read it through, and look up at Beamer.

"What the fuck?" I say.

19

CHAPTER

TODD EVERGREEN

REQUESTS THE HONOR OF YOUR PRESENCE FOR A NIGHT OF FORGIVENESS

THE

LET BYGONES BE BYGONES

PARTY

SATURDAY AUGUST 30TH

7.30 pm

RSVP CODE · TEXT 1966300033 · 88811

Todd Evergreen is throwing a party.

It was the talk of the town.

Todd Evergreen—*yes, that Evergreen*—was throwing a once-in-a-lifetime soiree. An extravaganza of such monolithic proportions that nothing, we were sure, would ever be the same.

We were right. *It wasn't.*

It will take us weeks, even years, to sort through the rumor and gossip, the decadence and debris. But we feel it is our responsibility—*duty even*—to give it that old college try.

Speaking of which . . . *is it true about Columbia? That they gave Crawford the boot? You would think, with the father's fellowship and all . . .but gun money is one thing, we suppose, and Illegal Possession of Firearms another thing entirely.*

But we digress.

Todd Evergreen—*is he going by Yum Caax these days?*—threw a party. And for those who have to *Wikipedia—Yum Caax [jum ka:ʃ]:* the Mayan god of plants. The phrase literally translating—*how deliciously kitsch!*—to "he who serves as lord of the forest."

Todd was a living Harry Potter book! *(We skimmed, but sounds about right.)*

Speaking of which . . . *did you hear about that jungle room? The one on the third (fourth?) floor. Peruvian monkeys and a baby jaguar (in a tiny Vuitton sweater, how adorable! We want them for our nieces).* Then there was the three-hundred-pound python . . . neon green, nonetheless, and the rain-forest vegetation (*illegally shipped, we suspect*). Our interior decorators are in an utter tizzy, they've been after that Amazonian mahogany for simply ages (*an armoire for the parlor?*). Yet somehow Yum—sorry, *Todd*—procured it overnight?

Some things seem so terribly unfair, don't you agree? And not seeing it ourselves? Unfairest of all!

But let us attempt to stay focused here, to impart what we know. To fit together the puzzle pieces, as it were, from our various sources; to mesh secondhand accounts of firsthand observation with the whispered conversations of Those in the Know. And if we've listened hard enough (*we have*) to just the right people (*you know it*), then we might just get the picture.

Beyond, of course, the ones that already exist!

Oh . . . *you haven't seen them?*

How could that possibly be?

Well, don't worry a bit (*worry*), we'll simply fill you in on everything! *(Since you obviously live under a rock.)*

Well, first things first. As OKP are well aware, scheduling is key, and our lifestyle dictates an order to things (*e.g., Botox before filler, Pilates before lipo, background check before nanny hire if wanting to keep your silver!*). But for the sake of brevity—and to get to the juicy part—we'll do a quick-as-can-be little rundown recap (*just like on TV!*).

There was that *Times* article (*Did we invest in the Rock Exchange? Get my accountant on the line. And I mean ASAP!*), then *The Set* launch party travesty (*we loved it*). How divine was that parting of the Red Sea thing? But oh, did that little Broadway heiress made an utter fool of herself (*well, her mother was rather dramatic, remember that Tony speech? She thanked her inner child, for godsakes!)*, that Southern-belle editor with a checkered past (*psychotic tendencies, tsk-tsk*), and the magazine itself, which was not at all bad (*that layout with the ne'er-do-wells dripping in diamonds? Divine!*).

But the highlight of the evening by far? The arrival of Evergreen's mother, from a faraway planet called Oregon. What an utter debacle (*we loved it!*)! What a horrific faux pas (*I mean, REALLY loved it!*). Seriously, we could not get enough.

Then came the media folderol, of course, the headlines on every page. *Golden Boy Tarnished*, so on and so forth, Hoff Media responds (*that Gerald is rather brash, agreed?*). There was that incendiary *Atlantic* write-up (*didn't read it*) and the *New Yorker* piece (*skimmed*), *Vanity Fair* hinting at eco-cult ties and FOX News proclaiming liberal bias. And topper? The real crème on the brûlée? That horrific interview Matt Lauer did via satellite (*Lovely man, though we hear his marriage is on the rocks. Confirm? Deny?*).

There she was, cross-legged in the proverbial grass. That same flowy robe and piled-on amber jewelry (*why is it always amber with these types?*). She denied the rumors, spoke of the commune mission (*some hippie-dippie nonsense involving trees*). Then she gave the tour, showing off her yurt, then led a granola-making lesson (*we kid you not*), the recipe of which we might very well try (*i.e., pass it on to the personal chef*).

Lauer can be such a bully, on that we agree, but that tree-hugging act? Simply inane. The woman hugged a tree. *Literally.*

And what about that hair! Nearly to her ankles, Lady Godiva–style. Have you ever seen anything more ridiculous on a grown woman? *(We're secretly a tad bit jealous.)*

And as for Evergreen? Another disappearing act. Probably escaped to Cuba, we theorized, or with that Branson fellow on his private island. *(He has a golden toilet for a throne! How very nouveau of him. But we do allow for concessions with those "artist" types. As for Trump's diamond door, well . . . he simply has the loveliest daughter, don't you agree?)*

Even without the man himself, the legacy endured . . . the debates, the leaked contracts, that rapper married to Kim Kardashian offering up yet another sound bite (*what was his name again?*).

The Associated Press wires, the worldwide media outlets, the onslaught of international press coverage . . . the whole gobbledygook of utter (*delicious!*) vulgarity.

Evergreen or not, the debates raged on. Intellectual property rights, child advocacy rights, eco-commune rights . . . (*yawn*).

What we really cared about? The part that was missing. Our little *Yum Caax* himself, Mr. Todd Evergreen.

Where could he possibly have gone? And will he ever come back to us?

(Our bridge team is in desperate need of new fodder to chew on.)

Then, like a miracle from above, the first invitation arrived.

The invites? Unexpected, exclusive. Who did this guy think he was? Jay Gatsby?

Evelyn Webbils's fourth cousin Claudia—we know her from the club—had gotten one. Claudia (*Bryn Mawr, anorexic, 2011 Deb Coterie*) seemed an odd choice, with her middle-to-lower-scale looks and sour disposition. And from what we've been told by a select few individuals (*practically ev-*

eryone), her hobbies tend toward the—how shall we say?—lowbrow in nature? *(Whiskey sours, lesbian experimentation, and that year she followed Phish around the country.)*

Now we had a source from which to gleam information, as Claudia would tell Evelyn, who would tell Ricardo at the hairdresser's, who'd then dial us up immediately (*we tip well*). Evelyn would have told us herself, of course, but we were on the outs that week (*she knows what she did*). Besides, it was much more fun this way!

According to Ricardo (*via Evelyn via Claudia*), the invitee had never even met Evergreen. And the invitation itself offered up few revelations, but once she'd texted the number (*untraceable, trust us*), she received very specific instructions. *Show up alone, formal dress required, no cell phones or smartphones or gate-crashers* . . . just on and on.

What was this, we'd wondered, a reality-show setup? *Survivor* for the Spence set?

Quite frankly, it made us nervous.

And *Bygones Be Bygones*? How odd. Our kind is not known for apologies, as we are rarely guilty of anything (*even when we are . . . which is never*).

Then again, Evergreen was never one of us. Not *really.*

And who knew if this party was real in the first place! Impostors, as we all know, are rampant. Remember that Long Island girl who'd posed as a Rockefeller, landing herself that Vermont tire heir (*Yalie, coke problem, plays a mean doubles*)? Once the PI had surfaced the truth, she'd been relegated to Boca with the white-collar criminals. For a while, she'd seemed content as could be (*the stylist, masseuse, personal shopper, and huge alimony check were of help*), but those secrets you keep in your walk-in closet? Bound to be revealed (*meth, two baby daddies, an arrest warrant . . . and forget Rockefeller ties, hers were more Sammy the Bull in nature*).

When these secrets come out—as they always do—we all know the key word is *discretion* (*meaning get out of town as fast as you can and hope everyone forgets in a few years . . . PS: They won't*).

A party admitting to your inadequacies? Celebrating them, nonetheless? We'd never heard of such blatant disregard for proper social interactions.

(Why didn't we get an invitation? If only we were twenty years younger.)

The party was to begin at seven thirty sharp, from what our sources have said (*meaning what our lawyer's third wife had overheard at the Bergdorf salon rinse station*), and the location was extraordinary (*or so said the ladies-who-lunch-if-you-count-picking-at-a-salad on their weekly Four Seasons engagement*).

The setting of the most hotly discussed society gathering since Truman Capote's Black and White Ball?

Brooklyn. We know. Exotic, to say the least (*but what of safety? Did the "come alone" thing include bodyguards?*).

But by this point in the hoopla, guests would have flown from Kathmandu to attend, that's how frantic the excitement had become, at what high frequency the buzz was buzzing.

This crowd certainly had access to private jets.

From those who were rumored to be attending, the demographic was clear: the 1 percent of the 1 percent. Or to be more specific, their children.

Todd Evergreen's party—on this we could all agree—would be the stuff of legends (*if you made it over the BQE without getting stabbed, that is!*).

The rich are different from you and me. We've heard it a million times. Some attributing the quote to good old F. Scott, others to his frenemy Hemingway.

As for us, we could not care less; having said it at all speaks volumes. The You and Me may say such things, but certainly not members of our circle.

Perhaps we are old-fashioned, but this is what we were taught, and we live it to the letter: when you have everything in the entire world, flaunting it is unnecessary.

Leave the peacocking to those with less natural wealth; leave it to Paris Hilton. Gaudy nouveau might get you on the cover of *Star*, but it won't get you prime seats at the Met Ball.

For People Like Us, every rope is lifted, every step we take is down a red carpet. And when bestowed with such a gift—*and, yes, we were chosen*—there also come certain obligations.

We know, we know. Terribly snobby, but rather the truth, don't you think?

On compound or yacht, manor or private island, we follow the lead of our parents and theirs before them: we lie low, indulge only in private, and are sure to keep our gossip to just under a whisper.

Be discreet with your indiscretions. It is simply that simple.

That is why—*and we do not exaggerate here*—these photos compromise our very existence.

Not that we didn't enjoy them!

We may have assets beyond imagination, but we are also human. And so long as our reputations are not on the line, curiosity is both healthy and encouraged.

(*And regarding the above conversation? Let's keep it between us, dear.*)

From what we gather, the party ended at noon (*the day after*). By seven-ish, the site had gone live.

By seven thirty a.m., there'd been twenty thousand hits (*give or take a few. Our husbands handle the numbers!*), the page views increasing with each passing moment.

By seven forty-five, it was official; this was a scandal of unfathomable proportions.

By eight, we'd called everyone in our Rolodex.

With frantic whispers and the aid of voice dial, we'd begun piecing it all together.

Epilogue

Todd Evergreen

I never ate bark. Or lived in a yurt, for that matter.

It was a normal house. Running water and everything. And, yeah, we didn't celebrate Christmas, but that was because everyone thought it was too commercialized. Which it is. And true, there was a lot of Goddess Mother Earth stuff happening, but that didn't involve blood or animal sacrifices. Mainly it was a bunch of old hippies meditating outdoors, calling on nature's love. It was kind of beautiful, actually.

Sometimes there was chanting and drums, but you see that on every college campus across America.

There was no TV, though. And homeschooling was kind of lonely. But you can live with all that. You can live without a lot.

Kids are pretty resilient. They don't know what they're missing.

That was before I touched my first computer.

My mom was a sweet woman. Totally flighty, whacked out of her mind . . . but sweet. Dad hadn't been around for a long time. I didn't even remember his face. Which is how we ended up there in the first place, in an eco-settlement in Oregon with a bunch of ex-hippies. I knew they were ex-hippies because they'd get stoned and tell me.

There was a lot of getting stoned. And that part wasn't great, I guess. I smoked my first joint at six.

Just like Mom, they'd all pretty much had it with life. So maybe it was just an excuse, all that live-natural, don't-use-up-the-resources, fuck-the-mall shit. A reason to drop out of a world that was in overdrive.

Not that I knew what a mall looked like.

I was always the one asking questions. And sometimes, after a big spliff, they'd answer them. It would always end with the line "And you couldn't pay me to go back."

I had no idea what paying anyone was like. We didn't use money. We grew everything we needed. And for everything else, there were the yearly trips to the Town.

I was never allowed to go.

But I wasn't abused or anything. I always had clean clothes, which Mom scrubbed in the lake. Dead of winter, she was out there, making sure I had fresh stuff to wear. Hand-me-downs from the older kids, but clean, and I didn't know different either way.

A washing machine would have been nice, I guess.

And Mom was a good teacher. I was reading at a fifth-grade level when I was seven. And there were plenty of kids to play with. Artemis and Pan and Bacchus. Some of them had different names before their parents showed up. Pan had been Richard when he came at four. By nine, he was more Pan than any Richard could ever be.

Since I had been born there, I was always Yum. I wouldn't understand how embarrassing it was until I was gone for good.

I left for the first time at ten.

Because here's the secret, the one I never mentioned to

anyone, not even Pan, and he was my best friend: if this place was paradise, paradise kind of sucked.

Paradise was boring as shit.

That first time, at ten, I'd hitchhiked to the Town. Everyone had looked at me walking down the main street—only a couple of stores, but it seemed like a huge city to me—like I was some sort of alien. "Son," said the Old Man. He owned the local convenience store. The only convenience store, but I didn't even know what one was at the time. "Do you know where you are?"

"Sure. This is the Town. I may live with a bunch of hippies, but I'm not an idiot."

"Well, might as well come in. Have some lemonade."

I didn't know about strangers being bad. Lucky he wasn't one of the bad ones.

When I got home, Mom had not been angry. "You want to see things," she said. "I understand that."

"I'm going back."

"We all have free will." But she looked kind of sad.

I was back in the Town by the next afternoon.

Old Man—Jerry, but I always called him Old Man, which he always liked—gave me candy. Hershey's bars, Snickers. They blew my mind. TV was even crazier. He only watched old movies, mainly the black-and-white ones, which didn't matter, since it was a black-and-white TV. And how was I supposed to know nobody used VCRs anymore? To me, they were magic boxes.

We saw all the classics. Garbo, Hepburn, Grant. The Esther Williams ones, a bunch of girls swimming in a pool, their moves like mirror images. There were the 1940s films, where everyone talked fast and lived in loud places. Cars honking, ambulances wailing, and everything dirty. Except the women, who wore long, sparkly dresses instead of faded-out robes. The City looked kind of horrifying. I couldn't wait to see it.

Then I saw my first musical, and I was hooked. Fred Astaire, dancing on surfaces you weren't supposed to dance on. Stages full of girls whose shiny legs kicked at the same time. It was big and crazy and I thought, *Wow, that must be what heaven is like.*

Old Man explained heaven to me. It was nothing like the Great Goddess After. There was no mixing with the dirt and growing into trees.

Heaven sounded a lot better.

When I left for good, Mom hadn't cried. She said, "I will see you again, I know I will."

I had cried, but I waited until I was a good mile away. Then I stuck out my thumb. This time, I was going to a Bigger Town, like the ones Old Man had shown me in his movies.

He had patted me on the head and given me a Hershey's for the road.

I was fifteen.

There was a lot of scraping by in the next few years, shacking up in trashed-out squats with all the other street kids. I learned to beg for dollars, then to steal them. But I only did that a few times. I'd rather be hungry than feel the guilt.

All the kids had big plans. They wanted to start rock bands and move to LA, where you could sleep on the beach.

I didn't know what a rock band was, so one of them played me a song on his headphones. "Fuck," I said. Because I couldn't think of anything else. It was too good for words.

"Bob Dylan," he said. "Guy is rad."

He was a friend, and there were others. But none are worth naming. They were the kind of friends who went in and out of my life. And when they went out, I knew I'd never see them again.

I got a job. Stocking shelves at a grocery store. I worked hard and fast, and the manager let me sleep on a cot in the back. It was a good deal, especially since there was a computer I could mess with at night.

That's when I discovered the internet.

On the hot summer days, I'd drag the screen and whole setup to the freezers, log on, and discover everything I had been missing.

An entire world was in that screen. I could go anywhere, see anything. I was still in the back of the grocery store, but not really, because I had the universe at my fingertips.

This blew my mind even more than the Hershey's bars, or even the TV.

I had always been good with numbers. Patterns, really. I used to find them in the dirt, the tree bark.

The bark I never ate. I mean, who eats bark? That shit is crazy.

Computers were just layers of patterns, and if I looked at them long enough, they would unfold and unfurl before my eyes. They would answer their own questions and tell me what they wanted to do, where to place them so everything buzzed to life.

Within a year, I had revamped the system for the store. They saved a lot of money. Then the district manager came to me and asked, "Can you do that for all the stores?"

"No problem," I said. "There's a computer in the back."

He'd looked at me like I was insane, then just laughed.

Nine months later, I had a staff of ten. I had an office and a car. I had even fucked a girl, Milly, who had thrown herself on me one day in the 7-Eleven line.

I liked her a lot. But in the end, it was easier being alone with the computer. Machines didn't ask questions, like why I'd rather sleep on the outdoor porch than cuddle, or why I refused to mow the lawn or cut back the trees.

I wasn't Yum Caax anymore. I hadn't been for a long, long time. But I was still Yum Caax inside, I guess. At least partially.

And I'd always be Todd, too. It was a perfect name. Completely ordinary, just like everyone else's. And the Evergreen? That was for my mom.

Just like those first friends, I knew I'd never see her again.

Rock Exchange just made sense. If I wasn't working, I was out hearing bands. I never cared what kind of music it was, country or death metal or pop. I just liked the excitement of the crowd, the way they pushed in as close to the stage as they could.

People started recognizing me. "Hey, Todd," they would say. They invited me backstage, to their parties. Got me passes to their gigs.

They seemed to like me. Most everyone who met me liked me. I didn't say much. Just listened to them talk. I knew how to be quiet and listen. Growing up with chirping birds and rustling leaves, you learn to appreciate the details.

People liked you when you listened.

They knew what I did for a living, called me the Man and made fun of my corporate job. "What do you do exactly?" they'd ask. "Just sit there and enter codes all day?"

"Yes," I'd say. Because it was true.

"Can you do websites?"

"Yes." If it had to do with the computer, I could probably do it. The keyboard was just an extension of myself.

After the first fifty sites, I realized how many good bands there were. Some great. And they'd get their website, and maybe a few gigs. If they were lucky, maybe even an album for their family to buy. But most of them would never get heard. Not by anyone other than their friends and, if they lucked out, a few fans.

That seemed kind of fucked to me. If you make something well, people should appreciate it. That's how it had been when I was growing up. If your birdhouses were great, people wanted them. If you cooked the best stew, you were the stew guy.

Shouldn't it be the same with songs?

It didn't take long to make Rock Exchange. I had the contacts already.

I figured people would like it. Just not *that* much.

It happened too fast. Too many people coming at me. Prospective investors, publicists, bands, advertisers. And that was just for starters.

"You have contracts, right?" asked Luanne, the girl I was fucking at the time.

I liked her a lot.

I had shaken my head.

"You have to have contracts, Todd. Someone could get screwed. Lucky my cousin is a lawyer."

Now I know lawyers work out of offices, not their kitchens.

Fifty-fifty split. That was what I told him. I guess I didn't read the fine print.

I didn't even know what fine print was.

Those contracts they released were fakes, by the way. The real ones were far worse.

By the time I figured it out, it was too late. The artists were already suing, and he'd skipped town. With $10 million he'd skimmed off the top.

And by then, I'd already sold to Hoff.

It was like a bear hug, meeting Hoff. He just jumped headfirst into my life with his big voice and excitement. He pulled me right into his embrace.

Yeah, I wanted a dad. Always had. But there's no sin in that.

He swept me up. Made plans for my future. *You'll make something big. You remind me a lot of myself. You got the goods, kid,* he'd say.

Now I was Yum Caax, Todd Evergreen, and the Kid.

I liked the Kid the best.

Now I don't like it at all.

I guess I loved Hoff. He was my friend. And this one, I decided, might stick around.

Then there was his daughter. Her boyfriend. The guy from Hollywood, the girl with the loud voice. The one with the smile. The one from far away who also made things well.

I liked them.

And they liked me, just like everyone else did. The only difference was *everything.*

They had stuff. Lots of stuff. Big shit I'd only seen on the internet, on TV. Whole boats and lots of houses, some you could only get to by plane.

They had planes, too.

I could buy some of this stuff myself after selling to Hoff. But I'd never needed stuff, and it just seemed weird. Spending all that money on more stuff than you could ever use.

I bought an apartment, though. It didn't have a porch, but it had a patio thirty floors up. Unless it was winter, I planned on sleeping out there.

I liked their things, don't get me wrong. Not for the things themselves, but how excited they got about them. How their faces lit up when they talked about them.

But I liked the people for other reasons. Better reasons.

Phillip could see beneath the layers of people, just like how I did with the computer codes. He wanted them to be happy. If they got hurt, he wanted to be the one to heal them.

Desy never said she was sorry for anything, and she made me laugh. Also, she could sing. Really sing. She could dance, too. I'd heard a lot of performers on Rock Exchange, and she just had that thing that makes you want to watch her, even if what she did was a little insane.

There was M.C., who gave a fuck. He wanted his life to mean something.

I got that.

Cordelia was the same way. I only met her a few times, mostly that first night in the Hamptons. But I could tell she believed the best in people. When they messed with her, it broke her heart.

I got that, too.

Christian was almost a stranger, but he knew beauty. He made beauty. And anyone who made things, I'd always believed, was cool.

Annalise? Well, she was Hoff's daughter, and I loved her for that alone. Just like him, she went after what she wanted. She refused defeat. And I admired that, because I was a survivor, too.

I loved them all. I couldn't help it. I'd never met people who were more lost.

I guess I was a little lost, too.

But each passing day with them, I was more found.

Then everything went upside down. It was that shitty lawyer, who probably didn't have a law degree.

Then the calls started coming. The threats and attacks. Did I have a comment? What did I think of the case?

Was I evil?

It sucked, but not like the I'm-gonna-die kind of suck. I wasn't in a squat anymore, I had enough to eat.

Most of all, I had Hoff.

Until I didn't.

Gone. Just disappeared one day. And it was like someone ripping out my operating system. I didn't quite work anymore.

Was this how my mother had felt? The day I walked away and never came back?

I wished I could call her. *I cried, too*, I'd say. *Just a mile down the road.*

Only I wouldn't call, even if she'd had a phone.

I shouldn't have gone to the magazine launch. I was stupid. I just thought, I don't know. That people forgive? People forgive, right?

Now I know better.

They had laughed at her. Not out loud, but I saw it in their eyes. All these people in their fancy clothes, laughing at my mom. She was a joke to them.

But I was an even bigger one.

And the people who made it happen? They were my friends. Friends I had started to believe—no, fully believed—would stick around.

You can't trust people, I know that now.

The headlines. My name everywhere. And now I started reading the articles. Seeing the lies. Those interviews on TV with people I knew. Had known. Pan, all grown up now. Wearing robes, just like the adults.

We were the adults.

He looked confused. Upset. It hadn't been paradise to me, but it was to him. And now I'd taken a big chunk from it.

I didn't mean to, but I did.

And then there was my mother. There's not much to say about her. Especially since she was with me every day in my mind. The image of her face as she searched the crowd for me.

Now they were laughing out loud at her.

It burned me up. My body was on fire with it.

I wanted to hurt someone. I paced the apartment at night, prowled like a coyote looking for prey. Only there was nothing to attack.

I wanted to destroy them, just like they had me.

I'd never felt this before. *Hatred.*

Yeah, I'd gotten frustrated. Even pissed. But hatred? That was new.

I wanted their raw flesh, their meat. I wanted to rip them to shreds, tear them to sheds. Leave the parts of them in so many places they'd never be whole again.

The problem was, they were protected. Hidden away in their padded cocoons. I couldn't touch them.

They had everything you could possibly want. If I took something, it wouldn't make a dent. They'd just replace it with a newer, better one.

That's when I realized. You have to take something irreplaceable. You have to take something from the inside out.

You have to take a piece of their paradise. The one they keep inside.

But how to draw them in? I thought about it for days,

then realized it was easy. Just give them what they cared about most.

In other words, stuff.

I rented a warehouse in Brooklyn. Ten floors. Ceilings so high you had to bend your neck all the way back to see the top.

I got the stuff. Lots of it.

Then I got the cameras. Installed them everywhere. And in case that wasn't enough, I hired a few people to get extra, covert shots.

The Bygones Be Bygones Party.

They came by BMW and Bentley, Aston Martins and limos. Some were chauffeured, and a few even drove themselves.

Nobody came by subway.

For my VIPs, I'd hired helicopters to pick them up in Manhattan. It took under four minutes for them to arrive, just as the sun was setting, to a helipad in Brooklyn.

Champagne was waiting.

Click.

▪

They all ended up—VIP and other—near the red carpet. A ton of people were waiting outside the ropes. Some whom I'd hired, others who had just come for the spectacle.

I knew who was on the list. I'd picked them carefully and hired tight security.

They were the unpredictable type, the ones who could explode at any moment. The ones who would make things—good or bad or both—happen.

And if they needed help? Well, crystal bowls were stocked

with powder, girls in pink maid uniforms offered up trays of pills.

The girls had been an easy hire. They'd been more than willing after that magazine launch. But just in case, I had them sign an NDA.

I had a real lawyer at this point. A team of them.

Besides the powders and pills, I had liquor. Every kind you could imagine. Some legal, some not. Some that even made you hallucinate.

That stuff hadn't been easy to get. I'd had to call in favors. But there are lots of guys out there like me, ones who lived behind a screen and spoke in code. They were people I'd never met yet I knew well. And even with the press, they respected me. Some even considered me a hero.

These were the kinds who could hack the unhackable, and their access extended beyond the screen.

They could get me whatever I wanted. And I wasn't just talking about the drugs.

Their reach brought what I needed to create alternate worlds. Whether it was imported from the Australian outback or a warehouse in Queens, I had everything I needed to create a maze of different universes, twisting hallways that led to rooms, each one more wild, more decadent, and more surreal than the last.

All my VIPs' fantasies were here, I'd made sure of that. And each one ripe for picking. If it could take them over the edge, they'd be sure to find it. And if that wasn't enough, there were always more drugs.

I wanted my VIPs to feel special. And that started outside on the red carpet.

All of them—Cordelia, Christian, Annalise, Phillip, Desy,

M.C.—ushered to the front, like movie stars. Now, for the first time, they were the real-life celebrities they'd always been in their heads.

As for the VIPs themselves? Their biting remarks and catty infighting? In that moment of being worshipped, all was forgiven.

When they'd reached the entrance, there was a brief photo op. Shot after shot of them posed while the onlookers—both hired and not—shouted their names and *I love you!*

One by one, their hands were stamped. Now they were ready.

Can we get one last shot? asked a photographer. *A fist pump would be cool!*

They were more than happy to oblige.

As for April Holiday, she just jumped the rope and stepped right in.

I could not control everything.

Click.

That would be the first picture, and last camera, they'd see for the night.

Of course, there were the countless others they couldn't. And I knew the location of every single one.

▪

From my hidden room on the top floor, I kept a close eye on developments.

In front of me, a whole wall of monitors.

This was where I belonged. Had always belonged.

And they were the same, only with the limelight. They'd belonged in the center of the action. They were meant to be adored.

And I was meant to be far away. Watching. Sort of a part of the whole thing and sort of not.

■

M.C. was the first to go. He found his mean streets after all. The underground club in the basement with the kinds of guys he admired. The ones who'd never give him the time of day unless I'd hired them to.

I'd even gotten LL Cool J to sing.

You can buy pretty much anything you want. People included.

There was top-shelf liquor and real criminals telling stories of their time served. There were badasses to spin, badasses to perform, badasses to tell him he was a badass himself.

There were hot, slutty girls in skintight short-shorts. They'd do anything he wanted.

There were drugs. Really hard ones. He had a tolerance, so I made sure to stock the hard ones.

When he was really messed up, could hardly see straight, the gift was delivered with a little note. *With sincerest apologies, Todd Evergreen.*

He'd loved that gun right away. Stroked it like you would a woman. Ran it down his flesh, pointed it like a killer. Shoved it in his waistband and posed, head thrown back, for the women to admire.

Click.

That would be the shot I'd use.

■

There'd been empty rooms with huge, floating balloons, silver like Andy Warhol's. White-fur tunnels led you to white-fur rooms, every surface covered like a soft cloud. There was a playground with swing sets, an old-fashioned merry-go-round, and a bar.

There was always a bar.

And if you began to feel tired, a maid would appear, her pink uniform glowing neon in the dark.

"Refresher?" she would ask.

Click.

▪

Christian and Cordelia had been a surprise, but not because of the room they'd chosen. The fact they were together at all.

Some secrets I didn't know. Though everyone in the world seemed to know mine.

The location had been expected, one of the hidden rooms on the third floor. The circular bed with crimson covering, the walls draped in lush fabrics imported from India and Nepal. Soft, bloated pillows scattered across the floor.

The only light a faint, warm glow from an oil lamp.

They'd circled each other for a while. Argued. She'd cried and he'd pleaded. Then they were tackling each other, laughing and rolling across the floor. His pants came off, her shirt.

They were both very, very drunk.

Her skin looked abnormally white against the crimson, and his jewels beautiful against her bare flesh.

Click.

▪

Later, I made sure she found the purses in the dead-animal room. She hadn't been afraid of their stiff, furry bodies or lifeless eyes.

On seeing the purses, her own eyes had gotten as wide as theirs, and even wider when she found my note.

All yours, with apologies. Todd Evergreen.

Click.

■

Later—a few hours? Many? Phillip and M.C. had found the hot tub full of models. Real models who I'd hired to sit there and drink champagne in the bubbles.

This was a good gig.

M.C. hadn't wanted to get inside. He didn't want his gun to get wet. And there was plenty to occupy his time without.

There was a pool table and rows of arcade classics, but that's not all the game room had to offer. There were people to play with as well.

Pin the pastie, and you couldn't miss. The targets were huge, as I'd hired a porn star to assist.

Later, Phillip surprised me as much as Cordelia and Christian. For such an enlightened man, he really took to the anal ring toss.

Click.

■

In the end, they'd gotten in the hot tub, just as I expected. You couldn't see them in the picture, though, as it was just a lot of slippery flesh.

Still, it was a good picture.

Click.

■

As for Annalise, she snorted and danced, popped a pill. and had a few drinks. Somehow she'd ended up in the bathroom. Alone. For hours.

Phillip had come to find her, but it had taken a bit. His

steps had grown wobbly, and he'd crashed into walls and fallen a few times.

When he'd finally discovered her, she was huddled on the floor, a crying, rocking mess.

He couldn't find a Kleenex. Just the only $100 bill he hadn't already stuffed down a bikini bottom. This one he'd saved for snorting.

Click.

■

I'd never know what made Annalise cry, as there was no audio feed. But maybe—or I'd like to believe—it was the demons of guilt inside her head.

On their way out of the bathroom, a still-wobbly Phillip attempted to carry the weight of his drunk, slightly drooling half sister.

A passing girl had laughed at them and stuck out her tongue.

Click.

■

Downstairs, in the cavernous center room, the disco ball spun over a packed dance floor. The music thumped and bodies writhed and people screamed from drugs and excitement. Michelangelo's masterpiece was projected from the ceiling. God and Adam, fingers touching, watched the fun from above.

Though Adam, it seemed, was touching the disco ball instead, almost spinning it with his finger.

Click.

■

The big finale, and this one for me. Or really, the Old Man.

All those Esther Williams movies we watched, his favorites, the identical girls in swimsuits, rising from the water, arms first, like graceful swan necks.

I had my girls rise from the floor instead. And water was great, but a champagne fountain is even better.

Click.

▪

It was late in the evening, or early in the morning, or late the next afternoon. Nobody seemed to care which. The pink maids just kept coming, the bowls of powder miraculously refilled, empty champagne bottles replaced with full ones.

Even the ones attached to hats.

Click.

▪

More hours. A lot of them.

For those still on their feet, the dancing was more of a staggering, and sprawled-out bodies needed to be dodged.

Nobody would OD. I had a team to make sure of that.

I wasn't evil, just angry.

In the end, a few stomachs would be pumped, but those weren't fatal. Besides, I'd hired on-site medics, so it would have been a shame not to use them.

▪

But where was Desy? Every monitor drew a blank. Then it occurred to me: right over my head.

The roof. After all, Desy always wanted to be on top.

I zoomed in.

The pool was now littered with empty bottles, but Manhattan shone just as bright. Desy took off her top and stood there for a moment, letting the warm summer breeze embrace her. She was finally where she belonged, the center of everything. She looked at the city, probably thinking, *I own this place.*

Then she backed up, did a running jump, and dove, headfirst, right in.

Click.

■

At some point, the place began to clear out. It wasn't empty until five the next evening, and even then my people kept finding them passed out in dark corners.

Then there were the cleaning crews, the dismantling team, the workmen to haul out supplies. I watched the progress on my monitors while making my final image selections.

Iggy Pop meowed, weaving between my legs as I worked. Rubbing up against my leg and purring while I decided fates.

Did I ever hesitate? Just for a second. Then I pictured my empty apartment, my mother's face from that stage. Mr. Hoff smiling at me and Annalise huddled in a crying mess.

These people had played by different rules, and now so would I.

That thought in mind, I entered a code and, at exactly 7:00 a.m. the following day, my anonymous site went live.

■

I had wanted to humiliate them. To expose them just as they had me. To lay them naked across a chopping block for the world to see.

What they cared for most? How they were seen. And after I was done, no one would ever look at them the same.

I succeeded. Only not in the way I had expected.

▪

Within a few days, everything had changed. Within a week, it had changed forever.

With his newfound street cred, Miller was inundated with potential investors. He'd found a space, hired an architect and a lawyer, and within a few months his recording studio would be up and running.

For his parents' sake, he'd stayed at Columbia, which had agreed to allow him back in. He never did an hour of the mandatory community service, and eventually, he would graduate without having attended a single class.

The first track he planned to lay down? Desdemona Gold. Or Berg. They were still working on the specifics.

As for Des, she had gone from It girl to *the* It girl. The pool shot had done it. She was recognized on the street, whispered about by strangers, and made Page Six every other week. Beyond her music career, she'd been fielding calls from reality-show producers.

Impressed with her audience draw, her father, Hymen, already had a cameo for her in his next Broadway show. Two scenes, one dance solo, a ballad, and just the quickest flash of full frontal nudity.

If it was for the sake of art, Des was on board.

Within a few days of the photos' going online, Cordelia was

fielding editorial offers. *Cosmo* liked her modern, Southern-belle style, *Vogue* her fresh perspective, and *Vice* her breasts. While her past's being revealed hadn't been easy on her, that, coupled with the topless, jewel-clad photos, had given her the allure of mystery, danger, and edge.

The fashion community had gone into overdrive with buzz. Cordelia Derby, they believed, had vision.

She was featured in the *Times* Style section as *The 5'5" Next Big Thing in Fashion* and became a cover girl in a national ad campaign, that of her on-again, off-again boyfriend's hotly anticipated jewelry line.

The world had been waiting for Christian's unique mix: artistry and regal sophistication with a rock-and-roll edge. Within three days, his signature piece, Cordelia's Crest, had received over a hundred orders, some from as far away as Denmark.

His mother had been the first to call in.

With his upcoming launch and new factory space, Christian was in need of help. Someone to guide the brand.

He had just the butler to fit the bill.

While waiting for his new apartment to be renovated, Johan crashed with Christian in his. In this open-air loft in SoHo, Johan, though not on staff, regularly brought Christian tea.

As for his love life, it's complicated. Though often at each other's throat, Christian and Cordelia were widely referred to as the hottest young power couple in New York, even going by the moniker Chrisdelia.

Phillip had been horrified by his photo, but not as much so as his mom. As an advocate for women's rights, she told him, in no uncertain terms, she needed to distance herself from such things.

He could have the deed to the Trump apartment, though. As well as an early release of his trust fund.

Phillip could not have been happier.

His father, Gerald Hoff, had been equally delighted.

Chip off the old block, he'd called him and was already thinking of Phillip for a managerial role at Hoff Films, the new movie studio Gerald had in the works.

Phillip still talked to his brother, who, though it was several years off, was already planning on NYU for college.

As for Annalise, by next spring she got her first-choice Ivy. And, after Gerald put his foot down, debuted at cotillion that fall.

Hoff dumped Candace Lilliput a few weeks after his daughter took her bow.

Even without M.C., Annalise's success was clear: she had gotten everything she had ever wanted. She didn't want him anymore. His new lifestyle choice, she believed, would not reflect well on her.

Which is why she kept her boyfriend, Pablo, on the DL. As soon as she got him into Harvard Law and he'd graduated with honors, she'd launch him onto the world.

Marrying a Latino would be hip, she had decided. After all, this was a new world.

And Annalise Hoff? She was just the kind of new money to guide it.

■

And what of Todd Evergreen, aka the Kid, aka Yum Caax?

I would just have to wait and see. With the lawsuit settled and plenty of Rock Exchange stock money rolling in, I could pretty much do what I wanted.

And the first thing I wanted to do?

Get the hell out of New York.

Acknowledgments

With tremendous gratitude and appreciation to the Gallery Books team, specifically Emilia Pisani, whose insight and unstoppable talent made this book possible.

Profound thanks and ongoing debt to the RKOI team: David Kuhn and the Kuhn Projects crew, especially the wonderful Jessie Borkan; CAA Publishing and the extraordinary Cait Hoyt; Stephanie DeLuca, publicity rock star; and copyeditor Steven Boldt, whose sharp eye was invaluable.

For those whose wealth of knowledge and insight aided in the creation of this book: Jack Siebert; surf guru Joss Kelly, and Justin Hogan. The brilliant Baron Cody Franchetti, this semicolon is for you; to Magnus Ranstrop, for taking time out from his busy schedule to answer silly questions. The elegant and sophisticated Johan Nissen and, of course, a "ciao ciao" to Justin Ward and JWHCS Hamptons Concierge Service.

To those who inspire every day: King Jerry Kalajian and IPG; Laurie Meadoff, who endlessly inspires; Liz Killmond-Roman, for her wisdom; Matti Leshem and Lynn Harris Leshem. To Will Smith I, whose support and friendship is a great gift. To Karen Burnes, one of the most exceptional and bighearted people in the world . . . you are loved. To Leslie Epstein and Skip Hays, who make this all possible. And to the late E. Lynn Harris, who is still around, helping the words to come.

To our family, whose emotional support means the world: Dr. Stephen and Roberta Sloan; Greg Sloan; Chris, Carla,

Calder, and Caleb Sloan; Jon and Julie Gold; Aaron Miller. Ina Lise Warming Larsen; Kai Warming; Tine Warming, Ronni Tias Nielsen and the Hobbits. And to our friends, who mean just as much: Emily Johnson; Margaret and Keith Frederickson; Jefferson Courtney. And, of course, Myles Grosovsky. To the inspiring Peter Mauceri. To Kenneth French and NYU SCPS; Katherine Burnes; Limor Aberman; Ned "Lyndon Walker" Shatzner and "Burn Brother" Zachary Karabashliev. To Nicole Vorias, brilliant producer and all around cool chick. Also to Neal Feinberg, a gifter writer, for his encouragement. Michael Patric Hall; Loretta Coney; Steve Waitt; Stephen Sanders; Xiaoyan Zhang; CGTextures.com; to the guys at the Grand and Graham Street Farmer's Deli; Caroline C. Woods; Mara Cazars; Terrell Jones; Tucker Hollingsworth; Brandee Dallow; Davy Rothbart; Malina Saval and Best Man Stephan Fowlkes. To the gifted Aimee Delong. To Ned Martin Shatzner and Renee Martin Shatzner, who is always in our hearts.

To all the RKOI kids, who are unapologetically themselves; in a world where so few will live out loud, you guys have guts, and for that you deserve admiration.